Jacob

Children of the Gods

EAMON BLAKE

Acknowledgements

Book 4

This book, **Jacob - Children of the Gods,** is the fourth in a series of books following the fantastical journey of Jacob. It tells a story about the children of the gods, and all the challenges they faced. For me, authoring the books was a labour of love that began in 2016. Little did I know that over time, it was to grow into a story to be told in the below series of five books.

Book 1 - Jacob - Journey of a God

Book 2 - Jacob - Walk of the Messengers

Book 3 - Jacob - War of the End Times

Book 4 - Jacob - Children of the Gods

Book 5 - Jacob - Battle for Olympus

These books would never have been written if it weren't for the support and encouragement of my amazing family and friends who listened to my relentless telling of the stories and the ideas I had. A special 'Thank You' to you all, you know who you are.

I would like to take this opportunity to thank those who took the time to read and proof-read this book in a genre that, in a lot of cases, is alien to them. They were the ones who particularly encouraged and cajoled me into taking this epic story to its conclusion. Thank you, a million times, to Teresa Carroll, Rita Foley, Sean Blake, Tom Lillis, Vincent Reynolds, Eamonn Maguire, Raymond King, Vanessa Keogh and Thérése McGarry.

To my friend Damien Carroll: What can I say. Your regular emails and phone calls were a great help in getting some of my Dublin 'isms' out of the story making it a far better read. I am filled with gratitude.

I am eternally grateful to a very special group of people, the Poets, and Authors in the 'All About Writing Group'. Thank you for assisting me in getting my book to print ready; this would not have been possible without your valuable critique and editorial assistance, especially with grammar, layouts, and storylines.

To my amazing niece, Niamh Blake, thank you so much for your wonderful cover designs.

I would also like to acknowledge PerpetuityPublications.com for their assistance in formatting my books and getting them ready for release. Thanks again Perpetuity Publications.

And finally – A special thanks to Blake's Food Service Ltd for their kind sponsorship of this book.

Author's Profile

Eamon Blake is from Crumlin, a Southside suburb of Dublin, Ireland, a place he still has a great love for. It was there, between 1970 and 1975, where he attended the local secondary school, Meanscoil Naomh Colm. During fifth and sixth year, he had the pleasure of being taught English by the late Michael Condon, an inspirational teacher who had an amazing teaching technique commanding the greatest of respect from his pupils. Eamon believes that as a result of that teacher's style and perseverance he developed an interest in writing. It was in that same school where he developed his passion for real and classical history. *The history and mythology learned during that time lingered in Eamon's mind and those early influences only resurfaced in recent years, inspiring him to pen a series of five fantasy novels recounting the tale of a Dublin schoolboy discovering his extraordinary powers, and who he actually was.*

A widower with one son, Eamon, over the years, has successfully navigated various employment roles involving procurement, sales and marketing. His professional journey included delivering marketing presentations to major wholesale and retail chains, as well as participating in monthly sales and planning meetings. He believes the wealth of experience garnered during those years helped him develop his own writing style, ultimately leading to the Jacob series.

Eamon's first foray into writing began with him researching and publishing a book detailing the history and genealogy of his own family in central Dublin, dating back to the 1780s. Motivated by a desire to share this heritage, he produced and published enough copies exclusively for his extended family.

The idea for the Jacob series came to Eamon in the late summer of 2016 after he witnessed a charming yet humorous incident in Temple Bar, Dublin. This event led to the realisation that a fantastical story could be crafted by intertwining major historical events from Africa, America, Europe, the Far East as well as the Near East, linking them, and drawing inspiration from worldwide mythological realms featuring Centaurs, Dragons, Elves, The Gods, The Little People, Mer-Peoples, The Yeti and Wizards.

Contact author:

Email: thejacobsaga@gmail.com

Prologue

Jacob, although well liked, quickly realised he was different. He never sought attention but for some reason that attention just kept targeting him. As a young teenager he was known for his formidable strength of character with morals to match, for constantly challenging issues he felt were wrong and for never flinching in his efforts to set them right. Unfortunately, it was also during this period when strange events and horrendous nightmares plagued him.

The nightmares intensified after his fifteenth birthday, prompting Shane, his best friend, to suggest him having a conversation with his mother, which he duly did.

Maria wasn't surprised, she was expecting him to seek her help. She began by telling him his story and the very personal story of her own fantastic life. She didn't hold back, she showed him how powerful she was, and then encouraged him to explore his own powers, some of which he was already aware. She brought him back in time, by two thousand years, to his ancestral home, the Temple of Olympus. There he discovered he was a grandson of Zeus, the King of the Gods. He found he had an identical twin and two stepbrothers. He also discovered his father was the most powerful Thunder God.

"Well then, it's settled," nodded Pegasus while summoning a nearby stallion, "take this trusted steed, the only black stallion in the herds, he's one of the Horse Lords, the very one who carried Thanases that time when he changed the ways of the north. He will take you to the furthest reaches of Olympus." He then quietened, just for a moment. "Listen, can you hear it? It seems a very young colt of mine carries a youngster towards the mountains, a powerful youngster."

"Obelius?" exclaimed Jacob while throwing his eyes to the heavens, grinding his teeth and clenching his fists, "it has to be Obelius. I'm going to kill him."

"Yes, it is Obelius. My instincts tell me he knows you will be leaving from there." said a sympathetic Pegasus. Pointing towards the western section of the shield, "I think you're going to have your hands full with that one."

"I best go," said Jacob as he mounted the stallion. "Oh, today my mother said, 'the apple never falls too far from the tree' was I really that bad?"

"Need I remind you of when you were in the realm of man? I was your hidden guardian and saw everything you got up to. At times I wasn't impressed. You were one naughty boy. Trust me your mother always speaks the truth."

Jacob bowed, then left to race towards the mountains. He was angry and determined to put Obelius back in his place, but first he had to find him. He then placed his hand on the stallion's head and asked, "Tell me, Horse Lord. Do you sense the colt that carries Obelius? Help me find my son."

The stallion raised his upper lip, sniffed the air then slightly elevated himself above the ground so as not to make a sound as he galloped towards a hidden ravine just beyond a nearby hill. On reaching the ravine, Obelius came into view. He was resting, belly down, on a boulder looking out through the shield into the realm of man.

"I know you're behind me, pappa," he said without turning, "you promised, so I'm here to insist you fulfil that promise."

Jacob looked down and, in his mind, all he saw were photographs taken when he was five, he was looking at himself and knew then his mother was right, his anger left him, and he just shook his head. He saw he wasn't going to win and recognised that Obelius was a lot more stubborn than he ever was. He noted Obelius was wearing a custom-made tunic and carrying lethal weapons.

"Who made your tunic?" he asked.

"Mother," replied Obelius, "I tricked her,"

"And, who gave you the weapons?"

"Ah, I borrowed them. Hephaestus was at the celebrations when I snuck into his workshop, Victor was with me. They were just there so I thought they looked good in my hands."

"So now you're a thief!" said Jacob trying to suppress his anger. "Did Viktor steal any?"

"I said borrowed," Obelius sternly replied, "and no, Victor took nothing, he's a coward."

"It's not right to call him a coward," said Jacob "it was brave of him to stand up to one who is a son of the God of Gods."

"I'm sorry pappa," replied Obelius after taking a few moments to think. "I know Viktor's not a coward, he's my best friend."

"You're exasperating," said Jacob while crouching and stretching across to give his son a hug. "What am I going to do with you?" He then while doing things you shouldn't be doing. I want to kiss your forehead and tell you everything will be all right."

Jacob placed his hand on the back of Obelius's head, tightening his hug. He suddenly felt a jolt showing him a vision. It was a vision of an old man standing in a foreboding place and surrounded by swirling mists. The old man was bent forward and had his hand resting on the shoulder of a young boy. Jacob continued watching and soon realised that the young boy was Obelius, and the old man was the Ancient One.

"It seems son," he said when the vision disappeared. "It seems your path has been laid by the Ancient One. It explains your powers and your defiance. You will need to meet with the Wizards and the War Gods. They'll train and prepare you for whatever the Ancient One is planning."

"Pappa," said Obelius while snuggling closer. "Hugs like this make me feel safe, I miss them." He paused for a moment, cherishing the love he felt, "when I'm alone, I feel the strength of my powers, and as each day passes, they're getting stronger. It's as if I'm being prepared for something bad, a menace that's coming. It hides in ... Shadow. It's watching you and I think it's also after me."

Jacob was troubled, he stood while still holding Obelius in his arms, blinked, to arrive back in Olympus just as the lunch bell tolled. Walking though the main doors Obelius said, "Eh, pappa! Let me down, my friends might see my pappa carrying me. They'll tease me."

He attempted to free himself, but the grip was tightened. "Pity about you," said Jacob, enjoying his little bit of power over his son, "if you keep struggling, I'll cradle you like a baby and then they will really tease you." Obelius stopped struggling.

Jacob made his way to the main table and sat with Eala, his grandparents and his brothers; he still hadn't let Obelius go, he was enjoying teasing him. Modi stretched across and tickled Obelius under his chin only to receive an unmerciful kick where it really hurt. Jacob was shocked and loosened his grip, giving Obelius enough time to free himself and escape the wrath of his uncle. Modi was already on his feet, but the pain was so bad he fell to his knees, struggling to breathe. "You little bol...," he yelled after Obelius, but stopped himself considering the company he was in.

"When the teasing was bad," said Odi trying to suppress a snigger, "even I would never have attempted that."

Jacob looked across at Eala, smiled, bowed his head, and said under his breath, "That's my boy." He then entered Odi's head uninvited, "I felt a ripple, very small but very clear. Obelius mentioned Shadow. Do I worry? Do I go on guard?"

"I too felt the ripple," replied Odi, "Yes, we definitely should go on alert.

ways destined to be. Go with my blessing and always stand by King Odi's side."

"It's a pity you won't be at the feast tonight," interrupted Zeus, "but I do understand. Look after my daughter; trust me, she will be your greatest ally."

"Maximus!" blurted Modi while backing away. He stopped, looking confused, he turned back and asked, "What did I just say?"

"You said 'Maximus'," replied Odin, "what did you mean?"

"I've no idea," answered a now very confused looking Modi. He blurted again, "Maximus!"

"You just said it again," said Zeus.

"I'm a War God not a Seer," replied Modi. "I don't like strange things, especially things I don't understand. I've just seen an image of a crying boy. His name is Maximus and he's calling out to me." He shook his head, and said as he turned to walk away, "I must be getting flash backs to the war and forgotten seeing those two little boys."

"Two?" said Zeus furrowing his brow.

"Yes two! I can clearly see two. They look like twins; I don't remember seeing them before. Strange."

"Did you feel it?" asked Zeus after waiting for Modi to go out of sight.

"Yes," nodded Odin. "I certainly felt it. It's good that Modi is a War God, he thinks his vision was from his past, if he realised the future is showing him something I wouldn't be able to trust him, he'd be distracted and Asgard would be in danger."

"Any idea who Maximus is?" asked Zeus.

"No idea" replied Odin, "but every facet of my being is calling out and telling me he is of Asgard."

"Well then," said Zeus. "It's decided. We leave as planned but we stay close by, hidden from the gaze of the young gods. We must be ready to return if they need us."

A few moments later Jacob arrived and sat opposite his grandfathers. "It's good to have some time alone with you both, there's much to talk about but before I begin, I must tell you about two strange things that happened today. My son Obelius, I could kill him. He tried my patience but, in the end, I gave in and took him on my trip. While there he used the wisdom, strength, and speed of a full-grown warrior. He showed no mercy when he slit the throat of a Dark Angel. When he dispatched the angel, he reverted to being a five-year-old boy. I didn't understand until the Light came and surrounded him. He insists he's my guardian."

"Interesting?" said Zeus. "A five-year-old War God. That's never happened before."

"Is he of Asgard or Olympus?" asked Odin.

"Sorry grandfather," replied Jacob. "What I saw clearly makes him a guardian God of Olympus." Odin was disappointed.

"The second strange thing..." said Jacob just as Zeus interrupted him.

"What of the Dark Angel?" he asked, showing his concern.

"I plan to discuss the Dark Angel in a few moments," replied Jacob. "Is that ok?" Zeus just gestured for him to continue.

"The second strange thing happened a few moments ago. I met with Modi and Eris just as they were mounting their chariot and an image entered my head, it was a distressed young boy, no more than twelve years old. The name Maximus entered my head; I know nobody by that name. What could it mean?"

"Modi already mentioned that name," said Odin looking for support from Zeus. "None of us know anyone bearing that name so I wouldn't give it another thought." Jacob just shrugged.

"Tell me of your trip," asked Zeus, "were you happy with what you saw?"

"I don't know how to answer that question. I was happy when visiting many of the hamlets, towns, and cities. To see the people working together; sharing their workloads, helping each other, solving problems, it was inspiring. What the five goddesses achieved was amazing. They brought back the seasons and allowed the dew to gather. They recalled wildlife from a deep slumber, bringing back a degree of normality, but I'm concerned about several old-style governments who seemed not to have learned any lessons.

"Tell me of these governments," said Zeus.

"They seem to think they have the right to impose their will on the people, they insist on doing things using the old ways and I noted intrigue and deception as well as pure corruption. It seems so unfair after everything they witnessed during the battle. They've forgotten the mercy we showed, and the reason the gods went to war. How can they forget our efforts in saving them from the power of Hell? I think we should intervene again."

"What do you have in mind?" asked Odin.

"I understand why we cannot directly interfere, I know it's our most sacred law, but can we influence? Can we identify individuals, take them to Olympus, train them, and then send them back to lead their people into overthrowing the bad governments?"

"What of the Dark Angel?" asked Zeus, totally ignoring Jacob's question.

"Obelius saw him skulking around my old school grounds," replied Jacob, still startled by the way Zeus changed the subject. "He acted without warning me, suspecting the Dark Angel was a spy. It was the way he was watching some of the pupils on the playing fields. I too was watching the pupils. One of them, for a fleeting moment, reminded me of my friend Shane, he looked so like him. Is it possible Hell left Dark Angels behind to target descendants of those that fought in the great battle?"

"More questions," said Odin. "So many questions, this is a worry."

"He recognised me," continued Jacob, "He knew exactly who I was. He said 'Ah, the Boy King. We always considered you, and that imbecile brother of yours to be fools. Your stupid question confirms you've learned nothing.' He thinks I've learned nothing, which makes me think something else is afoot."

Zeus stood to walk away, paused then turned back to face Jacob, "I'm pleased you said, 'we cannot interfere' and to answer your question! Yes, we can influence. Remember, not all senior gods are leaving; you will have the guidance and wisdom of Apollo and Chiron. You will also have the power and tactics of Ares and Athena." He then left.

"Zeus speaks and says so few words," said Odin while placing his arm across Jacob's shoulder, "yet in those few words he has given you much guidance. He's just told you how you can influence. Use his words of wisdom well. You are God of Gods; it all falls to you."

"Grandfather," asked Jacob, "what do you know of Shadow?" Odin shrugged and left.

Jacob sat for a few moments before leaving to sit on the sill of the south facing window. He rested for several hours before moving to his room to prepare for the feast.

❦

It was well into the evening when the bell tolled, summoning the guests into the Great Hall and for the first to arrive it was a spectacular sight. Exquisitely decorated tables situated from close to the throne of Zeus all the way to the steps at the main entrance. There were so many attending it was felt there was no choice but to place more tables behind the statues of the gods. The stewards ensured no god was excluded and they worked towards giving each one a clear view towards where Zeus and the senior gods were to sit.

What the stewards created was a most amazing banqueting event, with all the frills and flounces customary for such a most regal gathering. Each table was covered using pristine white tablecloths, all inlayed with intricate designs made from strands of golden threads. The place settings of crystal glasses, gold etched crockery and ornate cutlery were so sumptuous it was beyond magnificent. The condiments were encrusted with semi-precious stones that twinkled like stars as they reflected the light emanating from the many candles strategically placed throughout the temple.

Nothing was left to chance; even the entertainment was designed to cater for all tastes, needs, and cultures. There were acrobatic displays of great prowess as well as dancers from across the world bringing an immense joy to the senior gods. Mime and pantomime followed, creating the greatest laughs of the night. From the east, displays of martial arts were presented much to the excitement of the Asgard gods. Individual singers, from among the choirs, performed the most amazing arias taken from many of the great operas. The final segment was presented in the gardens where circus acts included many iconic wild animals of the south.

The banquet itself was a grand gastronomic affair. There were seven courses of the most exotic and decadently presented foods available. Chocolate fountains, gifted to the gods by the Olmec Civilization, were placed between every third and fourth column.

There were tureens filled with some of the most briny, spicy, nutty, and wholesome soups and casseroles. The fish courses of salmon, trout, sea bass and hake arrived to great fanfare; each one decorated with lashings of green herbs and tomatoes laced in a generous drizzle of lemon. The side dishes consisted of prawns, clams and mussels smothered in a lavish helping of the richest cream sauces.

What came next was the 'piece de resistance' and it was jaw dropping. Spit roasts of venison, pork and beef stuffed with all kinds of spices and herbs were the main event and eagerly sought after. An accompaniment of root vegetables, cooked to perfection, surrounded each joint. Potatoes - mashed, chipped, and roasted, continued the food fest that was a feast for the eyes.

The assortment of fruits and cheeses presented were unmatched anywhere in the cosmos. The variety of breads on display suited all courses by mopping up the residue sauces on each plate. Platters of the most amazing delicacies in the form of Tapas were continuously being passed around.

Dionysus surpassed himself with the quality and quantity of wines and spirits he provided. The beers and lagers seemed just to keep on flowing. When it came to desserts - raisin bread, sweet bread, fried pastries, honey cakes, and Noah's pudding, as well as an assortment of chocolate delights, formed the centre piece of the side tables. Overall, it was a feast that will be spoken of for years to come.

The only serious part of the celebration was when Zeus stood and requested silence. "My friends," he began, "this is a most wonderful gathering of the gods. So many answered my call I worried for my staff, hoping they'd cope. I think you will agree; they did." All clapped, acknowledging the demanding work of the stewards, cooks, and servants. He continued, "Tomorrow morning most of the senior gods will leave to travel across the universe knowing our realms are safe in the hands of a pantheon of young gods under the guidance of Jacob, who by decree of the Ancient One is now your God of Gods. Always remember that the most important of the ancient laws is the one about non-interference in the affairs of man. This decree is the most sacred law of the Ancient One. It must be obeyed at all times." He bowed and then sat.

Jacob stood, said nothing for a few moments while glancing over all the faces staring back at him. "It has just struck me how, when the chariots line up tomorrow morning, how everything will have changed and changed so utterly." He continued after taking a deep breath. "I'm sure I speak for all young gods when I say that your departure will be like a death in the family. For us it will take time to adjust, we will have all the fond and pleasant memories to encourage and help us. We will remember your teachings, tutoring and support and will treasure all you have shown us. I envy you the tremendous and great adventure you are now embarking up-on as you travel to what is known to be some of the most beautiful places in the universe. When I look on you, I can see how you have defeated time, I look around at the new and young gods and can see your gift to us - the fountain of youth; we will cherish it. When I lived among man I learned of a quote, its source still unknown; it said, 'The Ancient One's retirement plan is out of this world'. I will finish by saying; you are going out of this world in the knowledge that you have done everything that had to be done, and you did it well."

Jacob walked to the centre of the hall and clenched his fist; he placed it across his heart, went on to one knee and bowed to the senior gods. Every other god, steward, servant, and guard followed his lead. It was very emotional; all realizing it to be the end of an era.

Chapter 4

It was just after the next dawn when chariots from the various realms gathered near the main door of the temple. Jacob and the young gods were already there waiting for the senior gods to arrive.

First to appear were the African gods, led by Shango, Isis, and Ra Atum. Their arrival was announced by the pounding of the Djembe drums and the roaring of the white lions. It was a spectacular procession not that unlike their arrival for the Council of the Gods all those years ago. Isis and Ra Atum presented as two most powerful Egyptian deities, their golden garments and imperial headdresses ensured they stood out under the glare of the morning sun. Shango also oozed power; he appeared as a very regal God of Thunder and Fire, wearing vibrant red robes, with matching red and white beads decorating his wrists and neck. His headdress stood proud with tall black ostrich feathers surrounding curved ox-horn. He dismounted and greeted Oba, Jomo, and Jahiri.

"It feels strange for me to hand over my realm," he said while slightly bowing, "it's a place I've ruthlessly guarded since soon after the beginning of time. I look on all three of you, so striking, so powerful, and I believe it'll be safe in your hands, guard it well. I remember that time on the grass-lands and how you used your cunning and skills to protect my people. Their migration was traumatic enough and only for you they may not have lived long enough to see the west coast of my domain. That, I will be eternally grateful for."

He then turned to acknowledge Jacob before mounting his chariot, and alongside the African gods, he flicked his reign to begin his journey out into the universe.

Next to arrive were the gods of the Americas. There were seven and they too were dressed in vibrant robes and wearing the headdresses of their realms. Lord Cizan dismounted and joined Mulan, Garuda, and Girish.

"Since that day in the Mayan temple," he said while avoiding looking them in the eye, "I wondered if you had really forgiven me. I fail to understand how your spirits were so resilient the call of the Elysium Fields failed to break through. I pray you will assist in guarding our realm as our people move into the next age of man." They assured him they would.

He turned to bow to Jacob, then remounted his chariot. He flicked his reign and alongside the other Mesoamerican gods he left for the skies before making his way out into the universe.

Mulan, Garuda, and Girish remained on the lower steps, they were waiting for the arrival of Lord Buddha and the gods of Asia, and when they did arrive, it too was most spectacular. Each deity wore the vivid coloured robes of their pantheon – the Sherwani or the Kimono, all adorned with intricate sewed-on designs. Their headdresses were encased with colourful jewels, many so precious they could only be mined and fashioned by the gods, for the gods.

"Like all the gods who have already left this hallowed sanctum," said Lord Shiva, "we too feel our realms are safe in your hands. Be wise and benevolent but most importantly, enjoy your reign as Guardians of the East." He then bowed to Jacob, remounted his chariot, and led a procession of Asian gods out beyond the moon to wait for Zeus and the Olympus senior gods. Some eastern gods returned to their homelands.

It was now the turn of the Astrals to leave, and they were led by Lugh and Eriu. Behind them came the supreme leaders of the Elf realms, followed by Lord Polkan and Queen Zephyra. The wizards were next. "Please try and understand," said Apollonius, speaking on behalf of all Astrals. "Those of myth and legend will not be travelling across the universe. There's a Shadow lurking and it brings fear. We see suffering and have chosen to prepare, to be ready and waiting." He turned to speak directly to Jacob, "When we hear the 'Song of the Elves', we promise to answer."

They blinked and were gone. Jacob was stumped, he whispered to Eala, "I don't know the 'Song of the Elves' do you?" Eala shook her head. Zeus just smiled.

King Derwyn and his family, along with Andras and Mia arrived, they were still in their human form. They stood in a straight line along the lowest step while King Derwyn went to speak with Jacob. "Like all Astrals, I too fear what's coming," he said, as he bowed. "In me the scars of battle run too deep. It will take some time for me to recover from the death of my father. Be aware, I will not stand down the dragon armies; we too sense a Shadow and cannot trust the peace that seems to exist now," he reached in and placed his hand on Jacob's shoulder, "when we're needed, I promise we'll be there." He backed away and joined his family before they transformed into imperial dragons. They then took to the sky where they sent out their fire before turning to fly towards the west.

Twelve chariots arrived; it was time for the Olympians and the Titans to leave. For the Olympians in particular, this was going to be traumatic; they had lived in Olympus for many thousands of years and never expected to be the ones to voluntarily leave. For the Titans, they were happy to return to Elysium, they prepared to leave on the first five chariots.

Before leaving, Rhea approached Jacob. "Always remember," she said while hugging him, "I'm the first of the Earth Mothers and when you need me, you know where I'll be." While moving away she suddenly stopped, she was receiving a vision; she turned back to Jacob and whispered, "Beware Shadow." She looked across at Obelius and called him to join her. She crouched. "Such a beautiful face," she said, gently rubbing his cheek, "so handsome. The warrior within has already shown himself, allow him sleep until your sixteenth year then become what you're destined to be – a God of Olympus and guardian to the God of Gods. As she mounted her chariot she acknowledged Jacob but never took her eyes from Obelius. When gone Jacob said to Eala, "She gave me a warning."

"Never mind the warning," replied Eala, showing some concern, "what did she say to Obelius?"

Before he had time to reply Zeus joined them. "Heed Rhea's warning," he said, "I too have seen your future and trust me you will need what I've left in place. In the temple the statues are all back on their plinths, always remember that when you seek their assistance, they will answer. I'm leaving Apollo, Chiron, Ares, and Athena as your advisers. Worry not about what Rhea said to Obelius, his time will come but not just yet."

"Grandfather," said Jacob, showing a small decree of anxiety, "Olympus is beginning to feel quite empty. Shortly Asgard will leave and in a few days my friends will be gone. Eala and I will be alone, and this concerns me. Rhea's warning scares me, who will protect my children?"

"For one so powerful, how do you still show doubts?" asked Zeus while shaking his head and walking away. He mounted his chariot and with a quick flick of his reign he led the departing Greek gods out into the cosmos.

Odin sensed the distress growing in Jacob and decided to intervene. "Strange," he said, "how right now, here in Olympus, it's a King of Asgard who has become the God of Gods."

"Do you really consider me a King of Asgard?" asked Jacob.

"Of course I do!" replied Odin. "Like your brothers, you are a grandson of the All Father and that's what makes you a King of Asgard. You are also a grandson of Zeus, the greatest of all the Olympians and this makes you more powerful. You share all our powers, so put aside your doubts until Shadow shows itself. Trust me; you will know what to do."

Jacob attempted to respond but Odin raised his hand indicating there was no more to be said, he left and made his way to mount the first of two waiting chariots. Jacob and Odi followed and wondered who the second chariot was for, they didn't have to wonder for long.

"It's time for us to go," said Maria leaning in to hug her sons. "It's your time now and you don't need us causing you to second guess your decisions. Us going will allow you to become what you're destined to be."

"Mother," exclaimed a now upset Jacob. "I need you here."

"You're not going to win this one," said Odi, "look at their faces, the decision is made. Let them go, you've got me."

Jacob watched his parents mount the chariot, never taking his eyes from them. Eala held his hand knowing his grief would soon show. They were joined by Obelius, Demetrius and Helena.

Odi also showed signs of grief and was delighted when Panya joined him. She embraced him, he too needed comfort. She reached in to kiss his cheek, tasting the saltiness of a single trickling tear. He cheered up when Thora and Sunniva wrapped their arms around his legs.

Maria had difficulty turning back to face her sons but when she did, she saw them, their wives and her five grandchildren forlornly staring back. She caved; allowing her tears to flow, even Thor had difficulty comforting her. They then left.

Jacob and Odi remained on the steps until the last chariot disappeared over the horizon; everyone else went into the temple. It was now late afternoon, and the moon was becoming visible.

"Strange," remarked Odi, "how the moon looks down on us and still the sun shines. Why did they travel in that direction? I would have thought they should have gone the other way."

"I was just thinking that myself!" replied Jacob, "but do you know what, when it comes to the ways of the gods, I think it's best not to wonder. I need a drink."

Arriving in the temple they were met with the sight of their friends putting together some kind of celebration. Several tables and chairs were placed in a large circle, and all kinds of foods were being laid out. After taking his seat Odi announced, "Panya and I were taking earlier, we think we should stay a few more days."

Jacob lit up, "If you stay," he said, with a smile stretching from ear to ear, "the stewards will kill me."

"I don't think the stewards care," said Oba, "look around, and see how many of us are still here. I'm quite sure they know we're staying. Think about it, the dangers we've faced, the travelling over eighteen hundred years, the two-hundred-year sleep, the war of the End Times. I think we should just enjoy each other's company the way we did all those years ago. But before we do, there's someone I'd like to remember." Everyone stood and raised their glasses.

"To our dear, dear friend," she said trying to prevent a tear flowing. "Fafner, Emperor of the Dragons, and not forgetting his beloved empress, Heulwyn. Both are gone, never to be forgotten." They all clapped in their memory, then sat, except for Eala.

"I look around at my dearest friends," she said, while reaching to hold Jacob's and Panya's hands, "suddenly memories of that first time in the Lagoon flood back. I was still fifteen when I became a mother, madly in love with an insecure sixteen-year-old boy. We didn't get to party like teenagers should have at that time, so for the next few days let's make up for it. I refuse to worry about my children, the stewards said they'd look after them, and that offer includes all our children."

"Oh, this day gets better," exclaimed a now very excited Odi while getting up to stand before the statue of Dionysus. "God of Wine and Partying, buddy," he said. "I know you're watching, and I don't care. Your cellars are going to be raided and there's nothing you can do about it." He called Jomo and Faer to join him and together they hijacked several barrels of beer, and a few crates of the finest wine.

For the next two days they partied hard, replenishing as the hours passed. They enjoyed every moment but, although really enjoying themselves, Eala, Irina, Jamilah, Manasa, Oba, and Panya, were always discreetly watching their children. The boys never once thought about them.

On the third day, Jacob, as usual rose early and went out for his daily run. He was soon joined by Faer, Garuda and Odi.

It was mid-morning when they reached the upper slopes of the mountains taking them into the realm of the Yeti nation. There they met up with Yaz and a column of his warriors who were out checking on their protective shield.

"Welcome to the realm of the Yeti," said Yaz after opening the shield to allow Jacob through. "I apologise for leaving your celebrations so early, but you must understand a Yeti ear is very sensitive, hence living so high in the mountains. Never before did I hear anything like the music you provided."

"No matter," said Jacob trying to suppress a laugh. "It was important for you to be there for the feast and the speeches."

"Ah," said Yaz, looking a bit distracted. "I see more of your friends are on their way."

It was Baldor, Girish, Jahiri, Jomo and Thanases, and they were carrying bedding, casks of beer, and food containers.

"I think our plans are about to change," said Jacob on seeing what they were carrying.

"Lad's night out?" exclaimed Odi rubbed his hands together.

"I take it your visit is now fleeting?" said Yaz while jokingly throwing his eyes to the heavens.

"I'm afraid it is, my lord," replied Odi trying to be respectful. "We're going to the lagoon, and we need to get there before dark."

Yaz bowed and made his way back up the mountain.

The Lagoon that late evening was at its pristine best, no light breezes, no shifting sands, not a ripple crossing the clear and mirror-like water. The sun was now so low its last rays found themselves arguing with the approaching moonbeams.

Baldor as the light bearer of the north used his power to ignite a hastily built bonfire while, at the same time, Odi again raided the cellars and commandeered two more barrels of beer. Jacob in the meantime blinked, to arrive in the temple where he met with Eala and the girls. He informed them that the boys were staying out all night and ladies weren't welcome.

"As if we care," said Eala, much to Jacob's surprise. He left, wondering what they were up to.

The girls made their way to the ornamental garden to sit before the statue of David. The stewards had arranged comfortable chairs and tables, as well as the most sumptuous foods and the finest wines for them to relish. From there they could hear the boisterous and wild party being enjoyed by the boys and were happy for them. They too were having a wild time especially when Eala and Panya discussed the physique of Jacob and Odi, comparing them to the statue of David.

The following morning the boys made their way back to the temple, all severely hungover. Their moans and groans heard across the meadows. On the way Odi noticed Faer had backed away and was walking slowly. He joined him and then saw his tear-filled eyes. "We all miss him," he said, placing his arm across Faer's shoulders, "and like you we're broken hearted. I know he was your best friend so you must remember how you had him for all those years. You fought together, laughed together, changed the world together. Jacob too is broken hearted and has to live with the decision that led to his death."

"He would have loved last night," said Faer, struggling to hold it together.

"Yes," replied Odi, "He would've been the ringleader, but it wasn't meant to be. Come on, you should be happy, look at the legacy he's left. Look at your own life, Danu waits for you to take her to the Fair Lands, and my visions show me lots of little Faer's running about. Think about how Danu lights up your life. Now think about how Fafner would want you to move on and be happy. It's time to let go."

On reaching the temple the boys found the girls fully recovered from the night before, they were looking their radiant best but seemed a bit subdued. It had dawned on them that this was to be the last time they'd see each other for a very long time.

The boys quickly made their way to their rooms to prepare for their journey to their various homelands. On returning to the steps, they were surprised to see their chariots were already waiting.

"Trying to get rid of us?" said Thanases with a smirk.

"I decided," replied Jacob, "I decided it might be better to have a quick departure. Knowing you're all leaving is breaking my heart."

The first chariot to leave carried Jomo, Oba, and Zane, and it was followed by the one carrying Jahiri, Jamilah, and Sagal. There was no standing on ceremony, just very tight embraces, and when ready they travelled across the meadows and soon reached the portal that took them to the far south.

The next two chariots were destined to travel to the Northern Icelands before making their way to Asgard. Baldor travelled on one and Thanases, Irina and Viktor travelled on the other. Their departure wasn't as emotional - Odi, Panya, Thora, and Sunniva were due to join them later that day.

A short while later, those travelling to the east prepared to leave. Girish, Manasa, and Hemish made their way to Mount Kailash, while Mulan and Garuda departed for the five sacred mountains.

Faer and Danu were last to leave and before mounting their chariot, they insisted on a long embrace from Jacob and Eala.

"I'm still grieving for Fafner," said Faer hoping to help Jacob with his grief. "Odi tells me you too still hurt so can we do a deal? I'll stop grieving if you stop hurting. He tells me there are children in my future and that means both of us need to move on."

"It's difficult to stop grieving," said Jacob, "especially when, at times, I hear Fafner's voice, it's been in my head for the last few days and it's getting louder."

"What does he say?" asked Faer.

"He speaks of Shadow," replied Jacob, "and I hear him speak of poison. He worries about a young dragon, but I don't know any young dragons. It's strange that Rhea also spoke of Shadow."

"Last night," said Danu placing her hand on his cheek," I closed my eyes and in the mists of the Fair Lands I saw a Shadow, now I'm worried." Jacob acknowledged her concerns.

They mounted their chariot and before flicking the reign Faer yelled, "If you need us, you know what to do. Seek the Fair Land, there you'll find us."

Chapter 5

Jacob watched the seven chariots until they finally disappeared, he turned to Odi and said, "It's time for you to go and get ready, it's your big day."

"I'm dreading this," said Odi showing a bit of nervousness, "It's the kind of thing I always shied away from. Why did grandfather make me the Asgard King of Kings?"

"I'm sorry I can't be there," said Jacob reaching in to embrace him, "but I have to get used to running Olympus and rearing my three."

Odi left for his room and when he arrived, he walked in on Panya being dressed by two servants. "You look amazing," he said while watching a cape being placed across her shoulders. She smiled and performed an elegant pirouette allowing her flowing cream satin gown twirl before it settled to show its perfect figure-hugging shape. Eala and the servants then left to prepare the two princesses.

Odi approached and gently kissed Panya on the cheek. "Last night," he whispered, "before going out with the boys, I went to the workshops and made these for you." He placed a set of earrings in her hand.

"They're amazing," she gasped while trying to take in their beauty, "your skills never fail to amaze me, did you really make these?"

"Oh, you of little faith," he sneered, "I do have a softer side, but I admit I did have help, I called in a lot of favours. I want you to arrive in Asgard as a Queen our subjects will never forget."

He took the earrings back and placed one in each of his hands, he moved his hands close to her ears and using his magic he gently manoeuvred them to rest on her ear lobes. She placed her hand on his cheek and moved in for a kiss prompting him to say, "I wouldn't if I were you; all that make up, that beautiful dress, I mightn't be able to control myself."

"I love it when you lose control, but I suppose it's time you washed and got ready, you still smell of beer and bonfire."

He made his way to the washroom and began to undress. Panya followed and stood watching as he ran his fingers over his long-ago healed wounds. She continued watching as he made his way towards the bath, still infatuated by his naked, highly muscular, yet lean body.

"It's my turn to try and control myself," she said while watching him slide into the water.

"You had your chance earlier," he laughed, "but I'm still tempted, shame we have no time."

"When I look on you," she said while backing away, "I sometimes feel I need to pinch myself. I ask as to how someone like me can be so lucky to end up spending eternity with someone who is clearly a paragon of creation; I love you so much."

"Someone 'Like' me?" he gasped in disbelief. "Don't run yourself down, you should look in a mirror more often; you'll then see it's you who is the paragon." She smiled, was happy, then left to check on her daughters.

Odi totally relaxed as the soothing waters caressed his body allowing his mind to show all that was great about his life. He didn't want to move but his duty was now intruding. He left the bath and prepared to get dressed; but before he did, he noticed all wounds and scars had disappeared, his skin was again flawless, that of a god.

He chose to wear the calf skin breeches and the imperial dress tunic of an Asgard warrior, the very robes he wore when he first arrived at Olympus. He also chose to wear the cape made from the hide of the great elk of the north. He then placed upon his head the gem encrusted crown given to him by Odin. When ready he walked over to the window and raised his Gjallarhorn, calling for the imperial escorts to prepare for his departure.

He left the room and made his way through the corridors and into the Great Hall where he walked among the statues of the gods. He acknowledged their power as he passed and on reaching the doors he used a gentle movement of his arm commanding them to open. When he reached the top step, he stopped and looked out towards the lagoon, raised his staff, and called on the Light and it came. He sent it to open a portal, through which came the royal chariot and its escorts.

He looked down at Panya, slightly bowed then asked, "Did you look in the mirror?" She smiled back and nodded. He looked at his daughters and could see Thora wasn't happy, she disliked loose gowns preferring to be dressed as a warrior. He saw Sunniva was enjoying the glamour and knew then she was going to be the one to break his heart. He looked at Jacob and didn't wait for an invitation, he just entered his head, "Don't, if you do, I'll kill you."

"You've always known I'm a softy," said Jacob trying to hide his upset, "I will shed a tear, and I won't be able to stop them."

The royal chariot arrived, Panya took her seat, and her girls then joined her. Odi walked over to Obelius, Demetrius and Helena and said as he crouched, then wrapped his arms around them, "When he gets snarky, you know where to find me. I'll sort him out."

"We love you Uncle Odi," said a sniffling Obelius while climbing into his arms. Odi again struggled to prevent a tear from flowing.

After mounting the chariot, he reached across to kiss Panya and then sat to the left of his daughters. He pulled an Arctic fox-fur rug across all four of them and waited for the charioteer to flick his reign. He looked up at Jacob and Eala then waved his goodbyes. It was an amazing departure, watching one hundred and one imperial chariots processing towards the still open portal.

❦

On passing through the portal, they arrived out among the stars where they continued their journey towards a light shining from beyond the rings of a distant planet. Thora was mesmerised. "Pappa," she exclaimed, "one day I will be a Warrior Queen, a Goddess of War and this will be my domain."

"Mama," said Sunniva, "I see nothing for me here. There are suns in my dreams and they're calling me. What does it mean?"

"That future will not be for a very long time," said Panya while hugging both, "enjoy what you have now."

"Look around," said Odi, "have you ever seen anything as magical?" He stood to take in the view, a vast black canvas filled with numerous specks of light, stars of all sizes. It was the colours, cool blues and whites to warm oranges and reds, that held his gaze.

"It won't be long now so let me tell you a story," he said while taking his daughters onto his lap, "Soon after the beginning of time, the 'All Father' grew to become the greatest of the sky gods, at that time he met a goddess who was of the Earth, they became one and from them was born your grandfather. There were many others born to Odin and you will meet them when we reach Asgard. Your grandfather is also a sky god, but he's different, he commands the power of the storms and of the thunder. Throughout his life he met many goddesses. Among them are the mothers of your uncles, Magni and Modi, another is my mother, she is your grandmother. Their combined powers are now channelled through me, and Uncle Jacob. Your mother and I believe those same powers will one day be shared between you and your cousins even though you are all destined to be so different."

He turned to Thora, "You were named after your grandfather because you too will have his powers, you will become a Goddess of War, and the Hammer will answer to you. You will be a Queen of Asgard and command great armies."

He then turned to Sunniva, "My darling princess, your future is out among the stars, far away from Asgard, your destiny is shielded from both your mother and I, but we do see a prince, a Lord of the Earth, and he will always be by your side. He will become a Sun God to you our beautiful Sun Goddess."

"Odi!" exclaimed Panya. "Is that Asgard?"

"It certainly is," he answered with a smile that went from ear to ear, "I feel I'm now home. Welcome to Asgard, realm of the Norse Gods."

The closer they got the more excited Odi became especially when he saw the golden armour of Heimdallr, the guardian of Asgard. On reaching the Bifrost Bridge he acknowledged Heimdallr with a bow before leaping from the chariot to meet up with him.

"Odin spoke of your arrival," said Heimdallr, "he asked me to ensure you are welcomed home as our King. All is arranged."

"I need to ask you something," said Odi, "this might sound like an odd question, but I'm bothered. Have you sensed a threat? Has a Shadow appeared in your dreams?"

"Strange you ask," he replied, "In my mind's eye I do see a Shadow, I focus, and it's gone. The ancient ones always said, 'The slightest suspicion, put up your guard' I've put up my guard."

"Good," said Odi. "The dragons are already on alert."

Odi helped Panya and his daughters from the chariot; he decided he and his family would walk across the bridge into the city. His escorts remained at the entrance where they too watched their new royal family walk alone towards the city. Odi's intention was to show Asgard his humility.

For Panya and the girls, walking across the bridge was daunting especially when they approached the fifty-foot statues of the ancients. While passing beneath the statues they strained their necks to look up in awe at how high they stood, at times they were met by the statue's eyes staring back.

"They are the heroes of old," said Odi, "they fell during the first war of the giants. They are still revered, especially by those of us who've seen their eyes move."

"Pappa is this all for you?" asked an excited Sunniva. "The flags fly on every pole and all torches are burning."

"My beautiful princess," replied Odi while lifting her into his arms, "this is not just for me; it's for all of us."

The closer they got to the gates, the louder the cheers. From what Odi could see the crowds were six deep, lining both sides of the avenue leading up to the palace. He felt their energy grow and this dispelled any doubts he had. Their excitement and their cheers got louder, becoming contagious. He resolved to greet as many as he could.

On passing through the gate, a battalion of palace guards greeted them, all dressed in their imperial robes, they were waiting in formation to escort the royal family up to the palace. It was then when they saw familiar faces. Thora lit up when she saw Modi. Panya got more excited when she saw Baldor, Thanases, Irina, and Viktor, even though it was only a few hours since she last saw them. The relief on Odi's face on seeing his brother was palpable and as they greeted each other Odi whispered, "That was a long walk."

"It was a wise walk," replied Modi, "you made your people wait, giving them time to get used to the arrival of their new King and Queen."

"Ok brother," said Odi after noticing how Modi was unusually skittish, "what is it? You're smiling and have dancing eyes, it can't be because I'm here, you don't love me that much. Spill the beans."

"I'm going to be a father," replied Modi. "Eris is heavily pregnant and she's due soon."

"But?" exclaimed a shocked Odi. "You were only with her a few days ago?"

"Have you two learned nothing?" asked Panya. "Eris is carrying the children of two powerful gods; they too are gods and are rushing to be born. This day gets better."

"Shit," said Odi, taking a deep breath, and tightly holding Panya's hand, "I'm suddenly nervous again."

"You're worse than Jacob," said Panya, grasping him tighter and throwing her eyes towards the heavens, "get a grip and let us continue walking."

Modi and Eris held Thora and Sunniva and walked close behind. Baldor, Thanases, Irina and Viktor waved them off. Viktor hid behind his father's cape but couldn't help himself; he was caught sticking his tongue out at Thora. What no one saw was Thora using one of her middle fingers to return the insult.

They made their way through the long avenue greeting as many citizens as they could. From the balconies, showers of petals fell like confetti, helping to create a most magical procession of royalty. Odi was overwhelmed by how every vantage point was occupied by cheering Asgardians and was having difficulty holding back his tears. Panya as always, held and encouraged him.

It was when approaching the palace when Odi gasped, he turned to Modi and said, "Is that who I think it is?"

"I wanted to surprise you," said a cautious Modi, "she returned after the retreat of The Darkness, and has made her peace with Asgard. She hopes you will accept her."

"This day gets better," said Odi to Modi's relief, "of course I'll accept her."

"Who is she?" asked Panya.

"It's Prudr," replied Odi forgetting for a moment that he never spoke of her, "she's my sister, my father's first born. Her mother is Sif, Earth Goddess of the Harvest. Sif was my father's first wife."

"For crying out loud," said Panya showing her annoyance, "when exactly did you plan to tell me of her?"

"I'm sorry," replied a chastened Odi, "I don't speak of her; she abandoned me when I was three years old. Over the years I put her from my mind and come to think of it, I've never spoken of her with Jacob; can you imagine his reaction when he finds out. He'll probably kill me."

"You're worried about Jacob killing you?" snarled Panya. "Any more secrets and you'll die at my hand." Modi sniggered.

Panya looked up at those gathered on the steps of the palace. "Who are the warriors," she asked, "they look formidable."

"They're our uncles," replied Modi. "You will meet them soon enough."

On arrival at the terrace surrounding the imperial palace they made their way to sit on the two thrones placed strategically to be on full view across the Asgard realm. They took their seats while all those around them clenched their fists, crossed them over their hearts, and bowed to their new King and Queen. Odi then stood.

"People of Asgard, my friends, I stand before you as your King. See how Queen Panya held my hand as we crossed the Bifrost Bridge and know how together we were encouraged by the strength of the love you sent out to us. Do not fear for me. I know I am a young King but behind me is my father, my brothers, my sister, and my uncles. I also have my mother. Most importantly, I have the support, power, and wisdom of Odin, the All-Father. I will quickly earn your trust and promise to be just and fair. I promise to guarantee your free speech and freedom of expression. I pray I will be a wise king who will protect and cherish the amazing and formidable realm of Asgard. From the bottom of my heart, I wish to thank you for the love and affection you have shown this day to my wife and my family."

Odi again acknowledged his people before leaving the throne and making his way to speak with his sister, but every attempt to meet her was thwarted by the constant stream of well-wishers including his uncles who swore their allegiance to him.

Hodr, who was Odi and Jacob's blind uncle said, "I hear you have grown to be so much like your father, if you bear his skills, I know Asgard will be safe in your hands, but it worries me as to how you have been through so much for one so young."

Balder than spoke, "I don't share those worries. The Light surrounds you, proving you've been blessed by the Ancient One. Your uncles will be your generals, and your counsel. With our support Asgard will continue to prosper under your rule.

Hermod then said, "I too see in you your father, and wonder what it is about the line of Thor that brings the most amazing women into your lives. Queen Panya is most beautiful. How can an ugly lunatic like you be so lucky?"

"Thank Odin I'm my father's son," laughed Odi. "No girl has ever captured my imagination the way Panya has. She's one of Jacob's friends and stole my heart the moment I saw her. Wait until you meet my mother; she is more beautiful than Aphrodite. Father is besotted with her."

Odi checked on his daughters then looked around for Panya, and when he found her, he commented, "Look across at Uncle Vidar; he looks so like my father it's deceiving, even Panya is in awe of him. I best go rescue her." On reaching them he stretched in and kissed Panya on her cheek. "Uncle Vidar," he said, "did I do well?"

"You certainly did," replied Vidar. "Aphrodite must have been so jealous." They all laughed.

Panya's curiosity got the better of her when she looked up at the very regal ladies standing near the main doors. "Odi," she whispered. "Who are the three goddesses standing at the back?"

Odi looked and said, "Come, I'll introduce you." and while walking towards them he said, "One is my grandmother and the others are the mothers of my uncles: Their names are Frigg, Jord and Grid."

"Odin was certainly busy," she said while trying to suppress a giggle. She then asked, "Which one is your grandmother?"

"Frigg is my grandmother," he replied, "the one on the left."

Panya then noticed a very lonely looking, yet very beautiful lady, standing alone and enquired as to who she was.

"Ah," he said, "that's Sif, my father's first wife. She's Prudr's mother. It's said she still loves him. She's never been able to break through his love for my mother."

"This is going to take some getting used to," said a concerned Panya. Odi then introduced her to his grandmother and his grandaunts. At times he was distracted, conscious he didn't get to speak with Prudr.

Chapter 6

Odi had difficulty finding Prudr; he searched everywhere and then remembered her favourite place. It was the same place his father went when he too was lonely - the highest tower at the rear of the palace. His hunch was correct.

As he approached her, images of when he was a toddler flooded back. He remembered her not only as a warrior queen of Asgard, but a big sister who always found time to make his days full of fun.

He stopped for a moment to just stare at what he considered a vision. She wasn't dressed as a warrior and although her back was to him, he could see she was dressed as a beautiful goddess. She was wearing a loose-fitting full-length cream coloured gown, secured around her waist by a diamond studded belt. Her long wavy platinum blonde hair was held in place by a gem encrusted tiara. Even with her back to him he sensed all was not right.

"I was so angry," he said on joining her, "I was broken hearted. You fed me, cleaned me and you brought me everywhere. Then you were gone. Why did you leave me?"

When he got no response he continued, "I swore I'd never forgive you. I never wanted to see you again but when I saw you on the steps earlier my real feelings returned. I'm happy to have you back into my life."

"When I think back," she said on turning to face him, "I remember your hugs, they were so tight. For a child you were so strong, so handsome, your kisses always special. The spark of greatness was always there. The Light was guarding you. Your destiny was set at the beginning of time and now I can see it has happened. You must be so happy!"

"Yes," he replied, "I'm happy because I met Panya; she has swept me off my feet, what we have is true love. Did you see her smiling while she walked among the gods? Did you notice how she continuously checked on my daughters even while greeting our uncles? She's so protective of them. She's my rock, my Queen and she too has been blessed by the Ancient One. She is a Goddess of the Light."

"She truly is most beautiful," said Prudr, "I'm really happy for you. Your daughters are showing signs of great power. One, a War Goddess destined to be a Warrior Queen of Asgard. She's the image of you when you were a toddler."

"Her name is Thora," replied Odi, "I named her in honour of father. The other is Sunniva; she will be a Sun Goddess of great power." There was a momentary awkward silence then Prudr said,

"You've got to understand, I was in love. He was a most powerful and loving Sun God, and we fell head over heels. For the first time I had some-body who made me feel like I was the only women in the world. His name was Sol Invictus, and he was revered throughout Rome. They even dedi-cated the Circus Maximus to him. Games were held in his honour and as a reward he shone his light and bestowed his warmth so that Rome always prospered. It was during his visit to Asgard when he stole my heart; it was also during that visit when we both received a vision showing the advance of The Darkness. We knew our place was out among the stars aiding the sky realms in preparing for any attack. I thought it best to leave without saying goodbye because I knew you'd make my parting more difficult." Tears welled up and then began to flow; this surprised Odi because it was unheard of for a War Goddess to cry. She fell to the ground and became hysterical.

Modi was close by and on hearing Prudr's cries ran to her aid.

"What have you done?" he yelled, "She's been through enough, do you not realise how painful her life is? How could you?"

"I never said a word," said a shocked Odi, "we weren't arguing, I swear. We were just talking."

Modi comforted his sister until she calmed and when she composed herself, she said, "Look to the northern sky and seek out the brightest star, count six to the right and see how all around that sixth star is hidden from us, as though in shadow. That's where we built our home. Sol gathered many Sun Gods together and as protectors, they became formidable. They fought valiantly but The Darkness had an ally, a shadow and together they used all their might to destroy our defences, Sol had fallen. They were swift and ruthless; they came to my home and while my back was turned, they took my babies. My beautiful Arum and Eliana; they were only ten and eight years old...." She couldn't continue such was her distress.

Odi thought of his daughters, and it brought tears to his eyes thinking of how he would feel if this had happened to them. He knelt beside her and said, "I am King of Asgard, and I promise everything will be done to find your children."

"I've been so lonely," said Prudr after calming again, "I knew if I was to see my babies again, I'd need the help of my family."

"We'll all help," said Modi, "coming here was the right thing to do."

"Tell me sister," said Odi, "tell me about my nephew and niece."

Prudr was delighted he asked, she needed to talk about them, and it helped her feel they were close.

"Arum is a lunatic," she said with a smile crossing her face. He's just like his uncle Magni; I remember when he was his age. He knows no fear and that always worried me. He'd get up to all kinds of mischief and did it with a cheeky smile. He never went anywhere without checking on Eliana first, he acted like her guardian, and this made me happy. Eliana is incredibly beautiful, blue eyes and fair of skin with a very, very soft heart. Her blond hair danced in the sunlight as she walked, and she always brought a joy to those she met. From an early age it was obvious she was destined to become a Goddess of the Light, one just waiting to shine."

Odi felt his heart breaking; he was devastated for his sister and resolved to do everything he could to help. He asked Modi to fetch Baldor and when he arrived, Eris was also with him. "Good," said Odi, "I need the power of the light bearer. Send out your light and see if you can find Prudr's children."

Baldor placed his hands on Prudr's head and sought out her children and when he found their memories, he knew what he had to do. He asked Eris to help, and they both climbed between the turrets, producing their staffs to send their light towards where the children were last seen. Their power wasn't strong enough; it didn't penetrate the shadow surrounding Sol's home world.

"I don't understand," said Baldor. "I'm the light bearer yet my light is being deflected, what magic is this? It seems your children are shielded from us." To give Prudr hope he suggested trying every few hours.

"Let me try something else," said Eris, "There's one whose powers are so ancient they can break through even the most protected shield." She closed her eyes, faced the north, and sent out a message using her subconscious mind, "Father," she pleaded. "Hear my call and answer." There was no response, so she tried facing south and then east, but again, no response.

She faced west and this time flags at first billowed, then flapped violently. All torches extinguished causing Asgard to temporarily go into darkness. The squally winds were followed by a series of violent lightning bolts that lit up the heavens. They were announcing the arrival of Zeus's spirit.

"Tell me daughter," he asked, "Why has Chaos called on me?"

"There's a great sadness in the heart of Asgard," she replied, "two children from the bloodline of the 'All Father' are missing, taken by The Darkness. They are the children of Prudr and your old friend, Sol Invictus. Can you help?" Zeus thought for a moment.

"They still live," he said showing his compassion for Prudr's plight. "One is safe but only by the actions of the other. Even I cannot see where they're being held, a powerful magic shields them. Their light has not been extinguished but it's being tested. They're in all our futures; I have seen it." He then disappeared.

"Zeus has told us of a powerful magic shielding them," said Odi while embracing his sister, "there's no point in us sending out search parties until we find a way to undo the magic. I'll speak with the oracles and the wizards; they must be able to help. Zeus has given you hope, you will definitely see your children again."

Prudr got comfort from Odi's words but soon began to change. "Maximus," she said looking confused and puzzled. "Maximus," she repeated, "I hear you. Who are you?"

"What did you say?" asked Odi, "The last time I heard that name was when I was with Jacob."

"It's strange how I too mentioned that name," said Modi, it was just before I left Olympus. Zeus and Odin were there; they fobbed me off and said I should think no more of it."

Prudr was still trancelike when she continued, "There's a young boy, he's crying, he's one of two. His face is familiar, from when I was but a little girl." She remained quiet as her head turned from side to side, and then she said, "He looks like Magni, but he's not Magni."

"Should I send a search party?" asked Odi.

"No," replied Modi. "Odin and Zeus said we should ignore this."

Prudr said as she snapped out of her trance, "I plan to sit here, night after night, and listen for my children's call. Now that I know they'll answer."

"Not tonight, sister," said Odi helping her to stand. "Let's rejoin the celebrations, let Asgard see you and I are together again."

Prudr was unsure but agreed, she linked Odi, and they made their way back into the palace. She finally got to meet Panya who greeted her with a calming embrace lessening the effects of her great loss.

Chapter 7

While Odi and his family were settling in Asgard, the chariots carrying Girish, Manasa, and Hemish as well as Garuda and Mulan had passed through the Middle East, northern Iran, Afghanistan, and Pakistan to reach the border of India where four majestic ceremonial beasts were waiting. They were enormous bull elephants, each one fitted with a golden howdah, draped in the most exquisite of silk, edged by multicoloured frills and emblazoned with precious gems.

The gods mounted the elephants, and after several days they reached the upper reaches of the Indus River, following its course to its source on Mount Kailash.

During this time, they remained invisible trying to stay clear of the throngs of pilgrims visiting the abode of Lord Shiva. The closer they got to the foothills the more Manasa became alarmed; she sensed the presence of Shiva and found this confusing especially after watching him leave Olympus to travel across the universe with Zeus and the senior gods.

Her confusion was put to rest when they climbed the mountain and reached Shiva's grotto. He was present, and ecstatic to meet with them again.

"I wondered how long it would take before you got here?" he said. "I see you have brought guests."

"My lord," said Girish, "I'm confused, we saw you leave for the stars, what changed?"

"I did leave for the stars," replied Shiva, "but soon after I reached the moon, I heard prayers that spoke of the Ganges dying, how the waters slowed and then ceased. I couldn't allow that continue. I returned to find my matted hair, the lock I left to drip its life-giving water, had been stolen. While away a shadow entered my realm and did its worst, so I've decided to stay and jealously guard these sacred lands."

"I see you bring me another grandchild," he said while turning to Manasa and reaching in to embrace her, "this day gets better." Manasa was surprised; she didn't feel pregnant but was happy especially when she saw Girish's excited face.

Shiva then greeted Mulan and Garuda, "What is it about this day, the news gets even better. You too carry a little girl destined to be the 'Lioness of the Gods' who one day will wield great power. I see a boy and she will be his rock. He's already born and will grow to become a guardian of the gods. He is of Olympus and is one who is blessed by the Ancient One."

Mulan was thrilled, she and Garuda dreamt of being parents and this news was very welcome. Her day got better when Shiva continued with his prophecy, "Behind her will come twins, two boys, boisterous and rebellious, and they will break your hearts but when all seems lost, they will be the ones to save your realm. They too, with the help of Olympus, will become mighty gods of the east.

Shiva then took the lotus position and went into deep meditation causing the waters flowing from his matted hair to increase in volume. He also intensified the monsoons, releasing a deluge so great the plains of India were flooded deep into the interior.

Girish, in the meantime, used this time to plan his family's future. He made his way higher up the mountain searching for a glacial cave that was vast enough to become a palace suitable for him and his growing family. After two days searching, he finally found the ideal cave, one that was facing the southwest. With Garuda's help he put together his plans, and using their magic they began by raising the raw materials needed from the lower slopes up to the ridge.

Girish had a clear idea on how he wanted his palace to appear, especially as it was to be recessed deep into the ice cave. He wanted the main residence to be accessed through an ornately carved archway, made from the finest white marble. He envisaged two bulbous domes, one on each side of the archway. The main structure was to be uniform, with bedrooms and reception rooms running along each side of a vast hall. The ceilings were to be vaulted and emblazoned with colourful and delicate ornamentation. He envisioned the internal columns and floors finished using high quality, polished marble. The panels, ornately carved into the walls, were to be finished using decorative, geometric, and floral designs, surrounded by elaborate inscriptions in Indian and Persian. They worked day and night for four months to finish the palace and only relaxed when the enclosed gardens were completed. Garuda, as Emperor of the Birds, called on the nearby vultures and storks to carry in their beaks, all the silks and tapestries needed to soften the interiors. They then fashioned the surrounding glaciers in such a way that the palace blended into the mountain and was undetectable by pilgrims or mountain climbers alike.

The completion of the palace was just in time; Manasa went into labour and after a difficult eight hours, she gave birth to a beautiful baby girl whom she named Gaia. For Lord Shiva this was another great gift, especially when she quickly showed signs of being a future Earth Mother.

৩৯

Mulan and Garuda remained on Mount Kailash and assisted Girish and Manasa settle into their new home, but soon their desire to move on grew.

"I'm receiving visions of the five great mountains," said Garuda. "The very mountains revered by the people of China. They seek the Supreme Gods of the Heavens and pray for guardians to protect the central holy mountain. It seems it's us who are to become those guardians."

Mulan was delighted to be moving on knowing her unborn baby was rapidly growing. When she and Garuda were ready, they said their fare-wells then began making their way towards the Tibetan border to eventually cross into China. They travelled for many weeks and when they reached Mount Song, they were pleased to see that the Shaolin Monastery had totally recovered after the End Times battle. Everywhere else they travelled they'd discreetly materialise to help those who had nothing, they helped by donating a Gem of Beauty ensuring those they helped had enough to feed themselves for years to come. They also spent a lot of time planting tree seeds leaving behind fast growing saplings destined to become Flowering Trees of the East.

When passing any monastery, they always stopped just to listen to the tales been told by the elderly monks. They especially listened to the stories speaking of the gods who once dwelled on the five sacred mountains, and how back in the mists of time, those same gods ended the rule of the dark forces.

The monks always ended their stories by showing those listening the summits of the five mountains. They'd explain how those mountains were the birthplaces of the great rivers tasked with quenching the thirst of all in their path, especially the medicinal plants and healing herbs growing by their banks. They insisted all life be grateful for what the sacred mountains bestows on the natural world.

It pleased Garuda and Mulan to see how the people were listening and learning from the mistakes of the past, and everywhere they went people were living their lives based on the teachings of Lord Buddha.

They continued their journey, taking them high into the mountains where they found an ideal location to build their Yaodong. It was a cliff-face; set on a wide ridge, slightly indented so it can't be seen from above. What they planned was to be a modest home suitable for their status as Gods of the East. Their plans included a sunken walled courtyard with a perpetually flowering tree as its centrepiece; a tree they hoped would send its sweet scent out across the valley for all time.

As the days passed it became obvious the Yaodong wouldn't be ready for the arrival of the baby and this troubled Mulan prompting her to seek divine helpers, and within minutes five arrived, each bringing different skills.

They were the five reclusive and ancient Chinese gods of the mountains, and first to arrive was Táiháo, the blue/green dragon, and when he took his human form, he announced he was the deity of the Eastern Peak. He offered his skills as the wood carver, and he helped by creating the frames for the doors and windows as well as the supporting piles.

The next to arrive was Shaohao, the white dragon, and when he took his human form, he had with him all the metal beams, nails and scaffolding needed to prepare the site for the build ahead. He bowed to his brother god and then announced he was the white deity of the Western Peak.

A few moments later two more dragons arrived, they were the red and the black deities. The red dragon was Shenrong, and he was the deity of the Southern Peak. The black dragon announced himself to be Zhuánxú, also known as the warrior deity of the Northern Peak. Together they brought with them Fire and Water.

Garuda was delighted with their arrival but when the next dragon arrived, he was in awe. It was the yellow dragon, and he knew exactly who he was. It was Huangdi, the yellow emperor whom Girish and the Shaolin abbot met centuries earlier.

The five dragons helped Garuda and within two days the main structure was completed. This consisted of thick earthen walls, two meters deep ensuring full insulation helping to keep the Yaodong warm in winter and cool in summer. Those same walls were reinforced using the now ornately carved wooden supporting piles. The facade was finished using locally quarried stone, each engraved with intricate patterns depicting tales from across the five mountains. The roof was completed using Tongwa semicircle-shaped tiles completing the image of a traditional Chinese home. The tall, vaulted arches, and the high windows, allowed the sunlight to penetrate deep into the interior giving maximum light.

The interior itself included a great hall with a large reception and dining area, as well as four sizable bedrooms, all placed along the rear wall. Garuda designed a simple heating system using a large woodstove, connected by a concealed pipe system that travelled through all rooms to a hidden chimney. Each room was finished using sleek, highly lacquered wooden surfaces with geometric design latticework adorning entrances, windows, bed panels and cabinet doors.

Mulan came into her own by introducing Feng Shui for her interior design choices; she insisted all energy be channelled in such a way as to create harmony in every room. She started by introducing pale decorative lanterns to create a dimly lit atmosphere, and then placed her expertly hewn latticework furniture and screens into positions that optimised the positive 'chi'. When it came to her colour schemes, she blended warm neutrals with vibrant tones of red, black, and gold ensuring good luck for her family. She finished by decorating the living areas with ornate ceramic vases filled with blooming flowers symbolizing a new beginning.

While Mulan was completing the interior, Girish and the five dragons were outside putting the finishing touches to the sunken walled garden. It was an open space lending itself to maximum lightening and ventilation. The central tree, planted a few days earlier, was already in bloom and sending its sweet aroma out across the valley. Flower beds were planted, vegetable patches created, and seating areas set up. A robust wooden security fence was built with the main gate facing towards the only approach from the valley below. Added security was provided when Mulan and the gods used their magic to create an impenetrable shield tasked with protecting them from prying eyes.

Soon a baby girl, as foretold by Lord Shiva, was born and she was given the name Aria. She immediately showed signs of her power, crawling within days, climbing within weeks, and walking within months, she was showing that she was truly the Lioness of the Gods. All creatures scattered on sensing her nearby, but they soon learned she was no threat. She was in fact destined to become their protector and a guardian of the highlands.

Within two years of Aria's birth Mulan again fell pregnant. This time she gave birth to twin boys whom she named Hai and Li. From an early age they too showed signs of being Warrior Gods, they were strong and agile, they had no fear, and as each day passed their skills grew but needed taming.

For ten years peace reigned in the mountains, until one autumn day a strange tremor rolled between the five sacred peaks. Garuda took to the sky and no matter how hard he searched; he found nothing sinister. He used his powers as Emperor of the Skies, calling all birds into his presence, only to be told that they found nothing strange or sinister. He met with the five dragons who confirmed that they too felt the tremors.

Although still troubled Garuda returned to his family. "Strange how we felt the tremors," he said after greeting Mulan, "yet there's no damage. It's as though all is hidden in shadow. I'm not happy. Something evil is coming, its probing, it's sinister and I felt something like it before. I want us all on guard."

"I too feel a threat," replied Mulan walking over to look across the valley. "Preparing our children is now the priority. They need to know how to defend themselves. Aria will soon become a Goddess of China, part of the Light. My visions show her as the Lioness of the Gods, with a young and powerful god by her side. I can't see who he is, but he too walks in the Light. Our sons worry me, they're so innocent, ill-prepared to be gods," she linked Garuda's arm and rested her head on his shoulder. "They need your guidance and there's no better teacher than you to show them the ways of the gods."

"Well then," agreed Garuda, nodding in agreement, "it's decided, to-morrow morning we begin."

Chapter 8

The following morning Garuda rose early and left for a ridge higher up the mountain. There he took the lotus position and quickly travelled into enlightenment to meet up with Lord Buddha.

"There was a tremor," he said without opening his eyes. "It was unnatural and now I fear a new threat. I seek your guidance on how to prepare."

"I too felt the tremor," replied Lord Buddha, "it's hidden in Shadow. My visions show it getting stronger and it soon will be of concern. You're right to prepare. Teaching your children the ways of the gods is wise. You don't need my guidance; you have all the skills necessary to ensure they become true Gods of the East. Your sons will test you; they are already planning it. Be firm with them, they will need taming."

Garuda continued meditating and after two hours he was joined by his sons. They knew not to interrupt but Hai was curious. "Father looks a bit odd just sitting there," he said while winking at Li, "he's like a statue, will I pinch him?"

"You pinch his cheek," said Li, releasing a low snigger, "I'll pull his hair."

They moved closer and as they raised their hands they were taken aback; their father was suddenly gone. He disappeared before their very eyes causing them to panic. They ran from one side of the ridge to the other, checking behind every boulder. They couldn't find him. After a few tense moments they felt a tug on their ears and soon they suffered an unbearable pinching pain, and through their pain they heard, "The more I squeeze the more intense the pain. Tell me my wonderful sons, which is better, learning the ways of the east or suffering the pain inflicted by your father?"

"For Huangdi's sake," screamed both boys in unison, "let us go." Garuda obliged, then said, "We wait for your sister. Let this be your first lesson, PATIENCE."

The boys never had patience, always in a hurry. Like all twelve-year-olds all they wanted was fun, adventure, and to cause trouble, but this time they saw how their father had changed and for the first time they didn't know how to manipulate him. They waited for what felt like two long hours before Aria came into view, they got infuriated when they saw she had a grin from ear to ear. She was deliberately delaying her arrival by pausing and pretending to sniff the wildflowers growing all around her. Hai was not impressed; his temper had risen. He leapt up and ran towards his sister only to be tripped by a broken branch thrown by his father. Li was shocked, he had never seen anyone use such skills and never imagined his father would be so exact with the use of a broken branch. He chose to say nothing.

"Pappa," said Aria leaning in for a kiss, "mother took pity and insisted I join you; I planned to wait another hour."

"Your mother is a softy when it comes to her boys," replied Garuda, "they're the apples of her eye. You my darling will always be mine. Sit and let's wait."

Hai limped across, grinding his teeth pretending to be in pain. "No one cares about me?" he said looking for sympathy, "my knees are bleeding, and my face scratched."

"Your injuries will heal," said Garuda, "for your second lesson, learn to control your temper."

"Why do we sit and wait," asked Li, "what are we waiting for?"

"Patience," replied Garuda.

Garuda closed his eyes, so did Aria and Li. Their breathing was at first strong, and as the seconds passed it became almost inaudible. Eventually as their breathing completely softened everything went so quiet nothing was heard bar their heart beats. Hai was watching and soon lost interest. He tried to leave but found himself being levitated with his legs being forcefully put into the lotus position. He was placed alongside Aria and within seconds he too was softly breathing. He then heard a calming voice; it was Lord Buddha, "My friend Hai," he said. "Why so impatient? Why such a temper? You're a son of powerful gods and destined to be the God of the Seas, a protector of the Oceans. Like Poseidon, you will become a guardian of the waves and reefs, but your domain will be the eastern waters close to my realm. Listen to your father, for two thousand years he has walked with me, and there's no better teacher. Listen to his words for they will be your saviour."

Hai opened his eyes and looked at his father, sister and brother and was taken aback at how peaceful they looked. He looked at the rolling clouds, the snow-capped mountains and then listened to the sounds of the forest. His eyes closed and he was overwhelmed by a need to sleep. His hands moved to rest on his crossed legs, and he was surprised to feel them being gently helped to form the perfect resting position. He totally relaxed and made his way into the Dreamworld.

When he opened his eyes, he found he was in a quite different place, it was the place where only those who were followers of the teachings of Lord Buddha dwelled. He wondered why he was allowed in considering he was always questioning the ways of his parents. He saw his father up ahead and ran to join him. "Why have you brought us to this most wondrous place?" he asked.

"I brought you here, my son, for you to look upon this ancient forest and its magnificent trees. I brought you here to submerge into the pristine lake just so you can see the beauty oozing from the vibrant colours of the creatures that swim and feed in its crystal-clear waters. I brought you here so you would begin learning the ways of the east, the ways of Lord Buddha. You will learn of his peace and how to defend it. You are children of the gods and will wield great power. Here I'll teach you how to control and use that power for all that's good."

Hai, Li, and Aria brought their hands together and bowed to their father. They submitted to his calmness and waited for him to begin their lessons.

"There are five tenets in Buddhism you must always obey. Never kill human or animal. Never lie. Never take what's not yours. Never be promiscuous. Never allow into your body what changes you. If you obey these simple rules and lead a good and honest life you will always have Lord Buddha by your side."

They walked deeper into the forest, all the time gently caressing the high grasses, softly stroking the tree bark, and carefully moving so as not to inadvertently injure or kill any insect they meet. Garuda was pleased by how cautious they were.

"Tell me, my children," he asked, "Do you feel his presence?" They all indicated they felt something.

He then suggested they close their eyes and think of their home. They did and when they opened their eyes, they found themselves back in their own domain. They were shocked by how much time had passed; it was now twilight.

The following morning Hai and Li were first to arrive for breakfast and were, as always, boisterous, and unruly pre-teens. As soon as Garuda arrived, they immediately quietened and acted respectful. Aria arrived, grabbed some fruit, and made her way out for her morning walk.

"Where do you think you're going, young lady?" asked Garuda.

"I'm meeting with the mountain lions," she replied, "their cubs are due today."

"Nature looks after its own," said Garuda, "Remain here, your training with your brothers begins shortly." Aria complied, knowing it wasn't wise to defy her father.

After breakfast they went out to the courtyard where Aria, Hai and Li sat on the bench near the Flowering Tree. Garuda sat opposite them. "Yesterday," he began, "while in the Dreamworld, I spoke about the five precepts of Buddhism, do you remember?"

"Never kill human or animal; never lie," said Hai.

"Never take what's not yours," said Aria.

"Never allow into your body what will change you, never be promiscuous," said Li.

"I'm impressed," smiled Garuda showing how pleased he was, "you all remembered. That's a promising start. Tell me what else is important?"

"We must lead good and honest lives," answered Li, "and we must use our powers to assist with the conservation and protection of the natural world."

"We must walk the five mountains," said Aria, "walk as their guardians for it's there where Mother Earth and Father Sky always come together."

"Father," asked Hai. "I look around at the beauty of the five mountains: mountains unmatched anywhere in the world. How do we protect the plants and animals as well as the magic and sanctity of these lands when we've no skills?"

Garuda left his chair and walked towards the gate, he gestured for his children to follow and said while walking away, "Trust me, you have the skills, you just need to hone them. Today we continue your lessons. Let us walk through the forest and see what happens." He stepped back and allowed his children walk ahead. He watched their every move and for many miles there were no incidents until they heard, "Li. Freeze."

Li froze with one foot touching the ground and the other held above the ground. Garuda joined him. "Look down," he said, "Tell me what you see."

"I see a caterpillar," said Li trying not to move, "it's slowly crawling across the pathway. Father was I about to kill her?"

"Yes, my son," said Garuda placing his hand on his son's head, "you were about to kill her. Think about it. Within weeks, she will turn into a most beautiful butterfly. On the first flap of her wings a new wind will be created, a tiny and almost undetectable wind, but somewhere in a distant land that wind will join with all other new winds and a hurricane will be born."

"But father," interrupted Aria, "surely hurricanes are bad; killing the caterpillar will save many lives."

"No," said Hai meekly, "father is right. All creatures have the right to life. Only nature can take it away. Nature sends the hurricanes to destroy, and from its passing new life will grow. It's not the place of gods or man to end life; it is the sole responsibility of Mother Nature and Mother Nature alone."

"It seems," said a pleased Garuda, "one of my sons is learning the ways of Lord Buddha. Let us walk in silence and see where the path takes us. Listen carefully to the sounds of the forest and when we reach the clearing tell me what you hear."

They walked for many more miles and on their way, they began separating what they were hearing, they were learning the sounds of the forest. Their hearing became so acute they learned to distinguish from each other the sound of leaves falling, branches straining, twigs breaking, birds chirping, mammals foraging, bear scratching, rivers flowing and insects flying. As they passed through villages, they remained invisible, all the while learning to separate the different Chinese dialects. The further they walked the more their powers grew; they were becoming gods of the east.

"Father," said Aria while pointing at a nearby majestic tree. "I've never seen so many leaves, as each one falls two more grow. I see what looks like a light filled string and it's travelling from leaf to leaf. What is it?"

"It's rare for one so young to see the string," replied Garuda "it tells me you are not only a Lioness of the Gods, but you are also a Goddess of the Light, one who will be powerful. The string is the life force binding all life together, every bud, every leaf, every branch, everyone, or everything that walks, crawls, flies, and swims. It is an ancient energy that gets its power from the first source light."

"Father," said Li pointing towards the summit of the yellow peak. "It's the yellow dragon and he looks troubled."

"Father," interrupted Hai, "I sense something is wrong. Look at all five summits, the dragons are on alert."

Garuda looked up at each summit then reached into his satchel and extracted his staff to call on the Light and it came. He sent it out across the valleys but nothing sinister showed. He then raised his arms, transformed into the Emperor of the Skies, and King of all Birds. Aria, Hai, and Li knew their father had the power to shape-shift, but had never seen him do it, they were in awe.

He flew to meet with the yellow dragon only to be told of a sinister shadow travelling through the sacred mountains. He looked across at the other dragons and saw the same concerns showing in their faces. He took to the sky and flew much higher; this time he saw a shadow with no source. He flew closer but it just faded then disappeared. He rushed to land where he last saw the shadow and found a destroyed village, one that had just suffered horrific scenes of devastation. He walked through the gates to be met by listless grieving survivors who froze with fear on seeing a giant bird. He took his human form and immediately the people relaxed, they felt a god was among them.

Garuda stood there as a very tall and handsome man wearing a brilliant white, black lapelled and collared, loose sleeve Shenyi robe favoured by the ancient Han peoples. His long raven-black hair was tied up in the traditional style of those same peoples. What made him stand out were the gold-coloured embroidered symbols depicting the power of the ancient gods. By his side he wore his golden sword, and in his hand was his crystal tipped staff showing he was ready for anything that might come at him. He stood there and waited then said, "What took you so long?"

It was Hai, Li, and Aria; they had arrived on the backs of three majestic male mountain lions. "Father," said Aria. "I used my power as the Lioness of the Gods to call for help and look what came; they got us here as fast as they could."

She dismounted, wearing a most amazing midnight blue Hanfu robe with an underskirt that was a vivid jade, and embroidered with gold threads showing her true form. Her dark hair hung loose at the sides and back but was partially tied up into a bun. The villagers found it difficult to avert their eyes such was her beauty.

Hai and Li dismounted, acknowledged their father, and immediately moved to help the injured. For two twelve-year-olds they were very decisive. Li was particularly strong and used his strength to single handily lift heavy debris from the trapped. Hai had the power to use water for healing and spent his time taking the pain away. For both, seeing so many corpses was unsettling especially those that were half eaten with their visible bones showing signs of being gnawed.

"Do you see them?" asked Aria who hadn't moved from her father's side. "There are many and they have such speed, see how they move rapidly from tree to tree. Their red sinister eyes are unsettling, and they smell of death."

"I saw them just as I landed," replied Garuda, "there are no more than ten so worry not my daughter; together we will send them back to where they came from. I'm trying to figure out what they are, but they do seem to move in shadow. Let's wait to see what they will do."

"Do they fear the gods?" asked Aria, "I'm wondering why they haven't attacked. Is it possible they see our Light and fear us?" Garuda didn't reply.

"The dragons are coming," he said.

Within minutes the loud flapping of wings was heard causing panic to spread among the survivors while watching five dragon's land. The dragons took their human form and moved to stand alongside Garuda and Aria.

"The shadow people have left," said Huangdi. "While flying we saw them scurry into cracks in the outcrop of rock yonder."

"My lord," asked Aria, "do you know who, or what we are dealing with?"

"There are whispers in the wind," he replied, "and they grow louder as each hour passes. There's talk of a new menace rising, something unknown, it's a menace that seems to hide out in the cosmos."

"The Light announced the death of a Sun God," said Zhuánxú, "and that is a concern. We know not which one. Astral ships speak of the Titans, all twelve have been sighted, they are said to have come back together. If true we should be worried."

"Father," said Aria changing the subject, "you must be so proud of Hai and Li? Look how hard they work. They haven't stopped; they're bringing hope and peace to the villagers. Look how they build the funeral pyre and place the bodies in such a respectful way. They have taken on to themselves all the pain of the villagers." Garuda just nodded; he was pleased.

The five dragons walked over to the pyre, surrounding it. They raised their heads, and the Light came to join them together. When the circle was complete their Light shot into the pyre igniting it, allowing it to burn until nothing but ash was left.

The dragons remained in the village until the fire extinguished then made their way back to their respective mountains. Before he left Huangdi brought Aria, Hai, and Li together. "Follow the path," he said, "it will take you to the sacred Shaolin Monastery. Speak with the abbot and learn the ways of the crane, dragon, leopard, snake, and tiger. Only then will you be ready to become the gods you are destined to be."

"What my lord Huangdi speaks of is called Kung Fu," said Garuda. "It's an art form that spans hundreds of years, and it's alive. Lord Huangdi is right, Shaolin will teach you a style of defence necessary to be a true warrior. You will learn of appropriate weapons and common sounds, but most importantly you will learn the style and prowess of the five animals he spoke of."

There was no more to be done so they rejoined the path they were travelling and continued with the peaceful and calming ways of Lord Buddha. They carefully watched every step they took and learned to identify every sound they heard. After a while they reached the red doors of the renowned Shaolin monastery where on admission they were ushered into the Great Hall. While waiting they were excited to see a portrait of their father, hung alongside their mother and Girish. They were painted as Messengers of the Gods, dressed in their imperial Olympus robes and armour. On a brass plaque that ran the length of the three portraits was written in Chinese script - 'Messengers of the Gods - Saviours of Shaolin'.

They were brought through to the shrine of the Golden Buddha where the abbot was meditating. He never opened his eyes, but he was very aware, "Welcome my friend and saviour, it's written of how your return will usher in the rise of Shadow, is this why you prepare? My hearing tells me you've brought me three students."

"I've brought you my daughter and my two sons, and yes, I fear it's time to prepare for what seems to be the rise of a Shadow, whatever that is. My children need to learn quickly because something's not right. Can you do this for me?"

"Of course I can," replied the abbot after thinking for a moment, "Call back in three days and you'll be collecting three masters."

Garuda said his goodbyes and immediately left for home. He took to the sky and flew to reach Mulan as quickly as he could. On reaching his Yaodong he removed his Shenyi and stood at the door half naked, "I've a present for you and it's going to last three days, a three-day holiday. Let's make the most of it."

"It took you long enough," she replied with a wry smile. "I thought you'd have got rid of them long before now? I have this need only you can fulfil."

"That's some pressure," said Garuda while removing the last of his clothes.

"If I remember correctly," she said while gently caressing his back, "you're always at your best while under pressure,"

Three days of bliss followed.

Back in Shaolin the lessons began at once. They started with meditation that lasted two hours, followed by learning to master self-control. Then there was lunch. After lunch, tutoring in martial arts began under a renowned Sifu, an expert with many years' experience.

The first movement they learned was the dragon technique, and to learn it effectively they had to understand the Dragon.

"Consider the dragon as the highest of all animal forms," said the Sifu, "learn of its 'Shen' or 'Spirit' and you will have a clear and powerful mind. When you master your mind, you will then use the dragon form to sway and curve. You will learn to master smooth and soft movements without moving your feet. Mastering the dragon form will mean that for you, defence and attack will become the same movement. You will learn to use your hands as your weapon, used just for striking. It will be known as your dragon palm." For the rest of the day, they practiced and learned to allow the spirit of the dragon enter their minds, helping them to master the movements of the highest of all animal forms.

The following day they spent another two hours in meditation before learning the ways of another two animals. "This morning you will learn the way of the tiger," said the Sifu. "Allow him in and you will learn to strengthen your bones and core. A firm core allows you crouch with a strong posture to pounce and finish an opponent quickly. The whole purpose of the tiger form is to be sudden yet simple so as to complete a move with strength and power." For the next few hours, they practiced, and soon they managed to control the power of the tiger.

After lunch, the next lesson was all about the crane and how its movement strengthened their sinews and increased their energy. "Go to the lake and watch the crane," said the Sifu, "study their frame as they stand on one leg. Note how the crane is not one of aggression or one to strike first, it is one who knows how to block and counterattack. Watch and learn how they balance and yet can have fast foot movements while using circular motion to block attacks. Observe their beak and see how you can use your hand in a hook shape movement to successfully block any attack and focus on how that block should be the start of your counterattack. You will learn to use your full force to wound or disable a single point. As you learn the way of the crane form, you will realise how a medium cat stance will allow you use the power of your opponent against them. The tiger form is a technique suitable to use against tall opponents, but the crane form is more suitable for smaller and weaker people. The crane form can be used against the tiger form because to use it means you have mastered the art of combat strategy and will have developed speed, accuracy, and agility along with timing, balance, and coordination."

As instructed, they made their way to the lake where they spent the afternoon studying and copying the graceful movements of the crane. They were joined by their Sifu and together all four practiced as a cohesive group until they perfected each move. When the Sifu was satisfied they had achieved perfection he said, "Tomorrow will be your last day, and you will learn of the snake and the leopard form. When mastered, your training will then be complete. Go now and rest."

The following morning was special; many of the young monks had come to watch and join in on the final days training. The Sifu said as he presented a snake, "Always remember how the snake is the most cunning of them all, it can remain so still it deceives, its speed when ready to strike is so lethal it's devastating. It looks so trancelike that its breathing is shallow, hiding an internal power. Beware that power, learn how to use it. Observe my snake fist, see how my finger is the main point of the strike; it can be terminal when used on vulnerable areas such as the eyes, throat, or groin. Never underestimate the power of the snake form, for it uses slyness and softness rather than a hard raw power. It's the one that looks soft until it strikes hard. It has amazing speed but far more importantly, you must learn how it uses its smoothness and flow. Go now and practice."

They practiced for several hours and when they showed they had mastered the ways of the snake form they were told to rest before being called for lunch.

After lunch there was a brief respite from the continuous training while the Sifu greeted Garuda who had returned to collect his children. When he arrived, he was surprised at the changes he saw, especially in his sons. Two and half days and they were no longer boys but had the appearance of two strong youths. He was also shocked to see Aria no longer looked like an early teen but had taken on the appearance of a most beautiful sixteen-year-old goddess. He remarked to the Sifu, "I was always in awe of the way Time in Olympus worked, it seems it works in the same way here in Shaolin. My children have aged almost overnight." He stood back and watched the Sifu begin the final lesson.

The Sifu called his pupils together. "This afternoon we learn of the leopard, always remember that the goals of this form are three-fold. The first is to develop muscle speed for external strength. The second is to learn patience, and the third is to apply the primary weapon, the leopard fist. Its punch is useful for deep penetration and lower body springing power. Do not rely on rooted stances except while in attack mode, this makes it easier to launch at an opponent. When you see the leopard, you will note how its form focuses on fast and short-range attacks, and to fully practice this form, you need a mix of balance, speed, flexibility, and agility. In the wild you will see how the explosive bursts of strength and speed are used for low kicks, forearm, and elbow strikes. Always favour strikes on soft parts of the body such as the face, throat, ribs, or the pit of the stomach. Don't be afraid to use a leopard block which always strikes joints and then can be quickly used to protect yourself. Use the leopard strike for it is powerful and can be found halfway between the style of the tiger and the crane."

Garuda stood on the highest step watching sixty monks arrive to form six lines from the front gate up to the entrance of the temple, he watched his two sons, and his daughter join them by standing behind the Sifu, and then a most wonderful and perfect display of fluent Kung Fu movements began.

When practice ended Garuda indicated it was time to leave. All four thanked the monks for their hospitality and said their farewells. They left and soon reached a ridge just above the monastery where Garuda said, "It's a long walk home so maybe it's time I carried you just as I did when you were toddlers." He transformed into the Mythical Bird and gestured for them to mount his back. He took to the sky and soon they reached their home where Mulan was excitedly waiting.

Even though she was excited, she was troubled. "While you were away," she said, calling Garuda aside, "I received a vision. It showed Jacob summoning children to Olympus. He's planning a school to teach them the ways of the gods. Aria was there, and she becomes enormously powerful. She commands the lions."

"Today," remarked Garuda, "I felt another tremor and this one again silently rolled through the five mountains. It was more sinister yet, with all my power, I couldn't find its source. If Jacob is planning a school, it can only mean the Ancient One has reached out to him and is giving him a warning of something coming our way, something strange and evil."

Chapter 9

Meanwhile back in Olympus Jacob and Eala had become used to being alone, with only their three children and three stewards for company. It was a blissful time that seemed to just drift by.

Soon ten years had passed and for the last four of those, hormones were racing, causing the usual conflicts between parents and their children. Jacob watched Helena like a hawk especially when there were visitors with teenage boys. He was extremely strict with Obelius but a little more understanding of the gentleness of Demetrius.

Throughout the cosmos the children of the gods were also reaching their sixteenth year and many of them were beginning to recklessly use their powers. Some had great difficulty and even with the help of their parents they found themselves troubled and out of control.

In the temple, things were equally difficult; Obelius was getting more rebellious and arrogant. Demetrius was still gentle and kind but had no direction or purpose to his life, while Helena was ahead of them and had become a Mistress of the Light. She had the ability to create magical scenes using distinct colours and strengths of light, but her real power showed when she learned to bend that very same light. Jacob was forever on guard and watching over them to the point of being intrusive.

One day while sitting with Eala, enjoying the afternoon sun, and watching Helena race the white stallions across the meadows, he said,

"That one is going to give me nightmares, she will have them calling from everywhere and I'll be chasing them out across the universe."

"She is most beautiful," said Eala laughingly as she reached across to reassure him, "don't be surprised if the one she meets is the one you least expect."

"OK, ok, prophetess," said Jacob while turning to stare at her. "Who is he?"

"You are the last one I'd tell," she replied while walking away, "I can see you chasing away every boy who comes near her. The meadows will have skid marks and warning signs; you are too protective. Remember, she's a mistress of the Light and will soon be a goddess, she can handle herself."

Jacob, out of nowhere announced, "I've got an idea!"

Eala threw her eyes to the heavens. "Oh, here we go again. What is it this time?"

"If you're going to give me attitude," he replied, showing his annoyance, "I won't tell you."

"Well then," she sneered, "suit yourself!"

"I'm serious," he said unable to let it go. "I've been receiving messages from across the cosmos telling me of difficulties our friends are having with their young gods. Father Time is bringing their ages together and just like our three, they're all reaching their sixteenth year."

"It never fails to amaze me how Time works," Eala said after returning to sit with him and link his arm, "ours were born two thousand years ago. Odi's were born less than fifty years ago. Hemish was born over two hundred years ago. I can go on, yet their ages are all aligning. OK, what's your idea?"

"Now, this is it and don't laugh," he paused while waiting for a reaction then continued, "I want to start a lyceum! A school here in Olympus!" He again waited for a reaction and when none came said, "Look at that little prick, Obelius. I love him to bits, but he gets on my nerves, he has no control. He needs discipline, he needs schooling."

"Did you come up with that idea all by yourself?" said an extremely impressed Eala, causing Jacob to get annoyed, get to his feet and walk away.

"Are we going away in a huff?" she jokingly asked.

He stopped, turned around, and Eala immediately saw the glint in his eye, he ran back and grabbed her. He threw her over his shoulder and carried her, kicking and screaming towards the lagoon. When he reached the water's edge, he threw her into a deep pool, and she wasn't impressed. She let her feelings be known but he knew how to manipulate her, he slowly removed his cape, then his tunic and then began to undo his breeches. He paused before tying them up again; he enjoyed teasing her. She folded her arms and looking sternly at him said, "I know what you are after so get them off and get in here before I lose interest."

He didn't need much persuasion; he was soon naked and stood watching as she removed her saturated gown. He dived in and speedily swam towards her. For them these moments were magic, they loved their alone time swimming along the sea floor and visiting the oyster beds. They always included a swim along the torch colonnade bringing them close to the realm of the Mer-People.

When they surfaced Eala cupped her hands and flicked the gathered water in Jacob's face. That was the one thing he always knew was the signal for him to make his move and he did. He swam closer for a kiss before placing his arms around her. "Do you know?" he said, "its times like this when I'm at my happiest, I love my family but just you and me, alone in the lagoon; it takes my breath away. I cherish these amazing moments."

Eala reached up and eased his head towards her, softly kissed him then said, "Ever since that first time I set my eyes on you I've lived for these moments. The feelings I had all those years ago are the same as the ones I have now, I love you more than anything else…. well except for my babies, of course."

"You really know how to throw in a passion killer. Did you see that little fu..." he said as he pretended to push her away. "He deliberately does things just to get my back up."

"You surprise me," she said while pulling him closer. "I didn't know it was possible for anything to kill your passion. For me it would take a lot more than the thoughts of our three to kill the feelings I have right now, how about you do what you do best?"

They kissed again allowing for the slow and steady build-up of passion to continue; soon they couldn't take their hands off each other and they began drifting towards becoming one.

Back in the Temple, Demetrius and Obelius were watching, "Here we go again," Obelius sighed. "They're going to start wrestling."

"Really," Demetrius exclaimed while slowly turning to stare at his brother. "Wrestling, is that what you call it? You're sixteen and you still call it wrestling?"

"Wha... wha..." said Obelius getting very flustered, "What do you call it?"

Demetrius was unsure of what to say, he worried he too would get it wrong, he then said,

"Remember when Viktor last visited, he told me about his mother and father and how they were always humping, so I call it humping."

"That's a great word," said Obelius, "mother and father are humping out in the Lagoon. Yeah, I'm going to use that word."

The boys didn't realise Helena had arrived and was standing behind them. She gripped both their necks and said, "My innocent, innocent brothers, gossiping again, are we a little jealous?" She released them then continued, "Surely father had 'The Talk' or were you not listening? Mother had the talk with me, and she called it 'Making Love,' so I prefer just to call it 'Making Love'." She took them both by the arms, "I think it's time we left for the other side of the temple."

Obelius started sniggering causing Demetrius to try stifle a laugh and this got Helena curious, "Are you going to let me in on the secret?"

"No," they said in unison.

She insisted and Demetrius gave in, "Father tried, but that idiot made everything very difficult for him. He wanted to talk about the joining of a man and a woman, but all Obelius wanted to talk about was the holes he found on the trees in the woods, or on the ground, even in rocks. He would say, 'Why would I need a woman when all I have to do is walk around our realm?' Fathers face was priceless; he'd get up and leave, shaking his head as he left, but he always tried again a few days later."

"Just for the record," Obelius interjected. "I never used any of the holes, I was only teasing."

"Is that so," enquired Demetrius furrowing his brow, "where do you go for you lone time?"

Obelius went bright red and walked off without answering. Helena placed her hands across her ears and headed in the opposite direction.

Back in the lagoon Jacob and Eala continued kissing with a passion that had no end, their desires for each other fuelled each time their soft and silk-like skin came together. Their kisses were always of such a raw intensity that when their tongues entwined a breathlessness came, threatening to overpower them, but they had no fear, they knew their bodies fitted perfectly together and in such a way that ecstasy was always their destiny. Their feelings for each other were like something written about in an ancient love story. They were so madly in love they soon drifted into a space ensuring they were lost in time.

Jacob might have been a slow learner while living in Dublin, but in Olympus he became a master, he knew when and where to touch and for how long he should remain kissing one place, he had quickly learned how to stretch his fingers so far apart that when they travelled down her back, no part was left untouched. When he reached those sensitive places Eala gingerly arched, bringing her so close to him he had no choice but to slowly begin thrusting before quickening the pace. His skill as her lover meant he knew when to slow down, prolonging the build-up so as to bring her to the ecstasy she had become accustomed to.

For him, holding back was difficult, but when he finally let go it was always explosive, and he looked forward to being held when the weakness came. Today was no different to all other times, they became one and held each other in an embrace of pure love before starting all over again. Their lovemaking went on for many hours because each time was always better than the last.

It was as the bell tolled, when they finally left the water and made their way back into the temple.

"Father, you look very flushed," said Obelius, trying to stifle a smile. "Is everything Ok?" Jacob chose to ignore him.

"Gee father," said Demetrius, showing some concern. "Are your legs sore? You seem to be walking with difficulty."

Jacob bit his lip and again chose to ignore the sly comments. When he took his seat, he noticed the sneaky grins and the hand gestures, again he chose to ignore them; then, he announced, "While your mother and I were........."

"Humping?" interrupted Demetrius.

"Wrestling?" said Obelius with another sneaky smile.

"While your mother and I were in the Lagoon," Jacob continued, trying and keep a straight face and refusing to look his sons in the eye, "we decided to start a lyceum which we believe will help you learn to control your powers. You will have the wisdom of Apollo and Chiron available to you, and I know their experience and knowledge will be invaluable. I also have an option to call on the power of the wizards. What do you think?"

Obelius nearly had a fit and was first to react.

"Just because you were in the lagoon having the time of your lives," he yelled, "doesn't mean you can come in here to ruin ours. No way, I can manage, thank you very much."

"I'm interested," said an excited Demetrius. "I need help with my visions and the whisperings I hear from Mother Nature. I don't understand how, when so many things go wrong, she always seems to find a way. That confuses me more and more."

"I think it'll be good," said a very happy Helena. "Will there be boys?"

Jacob looked at Eala while at the same time, grinding his teeth; he wondered was Helena teasing him by mentioning boys, but he was more interested in staring at Obelius and giving him one of his famous disapproving looks. Obelius retaliated and stuck his tongue out. Jacob grinned and said, "Well then, it's settled."

Obelius was not impressed. He stormed off towards the dunes to spend some time firing stones into the water. When he calmed, he returned to the temple but didn't apologise for his behaviour. He was just in time to see his father use one of his many powers.

Jacob stood at the centre of the Great Hall and just as Zeus did all those years ago, he looked towards the rafters and focused on one of the friezes. It was the frieze holding the heralds of the Angels and he called on them to answer.

When they landed, they bowed and listened to his request. They raised their trumpets and sent out a most magical sound that travelled to all pantheons. It travelled across the universe and broke through the shields of the dragon realm. It announced to all that Olympus was opening a lyceum and inviting the children of the gods to attend.

There was immense joy across the cosmos, parents were so relieved they rushed to pack satchels. In Asgard Odi slumped back into his chair unable to betray how delighted he was. Panya was equally excited and was heard to say, "Can you imagine poor Jacob trying to keep the peace between Thora and Viktor, they hate each other. I'd love to be a fly on that wall."

"Never mind Jacob," said Odi. "Can you imagine Asgard without our six young gods, the peace, oh the peace. I can't wait. Please tell me the chariots are outside ready to go."

In Africa, Zane was ecstatic, the thoughts of getting away from his four toddler brothers was exciting. He was the fastest to pack and first to make his way towards the portal. On his way he met up with a very upset Jamilah and Jahiri who were already missing their daughter. He promised them he'd look after Sagal and make sure she'd safely arrive at Olympus.

In the east the young gods needed no persuasion. Aria's powers had grown, and she too heard the call of Olympus, she excitedly ran to her mother. "I Know, I know," said Mulan "I heard it too. Your satchel is already packed."

"Are you trying to get rid of me?" asked a surprised Aria.

"No, my darling," said Mulan attempting to reassure her. "I'm not trying to get rid of you. I saw a vision while you were in the Shaolin monastery and knew this day was coming. I'm not worried because I know you'll be safe under the protection of Olympus."

"Until you're in Olympus," said Garuda while preparing to leave, "I don't believe you'll be safe. I'll escort you to the borders of the Indus. There you'll meet with Hemish and Gaia and I must insist that all three of you travel together."

Without further delay Garuda took to the sky, carrying Aria on his back. He raced towards the Himalayas, flying high above the peaks. He increased his speed to rapidly reach the Indus River where in the distance he was delighted to see Girish, Hemish and Gaia were waiting.

"I've missed you so much," he said while running to embrace Girish.

"You seem tense," replied Girish. "Is everything ok?"

"Something's wrong," said Garuda, "shadow has shown its face again and many nearby villagers were killed. I want Aria in Olympus as soon as possible. Do we travel with them or trust them to look after themselves?"

"I've felt nothing sinister," replied Girish, "and although I trust my children to be careful, I remember how easily we were deceived. Maybe we should travel with them, at least until they reach the desert near Olympus."

"Well then, it's settled," said Garuda, "we'll travel with them."

"I don't think so," interrupted Aria showing her annoyance, "I've been looking forward to a student's freedom and I intend having it. You can both go home and leave us in peace."

"I agree," said Gaia, "I've had visions showing us arriving in Olympus and being greeted by Jacob and Eala."

"I'm not so sure," said Garuda turning back to Aria, "remember what you witnes..." he was interrupted when she angrily made it clear they were leaving at once, and they were leaving alone.

"Everyone relax," yelled Hemish, "I have a plan, and that plan will ensure we reach Olympus within two days.

"And your plan is?" asked Girish.

"It's my plan and you just have to trust me," he replied.

Hemish summoned three elephants and when they arrived, he, Aria, and Gaia, prepared to leave. They said their goodbyes and made their way across the border into Pakistan.

"Now that's something I didn't see coming," said Girish with a wry smile, "it seems my son can be quite assertive when least expected."

Garuda still wasn't happy. He insisted they discreetly follow them just to be sure. He transformed into the Emperor of the Skies and with Girish on his back they secretly followed while hidden behind the higher peaks. After twenty-four hours they watched Hemish open a portal and then disappear.

"So that was his plan," said Girish, "he is Lord of the Earth with the power to open portals. So that's how he intended reaching Olympus in two days."

"Did you know?" asked Garuda.

"Like all our children," replied Girish, "their powers are growing and need taming. Jacob's plan will work. Put Aria from your mind and visit Kailash."

"I'll fly us to Kailash but will only stay for a few moments," said Garuda. "It's not safe to leave Mulan and my boys alone."

"Manasa and Lord Shiva will be pleased to see you."

In the meantime, Galyna, daughter of Mia and Andras, was preparing to leave the Dragon Realm. She was one of the first to accept the invitation from Olympus, but she was travelling alone. Drayce, the son of King Derwyn and Queen Isabella, was already travelling, but not towards Olympus. He was troubled and wanted to be alone. Isabella used her powers as a dragon mother to telepathically reach him, directing him to change his plans and follow Galyna.

Jacob's school was soon to have sixteen children of the gods as its pupils.

Chapter 10

Two days had passed since the trumpeters sent out their sweet music and soon the sound of a chariot was heard coming from the north, prompting a steward to investigate and then alert Jacob. He and Eala quickly prepared and when ready they stood on the highest step outside the main doors in all their Olympus finery. Helena stood alongside them. Obelius and Demetrius took a position a short distance away. Together they watched the first chariot arrive.

"Obe," whispered Demetrius shooting his arm across his brother's chest, "I think something has stirred?"

"Something has stirred," said Obelius looking down at his brother's crotch. "Cover yourself, you pervert." Demetrius didn't care; he just kept staring.

"Do you blame me?" said Demetrius, "look at her, she's more beautiful than Aphrodite."

"Never mind her," gasped Obelius. "Look at him, its Viktor. He's over six foot tall and broader than the God of Thunder. Once he was my best friend, now look at him? He stands before us as a most powerful Norse warrior. I can still see the free spirit that dwells in him. I bet he's now the conqueror of all he touches, look at his muscles, they're bigger than fathers."

"Enough of this muscle worshipping," laughed Demetrius, "just feast your eyes on her, she must be Lovisa, his sister. See how she stands before us as a most beautiful and powerful Warrior Goddess. I think father's idea for this lyceum is going to get very interesting."

Viktor took his sister's hand and together they bowed before Jacob and Eala. They were made very welcome. "My parents send you their regards," said Viktor, "they heard your call and seem really happy to be rid of us. They've sent us to learn the ways of the gods."

"It's lovely to see you again," said Eala while reaching in to hug him. "I can't believe how you have grown, and trust me, if I could find a way to get rid of a certain one of mine, I would." She looked up at Obelius who in turn stuck his tongue back at her.

Obelius then ran down the steps and said as he gripped Viktor, "You've definitely grown since your last visit, remember the time we raided Hephaestus's workshop."

"We were only five," laughed Viktor, "and for the record, you raided, I watched." Obelius brought Viktor to join him while Lovisa moved to be next to Helena. "Hi," she said "we've never met. Thora speaks of you all the time. She'll be with us shortly."

"Look out towards the tree line and tell me what you see," said Eala getting more excited.

"I see three tuskers," said Viktor straining to see into the distance, "they're carrying two goddesses and one who looks like a mystic god. He sits in the lotus position and hovers above the elephant."

"That's Hemish," said Jacob, "but who are the goddesses? Interesting?"

When the elephants arrived the three young gods dismounted and bowed before Jacob. "Hemish, Lord of the Earth, you are most welcome," said an ecstatic Jacob. He turned to the goddesses, "My ladies, forgive me, we haven't met."

"I am Gaia," said the nearest one, "sister of Hemish, daughter of Girish and Manasa. Lord Shiva has foretold that I, one day, will be an Earth Mother and goddess to the Indus. My parents send to you their regards." Demetrius's mouth dropped, his stirring got stronger. He forgot all about Lovisa.

Obelius was heard to say when the second goddess stepped forward. "Deme? that stirring you spoke of; I know what you mean. I've just wet myself. Look at her, she is the Lioness of the Gods and already she's got her claws sunk deep into me. I see her doing things to me; I think I need to go to the dunes. I'm the pillar of strength that will forever guard this temple, but my weakness will be her."

"My lord Jacob," said the second goddess. "I am Aria, daughter of Mulan and Garuda. For some reason they couldn't wait to get rid of me, they wanted me under the protection of Olympus."

"Tell me," Jacob asked, showing his concern, "what is it your parents have seen that makes them want you under the protection of Olympus?"

"Father has seen a Shadow," she replied, "and it troubles him. When we reached a village deep in the five sacred mountains, Shadow had showed itself by killing many. What we found was death, destruction, and grief. The bones of those who fell were gnawed upon. When the five dragon gods arrived, the Shadow disappeared. My father felt a tremor, so did they, a rolling yet soft tremor. Father again took to the sky, and with the five deities, they found nothing. He's on alert and has trained me, and my brothers, to be Warrior Gods of the east."

"This strange Shadow has been mentioned by Lord Shiva," said Hemish, "he spoke about a lock of his matted hair being stolen causing the Ganges to cease its flow. That's why he returned to Mount Kailash."

"We'll talk of this later," said Jacob, again showing his worry, "if Lord Garuda is concerned then I must go to him."

"Enough of these concerns," said Eala, "today is a day to rejoice and welcome those who have come to attend your school." She turned to the latest visitors, "Your parents are four of my closest friends, how are they?"

"They're well," said Hemish answering on behalf of all three. "They seem very happy to get rid of us."

Jacob returned to the top step; he was straining to isolate a low rumbling sound. It was coming from the north, he then announced, "Ah, I know that sound, more chariots, I wonder who it could be? Or should I say, prepare for chaos."

"I see the first chariot," said Helena getting very excited, "it's Sunniva and Thora and the second chariot has to be carrying Tristan and Sofia,"

The chariots had barely stopped when Jacob ran down the steps to excitedly greet his nieces and nephew. He gave Sunniva and Thora a tight embrace showing how much he missed them. He then turned to Tristan and Sofia whom he was meeting for the first time. He held them equally as tight, "Your father told me of your birth," he said, "I'm so sorry I didn't make it to see you before now. How's your mother? Is Asgard still running scared of her?"

"Uncle!" said Sofia with a sweet snigger, "I think Asgard is more scared of my brother than our mother, he's a God of Tumult and Chaos, and his powers have no boundaries. Father believes your idea for this school will surely tame his lack of order."

"Says my sister," interrupted Tristan, "goddess of wisdom who's hiding many untested and chaotic skills."

Jacob then turned back to Thora and Sunniva, "I've missed you both," he said, "are you still tormenting you know who?"

"Don't worry about our father," said Sunniva while still giggling, "he's the Asgard King of Kings, and he's putty in our hands. He calls me his gift from the sun and knows how one day I will be a Sun Goddess. I haven't told him of how I am now actually a Sun Goddess because I refuse to talk to him, he chased my boyfriend away and I won't forgive him for that."

"Reminds me of someone standing not too far away," said Eala while hugging her and squinting at Jacob.

"Uncle," said Thora while giving Jacob another hug, "it really is good to see you again. I hope you don't treat Helena the way our father treats us, he watches us like a hawk and no boy is safe in Asgard. He's so busy frightening off our boyfriends he hasn't noticed how I have become a Goddess of War, and I dread to think of his reaction when he finds out that I can bring on the thunder, and just like with him and our grandfather, the Hammer also answers to me."

While Thora was speaking, Viktor, out of her earshot couldn't hold back, "Bitch," he spurted, "I fucking detest her; she's my worst nightmare, a tease and a whore." Demetrius and Obelius were standing beside him, they were shocked at his venom; they leaned forward and turned to stare at him.

"Where has this come from?" asked Obelius. "That's our cousin you're calling a bitch."

"I don't care," replied Viktor through gritted teeth, "she is a bitch, and I swear I'll kill her one day. For years she has treated me like dirt. She uses every opportunity to embarrass me."

Helena was also within earshot and gently nudged against Viktor, "Now, now, less of this venom. You're mad about her. You dream of her all the time. Isn't it time for you to take control and show her how much you care?"

"Care?" replied an irate Viktor. "That's not true," he continued through gritted teeth, "I can't stand her."

"You can't hide your feelings from me," said Helena, "I'm the torch bearer of the gods, I see and feel everything. It's good you've come here for schooling because you need to control those boyish urges, especially when alone. Thora won't be happy with you using her image to satisfy those urges."

"I don't know what you're talking about," said a now flustered Viktor. Helena backed away but not before giving him a knowing smile.

Obelius put his arm across Viktor's shoulders. "Don't mind her," he said, "just as a matter of interest, these alone time urges, are they as good for you as they are for me?"

"Fuck off," said an angry Viktor, pushing him away.

Demetrius remained quiet; he was moving his head from side to side. "Father," he said, "I hear flapping wings, and pattering paws, more are coming."

In the distance what looked like a powerful dragon came into view, it was flying alone.

"Something's wrong," said a surprised Jacob, "I was expecting two dragons."

When the dragon landed, she transformed into Galyna, daughter of Andras and Mia,

"It's a great honour, my lord," she said as she bowed. "Attending your school means everything to me. My parents always speak of your compassion when our emperor was taken from us."

"Fafner was one of my closest friends, and he's sorely missed," said Jacob lowering his head. "Welcome my lady to the realm of Olympus. Your father and mother, are they well?"

"They're fine," she replied. "I think my incessant talking wore them down but since I became the bringer of calmness, a dragon goddess, they've been a lot happier."

"There should be two of you," said Jacob. "Where's Drayce?"

"He should be here," she replied, "he left the dragon realm a month ago, claiming he was hearing things and wanted to find out who was calling him. His mother, as a Dragon Queen, used her powers to contact him, she instructed him to make his way to Olympus. He's not happy, he's one angry Dragon."

"This is worrying," said Eala, "we should start a search."

"No, my lady," said Galyna, "he's a Dragon Lord, he just doesn't know it yet. Let's wait and see what happens."

"I will say no more," nodded Eala.

"Look," yelled Demetrius pointing out towards the tree line. "Two monstrous white-mane lions, they must be from the dessert prides. They're carrying gods of the south."

The lions reached the steps, lowered their heads, allowing the two gods to dismount and there they stood for a few moments before bowing.

"I'm so pleased," said Jacob, "how you've both grown, so striking."

Zane stood there wearing nothing, but a tight calfskin skirt, held in place by a gem encrusted golden belt. Layers of red and white beads draped from his neck and around his biceps. Just below his knees, he wore golden bracelets, clasped by grips made from white gold. On his head was a crown of phoenix feathers showing his noble birth and his status as one destined to become a god of Africa. He was brutally large, muscular, and extremely handsome.

Sagal was stunning, and although slight of frame, she had a perfect hour-glass figure. She was dressed in a most vivid silver and gold gown, embroidered using strands of platinum. Her headdress was equally as grand as Zane's, but it failed to hold in place her magnificent afro hair, even so she presented as one of high status and a goddess of great beauty.

Obelius and the boys were enthralled by her and found it difficult to stop drooling.

"Close your mouth," whispered Eala while elbowing Jacob, "you're too old for her. Stop drooling."

"Excuse me," rebuked Jacob, "I may be two thousand years old, but I still look like a twenty-five-year-old. Fear not my Queen, you're my beloved and the only one for me. Look at her, see how she draws all men in."

"Typical," said an exasperated Eala, "always the mothers who have to sort out these girls." She stepped forward and said, "My lord Zane, my lady Sagal, you are both most welcome into the realm of Olympus."

"Zane," asked Jacob, "Oba and Jomo, are they well?"

"They're fine; they spend their time looking after my brothers and sisters. My sisters show signs of being Earth Mothers, already nature bows before them. My brothers are still too young, they're pests, but soon they too will show their powers and maybe you will find a place for them in your lyceum."

"Trust me," replied Jacob, "there'll be many more gods and goddesses welcomed into my domain, and they will be among them." He then whispered to Eala, "It seems our friends Jomo and Oba have been very busy."

"Tell me, Sagal." continued Jacob, "Your mother and father, are they well?"

"Yes, my lord," she replied, delighted he asked, "they're well. My father intends visiting in the next few weeks, he's not happy; he sensed something strange and wishes to discuss it with you. He and Lord Jomo will travel together."

"No," said Eala, "we must send a message and invite them all. It'll be like old times, except with lots more children. Oh, I can't wait."

All the visitors then made their way into the temple where they renewed old friendships and made new friends.

Jacob now had fifteen children of the gods for the opening of his school.

Chapter 11

It was late in the afternoon when once again a portal opened and finally, the last of the expected pupils entered the realm of Olympus. It was a teenager who could only be Drayce. He showed by his demeanour that he was at war with the world and just didn't want to be there. His contempt for life was obvious and this became more acute when nobody was present to greet him. He was so annoyed he chose to break protocol and avoid going into the temple. He walked towards the ornamental gardens where he approached the only person who was about the grounds at that time. It was Apollo, who was minding his own business and enjoying the peace and quiet of the afternoon while relaxing near where the statue of David was placed.

"The school is that way," Apollo said as he pointed towards the rear of the temple, he then asked, "Are you lost?"

"No," snarled the boy, "I'm not lost; I just don't want to be here. I've been sent to learn the ways of the gods, something I'm not in the least bit interested in. I've other, far more important things on my mind."

"Ah," said Apollo as he stood, "you can only be Drayce, son of Derwyn and Isabella. We were warned about you, your reputation arrived earlier today. We wondered, and were concerned as to where you were?" He folded his arms waiting for a reaction, and when none came, he continued, "Drayce, a powerful and honourable name, given to one who is destined to be mighty and intelligent. Isn't it a pity it's wasted on you?"

"Who," responded a shocked Drayce. "Who in the name of Zeus, are you? Who the Hell do you think you are? And what gives you the right to think you can get away with insulting me?"

Apollo wasn't impressed, he took his twenty-foot colossus form to look down on a startled Drayce. "I know exactly who I am," he yelled in a very strong and thunderous voice, "I am Apollo! Trust me, by the will of Zeus you will show me respect."

Drayce stumbled back and fell to the ground; he looked scared and repeatedly said as he used his legs to push himself backwards along the ground, "I'm sorry, I'm sorry. I didn't mean to be rude; I do respect you."

Apollo then retook his human form and held out his hand to help Drayce back to his feet. "It worries me when I see so much anger in one so young," he said, "you are a prince of the Dragon Realm and have everything. Even then you're not happy, is there no pleasing you? I'd prefer you didn't enter the temple today; you would be a bad influence on those who are already there."

Drayce again felt insulted and wanted to react, he bit his lip choosing to remain quiet.

"Walk along the lagoon," suggested Apollo, "take in the calmness and serenity of Olympus, see if it will help you find what you are looking for."

Drayce lowered his head and left to walk along the beach. He found a spot where he sat, very alone and lost. He began tossing small stones into the shallow waters showing how bored he was with life. He oozed unhappiness and just seemed like someone who needed to be hugged and loved. Never once did he sense or feel the invisible hand resting on his shoulder and it wasn't a guardian angel. He continued throwing stones and without watching what he was doing he inadvertently lifted an egg from a stone camouflaged nest of the very rare beach curlew. As he was about to fire it, he was gripped by the arm and held firm until he slowly released the egg into a waiting hand.

He leapt to his feet and withdrew his sword but was quickly disarmed by a much stronger and faster adversary. It was Jacob and he just happened to be resting nearby.

"First things first," he said, "you can only be the late comer. Drayce, prince of the dragon realm. Now, let us place the egg back into its nest. Be aware that all life in these lands is sacred. Secondly, you are going to move away and allow the mother return before it's too late."

"Piss off!" said an unimpressed Drayce, "I'm going nowhere."

Jacob was shocked by the aggression before him. He reacted so fast, his hand, on impact, gripped the back of Drayce's neck causing him to fall forward and end up drenched in the lagoon.

Jacob felt guilty when he looked at what he saw to be a very sad and vulnerable boy, who just seemed to be lost. His guilt didn't last long; he was subjected to a series of expletives he hadn't expected, vulgar words he hadn't heard since he lived in Dublin.

Drayce leapt to his feet, lunged from the water, and tried to grapple with Jacob but was no match. This time he was sent tumbling towards an unstable sand dune. On impact the sand at the summit began trickling, then avalanche down to cover him. On freeing himself, he yelled, "What is it about this place? Apollo slaps me down and you half drown me. Now you try to bury me, who the Hell are you?"

"I have no doubt you will find out soon enough," replied Jacob.

It was then when Jacob bent forward and took the sword Drayce had dropped, he examined its etchings. "This is the sword of Fafner," he said turning back to Drayce. "Tell me boy, how is it you bear it? Did you steal it? Did you raid his tomb?"

Drayce was disgusted at the suggestion of theft. "My family are honourable," he said, "they would never take what's not theirs. That sword belongs to me, give it back."

"No!" snapped Jacob. "Why would I give it to you? It belonged to the Emperor of the Dragons and should have been buried with him. Answer me, did you raid his grave?"

Drayce tried to grab the sword but again Jacob was too fast. "That sword was given to my father," he said, "It was given by the Titan guardian of Elysium, Lord Cronus. It belongs to my family, and I want it back."

Jacob took the sword by its blade and handed it to Drayce. "That handle was made by the handprint of Fafner," he said, "it's as though it was also made for you."

"Fuck Off," was Drayce's response as he walked away towards the far side of the lagoon where the highest dunes had settled. He was wet, angry, and mumbling to himself; he didn't realise Jacob heard the expletive.

Jacob watched Drayce swinging the sword from left to right and then using it to chop some reeds that were growing close to the water's edge. This was like a red rag to a bull, so Jacob went after him, grabbing him by the neck.

"What is it about you," he yelled, "that allows you to think you can vandalise these sacred lands. Those reeds did you no harm; they are the homes of the dragonflies, the dwelling place of the mayflies, and many seabirds' nest there. I have the strength to throw you twenty feet out into the lagoon and leave you there until you calm down. Is that what you want?"

Jacob raised him off the ground and while holding him high he noticed a tear gathering, he again felt a bit guilty until he realised Drayce was doing everything in his power to stop the tear from flowing.

"If I let you down," he asked, "will you continue your walk as Apollo suggested and try calm yourself?" Drayce just nodded. Jacob saw he was frightened and let him go.

Drayce placed the sword in its scabbard and turned to walk away. He stopped and said while staring at Jacob, "Don't you understand, I don't want to hear anything about 'The Great' Fafner or the powerful Derwyn. They're part of my past and I don't want them in my future. I'm not like them and never will be." He fell to his knees and placed his hands over his ears. "Stop, stop - leave me alone," his tears finally flowed. "All I want is for the voices to stop calling me, why won't the voices leave me alone? Please leave me alone, I can't take much more. What is this Shadow?" He then ran away.

"Drayce," yelled Jacob, "what Shadow?" Drayce kept running.

Jacob watched him for a little while longer and then stared out across the lagoon fully aware there was a spirit about.

"Fafner," he said, "Fafner, my friend. Is it you who's calling him from beyond the grave? Tell me friend, was it your hand I saw resting on his shoulder? Why are you calling him?" There was no response.

After a few miles Drayce reached a section of the lagoon not visible from the temple. He climbed the highest dune and stumbled upon a teenager who was hiding behind some low growing scrubs. The teenager was enjoying himself while spying upon a naked girl swimming close by.

"Hey, dirt bag," Drayce yelled, showing his disgust, "what do you think you're doing?"

The boy turned and showed no shame, "Piss off," before returning to spying only to find himself being dragged away by his feet. When he freed himself, he leapt up and landed a powerful punch into Drayce's chest.

Drayce was winded but when he recovered, he lunged forward and grabbed the boy around the waist causing both to roll down the dune. On reaching the base it was then when fists became lethal weapons, slamming and punching into each other's faces, chests, and stomachs. Soon after, the kicking started, and a real brutal savagery took over. They were equally matched and fought viciously, both hoping that the other would make a mistake, which soon came, causing Drayce to fall backwards allowing the boy to jump across his chest and hold him down. The boy threw his full body weight behind the torrent of punches he unleashed. Drayce was being beaten so violently blood began pooling in his mouth causing him to start suffocating.

Drayce managed to release one of his arms and use it to protect his face, but he was now in so much pain he was losing consciousness. It was as the boy stood and was about to release a full force kick into Drayce's stomach when a loud and shrill voice was heard. It was Helena. "Viktor!" she screamed. "No, let him go!"

Viktor paused, looked up a Helena then stepped away, he then looked down at the damage he'd done. He was horrified by his ruthlessness and tried to justify himself.

"Helena," he said, "he attacked me first, I was at the top of the dunes, and he came from behind and grabbed me."

"I saw you" she yelled, "you had subdued him and yet you still attacked, that is no way for a God of Asgard to act. Go away. Seek Apollo and allow him look after your injuries,"

Helena ran to Drayce's aid. She gently placed his head on her lap and softly rubbed his face, using her powers to begin healing him. He struggled to open his eyes but when he did, he was mesmerised by her beauty. "Are you and angel?" he asked.

"No," she replied shaking her head, "I'm Helena. Who are you and what are you doing walking alone in Olympus?"

"My name is Drayce, prince of the dragon realm." He struggled to sit then continued, "I never imagined Olympus to be such a dangerous place. First, I make a fool of myself before Apollo and then I get thrown into the lagoon by an angry god. Well, you saw what happened just now - I get beaten up by a lunatic God of Asgard; can this day get any worse? Do you know I caught him spying on a naked girl in the lagoon, I thought he was being a pervert."

"He's not a pervert," she replied trying not to laugh. "He's hasn't even reached his second day in Olympus and he's already showing us how he really feels. Most of us already know about his spying, he's mad about her, and hasn't the nerve to tell her, he's a coward."

"He might be a coward, but he packs some punch," replied Drayce while still trying to straighten himself. "I was doing OK until I slipped, and he got the advantage."

"Of course he packs some punch," said Helena, gently massaging his neck, "he's the son of Thanases and is a Warrior God of Asgard. The girl he fancies is my cousin, Thora. She's a daughter of King Odi of Asgard and, if the truth be known, she's already a War Goddess."

"I kicked the living daylights out of a Warrior God of Asgard?" exclaimed Drayce, "maybe I'm stronger than I think."

"Enough of the doubts, you're now with me and I'm of the Light. Let's make this a better day for you. But before we do, you need to go to the water's edge. You smell of the long road and need a good wash."

Drayce limped towards the water's edge and nonchalantly stripped before slowly wading into deeper waters. Helena sat and watched him wash then dive to swim along the seafloor. She'd seen her brothers naked and felt nothing, but when she saw Drayce, something inside stirred and it was a pleasant feeling, a feeling she really liked. When he surfaced, he swam to sit in shallower water just to get comfort from the gentle lapping of the warm waves rolling over his still suffering body. He slowly moved his hands over the cuts and bruises wondering when they'd heal. He eventually left the water, dried himself and dressed.

Thank you," he said, "thank you for being here for me, you've no idea how you've helped." She reached up to gently touch the side of his face.

"Touching your face," she whispered, "shows me a great deal of pain, and it isn't the pain of the fight, it's much deeper. Do you want to talk?"

"You wouldn't understand," he said lowering his head, "I don't think anybody would understand."

"Probably not," she said while still touching his cheek, "but I'm a good listener."

Drayce was about to talk when he noticed the shadow of a large nearby boulder approaching his legs; he leapt up and looked terrified.

"What is it?" cried Helena. "What's wrong?" She saw and felt his fear, pulled him closer and was horrified at how he was trembling. She tried to calm him but even her power couldn't break through his fear. "Let me in," she pleaded, "I can help, but I must understand what's doing this to you. Will you let me in?" He managed to nod then say yes.

"It's the Shadow people," he said with a trembling voice, "they're after me; they're everywhere."

Helena tried to calm him. "You are safe in Olympus," she said. "No evil can enter these sacred lands."

She placed her hands on both sides of his face, slightly squeezing. She closed her eyes and entered his head, "You're a Dragon Lord," she said, "yet, in you, I can't find the dragon."

She went deeper into his mind and arrived in the dragon realm where she saw him playing with his three younger brothers and several of his friends, he was the oldest among them. She saw the change come, at first to his younger brothers and then his friends. She watched as, one after another, they became young dragons. She then watched him, and his older sister who also hadn't changed, walking out near one of the three exits from the dragon realm.

Helena backed away for a moment, looking confused. She thought she saw something else but couldn't quite but her finger on it. She also noticed how Drayce kept moving further away from the gathering shadows; he was still trembling but not as violently.

"I need to get back into your head," she said. "There's something bothering me."

On again entering his head, she saw his sister was gone, as though by some kind of magic. She remained to watch Drayce run back to the palace and hide in his room. It broke her heart to see him in such shock, rocking back and forth, unable to speak. Through his mind she saw his parent's frantically searching for their missing daughter.

Her concentration was broken when the dinner bell tolled. They parted, both feeling drained. "Her name is Isidra," he said, "she's my sister and I blame myself; I'm a coward. I really miss her, and I failed to protect her."

"You might be many things," replied Helena, "but the one thing you are not is a coward. Remember your fight with Viktor? You gave as good as you got. Come, the dinner bell has tolled; we must go to the temple."

"Apollo has banned me from the temple," he said, "he said I'd be a bad influence."

"Linked to my arm," laughed Helena, "no one will stop you entering, I'm the daughter of Jacob, the God of Gods."

"You'd do that for me even though I'm not worthy?" he replied.

"Stop putting yourself down," said Helena, getting annoyed, "the dragon is hidden from you, but it will soon show itself and yes, I would do this for you. Earlier I got a glimpse of my future and in it, you're every-where."

In the meantime, Apollo and Jacob were talking near the temple steps when Viktor arrived. He was in a terrible state and tried to slip by without being noticed but was caught and questioned as to why he was in such a condition. He refused to say and asked to be excused, which wasn't grant-ed. He was told to wait near the main doors.

Helena soon arrived, still linked to Drayce. Jacob wasn't impressed and was about to react until he saw the state Drayce was in, he concluded that he and Viktor had met, and it didn't go well.

"There seems to be a major rush of hormones about this day," snig-gered Apollo, "Eros must be about."

"There can be any number of hormones rushing around as long as they stay away from my daughter," said an irate Jacob.

"Says the one who got Eala pregnant when she was not yet sixteen," responded Apollo loudly laughing.

"Ah, my friend Drayce," said Apollo as Helena and Drayce walked up the steps. "We meet again, Dragon Lord."

"It seems today isn't your day," said Jacob, "how is it you can attract so much grief?"

"Father," rebuked Helena, "leave him be, he's my friend and I've seen my future, it's a future showing him to be everywhere."

"He's your father?" asked a shocked Drayce, "I drew my sword against the God of Gods!" He then fell to his knees begging forgiveness. In the back-ground Viktor was heard to snigger, "Twat, fucking prick."

"Get up," said Jacob while helping him to his feet, "don't make a fool of yourself, when we met earlier, I knew exactly who you were. When the Ancient One created the mould, he never threw it away; you bear the likeness of someone who was very dear to me, your grandfather, Fafner. Because of him you will always be welcome in Olympus."

It was then when the shadow of a nearby pillar crossed Drayce's path, he froze and began to tremble again. He backed away in terror to rest against the temple wall where the sun was still shining. His fear was felt by all watching, taking them by surprise. Viktor was first to react, then Helena. They both ran to comfort him but there was no helping him.

"I'm really sorry for hurting you," said Viktor begging his forgiveness, "I never imagined a fight like we had could cause you so much damage, I'm sorry. I'm sorry."

"It's not you," said Helena while pushing him away, "he keeps talking about the Shadow people; he believes they're all around us and that they've taken his sister. He's suffering because of his inability to become a dragon meant he was useless when she was taken and for that he now blames himself."

"Father," she said, "I saw them, they were there. Drayce speaks the truth. Something is wrong, there's a new threat coming."

Jacob and Apollo remained quiet for a moment; they felt nothing. Drayce tightened himself against the wall showing his panic. Jacob approached him, placed his hand upon his head, and searched his mind. He quickly withdrew his hand and turned back to Apollo.

"Waken the guards," he said showing a sense of urgency, "place them around the temple, tomorrow we inspect the shield, I fear a breach."

He again placed his hands on Drayce, "What are we going to do with you?"

"What do you mean?" asked Drayce as his panic grew. "Are you going to kill me?"

"Kill you?" asked Jacob. "Why would I kill you? You're a hero, Dragon Lord. You've just saved Olympus. To be forewarned is to be forearmed. You're not the first to speak of Shadow. The gods of the east have brought news of a shadow prowling across the Indus realm; this shadow has also been seen close to the five sacred mountains."

"Take Drayce to your room and look after him," said Jacob, turning to Viktor, "make sure he's safe and feels protected. Light a sanctuary lamp above his bed and ensure there are no shadows. Call on the help of Zane, Obelius and Hemish. Do not sleep!"

Viktor and Drayce walked through the temple and soon arrived at the bedroom wing. It was a very tense walk, and nothing was said. They met Zane and asked him to fetch Hemish and Obelius. It was while waiting for the boys when Viktor finally spoke, "You really beat the crap out of me. You're some warrior, where did you learn to fight like that?"

"It must be something in the genes?" replied Drayce, "I didn't know I had such skills. My father is Derwyn, Emperor of the Dragons and boy is he strong. He's never trusted the peace that exists now and has insisted the Dragon army maintains its readiness. He decreed that all younglings begin their training as soon as they change. I've never changed but I watched as my younger brothers and my friends did. I secretly watched them and learned the ways of our warriors, but I never imagined I had developed their strength or power."

"Trust me," gasped Viktor while gently rubbing his heavily bruised ribs, "you certainly have the power, you really hurt me. If my father finds out I was fighting a dragon he'll kick me halfway across the cosmos. He has the greatest of respect for the armies of Fafner."

Zane, Hemish and Obelius arrived and with Viktor they took up positions around Drayce hoping he'd feel protected. Hemish noticed him heavily yawning but fighting sleep. "Hi friend," he said, "They call me 'Lord of the Earth', I'm of the east and I've been taught ways to help those struggling. I can help you relax and fall into a deep sleep. Let me help."

Drayce still had trust issues but the calmness of the room, the brightly burning sanctuary lamp, and four strong looking guards helped overcome his fears. He was so tired he couldn't resist any longer.

Hemish sat with him, and then placed his hand across Drayce's cheek, "Keep your eyes closed, and trust me. Breathe softly, slowly inhale, and slowly exhale. Breathe gently in through your nose and release the air through your mouth. Slowly, slowly, breathe until you feel the pangs of your pain lessen and then pass. Keep your eyes closed, remember you have me, a 'Lord of the Earth', and three War Gods protecting you, breathe slower and let the sleep in."

Drayce's head slightly turned to the right as it sunk back into the soft pillow, he quickly fell into a long missed deep sleep. Viktor maintained the sanctuary lamp ensuring its light glowed so brightly no shadow could appear.

The following morning Jacob arrived and was pleased to find the boys still awake. He checked on Drayce only to find him still in a peaceful and deep sleep. It was over an hour before Drayce began stirring, sleeping very lightly and mumbling. "Helena.... Helena...." he said before going quiet again. He twisted and turned and again started mumbling. "The mountains look nice, will you walk? Come with me." He went quiet again then said, "...a baby?" He opened his eyes to find Jacob staring at him, wide eyed. "I talk in my sleep; did I say something I shouldn't have?"

"You said enough," said Jacob trying to hold a stern face, "something about, mountains, walking, my daughter and more worryingly, a baby?"

Drayce raised his hands to cover his eyes. When he lowered his hands, he caught Hemish, Zane and Viktor giggling, He also saw Obelius's face; a stern and at times furious one.

"Just to let you know," said Obelius, letting his feelings be known. "Helena is my sister and I'm very protective of her."

"Yesterday was bad," said Drayce falling back on to the pillow, "it seems this day is going to be worse."

"Now it's time to be serious," said Jacob, "there has been a breach of the shield and thanks to you alerting us, I've ordered Olympus to leave this place. We're going to rest out among the stars until we figure out what's going on."

"You believe me?" asked Drayce.

"Yes," replied Jacob, "we all believe you. Like Helena I saw something when I was in your head. Once before I met a Shadow, and I can see how it brings terror. Oh, before we leave, I want to take you to a special place. I believe it's this place that'll take away your pain. Will you allow me?"

"Where is this place?" asked Drayce getting curious.

"It's protected and hidden in the far west; it's a very restful place I know the answers you seek lie there."

Drayce looked around at all the young gods, taking in their serious faces. "I'm confused," he said turning back to Jacob, "I haven't asked any questions."

"Trust me," replied Jacob, "the answers you seek lie there." Drayce just nodded.

"Hold on a moment," interjected Obelius. "You detect some kind of evil and at the blink of an eye you decide to travel in the company of an ill-trained teen, are you mad? You're the God of Gods and should only travel with guardians."

"Son," said Jacob, chuffed by his concern, "you sound like your uncle Odi. Relax!"

"Obelius," said Viktor, "trust me, he's not ill trained. He's a dragon lord, better skills than you or I. He beat the crap out of me and only for his slip I'd still be nursing my wounds."

Chapter 12

Jacob stretched across and gripped Drayce by the shoulder, he blinked, and they both disappeared. Within a second, they materialised on the beach of the Elysian Fields and much to Jacob's surprise there stood all twelve of the Titans. They were in their colossus form and staring out to sea. Jacob sensed their tension and enquired as to what was bothering them.

Rhea smiled when she saw him and said, "Worry not, we'll handle this, even Shadow cannot defeat our power."

"You know about the rise of Shadow?" Jacob said while furrowing his brow.

"Yes," she replied, taking her human form, "we've known for some time. The Shadow People are moving on all realms, aided by some kind of menace, but we cannot see or feel the menace, we just know it's there," She waited until she was fully human before continuing. "Have you noticed anything?"

Yes," replied Jacob after looking around, "I see there are twelve; all Titans are together again. It's written that when all twelve are together, nothing can stand against you. Is there a war coming?"

By now Cronus had taken his human form and moved to greet Jacob but he was more interested in Drayce. "Ah," he said while offering his hand. "Grandson of Fafner, welcome to the Realm of the Titans, Dragon

Lord." Drayce was showing signs of reacting and was about to express his annoyance.

"My lord Cronus," interrupted Jacob, "how did you know Drayce is a Dragon?"

"I know because..." He hesitated then said, "I think its best I show you."

He took them to the mausoleum and led them down towards an arch set deep in the vaults. Drayce was walking at a slower pace; the voices in his head becoming unbearable. He placed his hands over his ears, but the voices still got louder. On reaching the arch of the dragons he saw two ornate sarcophagi, each with stone effigies lying upon them, it was then when the voices faded. Standing beside the sarcophagi was a tall warrior, wearing the gunmetal grey scaled armour of a royal dragon. From the warrior was pulsating a neon blue light, a light that was illuminating the surrounding tombs. Tombs that were showing Drayce his line of ancestors stretching back to the beginning of time. He quickened his pace, and on reaching the warrior he drew his sword, "Why me?" he yelled, "Why call me? Weeks of chatter, whispering, and no sleep, why? Keep your dammed voice from my head."

"I recognise him," said Jacob getting emotional, "how can this be?"

"His spirit appeared six weeks ago," replied Cronus, "it's as though Fafner has risen to stand guard over the resting place of the dragons. Is he warning us of a new calamity? He has not spoken, he hasn't moved, but we think he soon will. He's waiting on something." Cronus looked at Drayce knowingly, "or someone."

Drayce wasn't interested, he backed away and let it again be known he didn't want anything to do with those from his past. He made his way to the beach and sat watching the Titans who were still staring out to sea.

Jacob remained in the tomb just staring at the spirit of his friend. He recognised the staff Fafner was holding and was pleased to see it still held the crystal, to him, he looked as powerful a warrior as he did in his last battle.

"It's been too long my friend," he said. "How can this be? Are you helping us from beyond the grave?"

Fafner didn't respond but he did make a slight movement showing he felt something. Jacob tried again, "Fafner, my friend, it is I, it's Jacob." There was still no response, so Jacob put his hand on his shoulder and said before backing away, "I'll leave you in peace."

He left the tomb and went looking for Drayce only to find him sitting and talking with several of the Titans who had taken their human form. He was pleased to see how he was happy, for the first time he had a smile on his face and was enjoying himself. Jacob also noted Rhea had her hand resting on his shoulder and could see she was using her 'Earth Mother' powers to bring the calmness.

Cronus re-joined him. "He's still at war with the world," he said. "The terror he experienced has penetrated deep into his consciousness and prevents him from recovery. He looked upon the face of Shadow and is still in shock. He needs the power of his ancestors to help him find his way, and that power will be channelled through the Emperor of the Dragons. Now I understand why you brought him to this most sacred of places."

"I've no idea why I brought him here," responded Jacob. "I tried to reach him and found a wall; it was blocking my view but, in my head, I too heard the voice of Fafner. I've been hearing his voice for many days now, meaning there's something else at play and it seems the dead are calling out for us to listen."

Jacob was happy to see Drayce so calm and was pleased when he extracted a Lyre from his satchel to create the most haunting music. The remaining Titans, after taking their human form, listened to song after song, sung by the voice of a tenor, the voice of an angel. It was when he sang the 'Song of the Dragons' when Jacob got very emotional, it was a song Fafner always sang, and it always plucked the strings of his heart. He thought of Faer and Garuda, Oba, and Mulan, he thought of Thanases and Baldor, Girish, and Panya, he thought of his beloved Eala and his brother, Odi. He then thought of Jahiri and Jomo and decided to bring them all back together. He turned to Cronus, "The mould wasn't broken when Fafner was created; it was kept. Look at him; I'd swear I'm looking at Fafner all over again."

"Jacob," said Cronus, getting very serious, "you do realise Fafner is an immortal. He wasn't decapitated, wasn't quartered, he chose the death he met and was happy to go and lie with the only woman he ever loved. Heulwyn is also an immortal, I checked her coffin, there's no decay, she's being held by the poison of a Prince of Hell. I feel Fafner knows this and will not leave her side."

Jacob stood tall and puffed out his chest. "The Ancient One made me the God of Gods and that must mean something," he said while moving towards the water's edge, "there has to be a way, I will find a way." He turned to Drayce and asked, "Do you know the 'Song of the Elves'?"

Drayce said he did and began playing its sweet sound. He played notes that travelled across the sands, over the seas and into the west to awaken the wizards. Within seconds a bright light appeared in the distance, and soon Apollonius, Merlin and Mygon arrived. "What is it that troubles our God of Gods?" asked Merlin.

"Olympus has been compromised, a kidnapping has happened in the dragon realm, the east has been visited by dark shadows and all twelve Titans have come together. There's a strange and sinister threat in the cosmos, we know it's there, we know not what it is for it still hides from us. We need your help, your wisdom, and your power."

Undetected, Drayce discreetly left and made his way back to the Mausoleum where he grabbed a flaming torch before making his way down towards the tombs of the dragons. He was unaware Jacob had followed, watching his every move while hiding in the nearby Celtic tombs.

Drayce stood before, and then circled the spirit of Fafner, drawn in by the neon blue almost white light pulsating all around him. He extinguished the torch light; Fafner's light was now so bright there was no need for any other light.

"Why have you been calling me?" he asked. "Surely you can see I'm useless; I even lost your sword to Jacob. I challenged him not knowing I was before the God of Gods; I made a fool of myself."

"Jacob knew exactly who you were," said Fafner, finally responding, "he saw me by your side when you threw those stones into the lagoon. I tried reaching out to you, but you were blind to me. When Jacob arrived, I disappeared. Drayce, I've been waiting for you to work your magic. It's you and you alone who can release my beloved from the grip of Hell."

"Are you for real?" said Drayce getting exasperated. "What is it about you people? I have no powers. I have no idea about what you are talking."

"I heard you," insisted Fafner, "I heard you sing for the Titans and then I heard you call for the wizards, the 'Song of the Elves' is a song very few can sing, you did. That's your power; you must sing once again the 'Song of the Dragons.' Let your voice echo through the tombs of our ancestors, let the words repel the poison from your grandmother, sing it now."

"No," replied Drayce, "I won't sing, I'm useless and have no powers." He went to his knees, extracted his sword from its scabbard, and placed it across his raised hands, "Take back what's yours; there has to be one who is more worthy."

It was then when Jacob came out of the shadows. "Drayce," he said, "get off your knees! Stand up and sing the 'Song of the Dragons.' We all heard your voice break through the barriers of the Astrals bringing the wizards back into my presence. Your voice disarmed the might of the Titans. Sing the song now and allow your grandmother walk again."

Drayce reluctantly replaced his sword, extracted his lyre and begun to sing. His voice brought on a soothing quietness throughout Elysium and then it called a mighty wind. The wind came and entered the tomb with such force it raised the lid from Heulwyn's sarcophagus revealing her very well-preserved body. His voice strengthened as the song progressed, and it began expelling the poison holding his grandmother. The poison exited as a foul-smelling mist that thickened to take the form of a hideous sniggering Dark Angel.

"Ah," the angel rasped, "the boy king who has become God of Gods and Fafner, dead Emperor of the Dragons. Fools, you know not what's coming. The power of Shadow will be your undoing. It's unseen, uncaring, and unbeatable." He then whisked himself out of the tomb.

Through all this Drayce continued singing, all while intently watching the first signs of life return to his grandmother. He watched her slowly levitate then drift from the coffin to stand next to her beloved. He continued singing while watching the spirit of Fafner transform; he too was coming back to life. When restored he and Heulwyn rushed to hug each other before stretching across to embrace Drayce.

"In my dreams," said Fafner, "I watched you grow even when your dragon powers failed. Look at you now, so tall, strong, and handsome. King Derwyn must be so proud."

"Why would they be proud," replied Drayce, shaking his head in shame, "I was there when Shadow took Isidra, I failed to protect her. I failed as a dragon and now I'm so scared. I'm useless."

"My handsome, handsome grandson," said Heulwyn, placing her hands on his shoulders, "your time is coming and when it happens, we'll be with you. Then together we'll seek her out."

Drayce was showing signs of discomfort. Beads of sweat gathered across his forehead; he then loosened his tunic and stepped from his sandals. He expressed his desire to leave the tombs but found his feet refused to move. A choking tightness gathered in his throat, and he began to retch. He didn't understand why his grandparents just stared and did nothing.

Heulwyn took pity on him. "Before we leave," she said, "there's something magical yet to happen."

"What do you mean?" he asked.

"Wait a moment," said Fafner, "I feel its power."

It was then when Drayce suddenly bent forward, calling out in pain. He was in agony, aches everywhere, and his breathing became erratic. He ripped his cape and tunic from his shoulders revealing his bare chest and back, he scratched and tore at his legs, arms, and head, seeking relief. His skirt ripped, then fell away. He knelt hoping to relieve some of the pain, but it was not to be. His head stretched back as though being pulled by an invisible hand allowing pawls of smoke escape from his mouth. He fell to the ground and rolled about screaming for help, but he had to go through this alone. His feet and hands grew claws, and from his back wings appeared, completing his transformation. He was now finally a dragon.

"Drayce, my boy," said Heulwyn, "come back into your human form and rest, the worst is over."

He looked at his grandmother, then Fafner and then Jacob, he was in turmoil. He'd waited so long for the change to happen; he didn't want to let the moment go. He flapped his wings flew up the stairs, and out the door. He took to the sky showing all watching how he was now a powerful dragon. He released his fire and was finally happy. He landed on the beach and took his human form before running back to the tombs to hug Jacob. "You did all this for me?"

"I did," replied Jacob. "I sensed your time was coming and felt you just needed a helping hand."

"I now feel ready to continue my search for Isidra," he said while being embraced by his grandparents. "I miss her so much. She was the one always there for me; I feel I let her down."

"For centuries, I lay cold and alone in my coffin," said Heulwyn, "there was no reprieve from the poison that bound me until one day I felt a warmth that gave me hope. It took me to a strange and sinister place. It wasn't Hell, it was somewhere else. It was there where I saw a terrified young girl. A vision told me it was Isidra. She's alive. She's being held by Shadow people. Your grandfather and I will find her. You must stay in Olympus and learn the ways of the gods." She placed her hands on his cheeks.

"Ah," she said reaching up to kiss his forehead. "I see you've found love, she's very beautiful. A Goddess of the Light, I'm so happy for you."

He lowered his head, and his cheeks began to blush. He coyly looked across at Jacob causing Fafner to look back and forth between them. "Jacob!" said Fafner, "is it true? Your daughter and my grandson; who would have thought?"

"She's sixteen," said Jacob, about to let his feelings be known. "She's too young to be with boys. I'm warning everyone, I'll be watching her like a hawk."

"If my memory serves me right," said Fafner trying to stifle a smile, "two thousand years ago I watched you walk into the lagoon, you were as naked as the day you were born. You had just turned sixteen and were nervous about showing all you had. Eala was still only fifteen and unable to avert her eyes. You approached her, touched her and within days you had her pregnant. Your love endured so why can't theirs? I think you should let them find their own way."

Jacob was about to reply when he was interrupted. "Eh, excuse me," said Drayce showing his annoyance. "You do realize I'm standing here. I respectfully ask you both to stop talking about Helena and me. We will make our own decisions." He turned to Jacob, "When Helena came to my aid, she entered my head and brought the calmness. There, we both saw our future, and it clearly shows us spending eternity together. One day I will ask you for her hand, so start getting used to the idea." Fafner was rendered speechless by his grandson's assertiveness, Jacob was shocked and wasn't happy, but chose to say no more.

There was an awkward silence so Fafner and Heulwyn thought it a clever idea to take Drayce out of the tombs, leaving Jacob alone. Jacob was happy they left; there was something he wanted to do. He moved towards the Celtic arch and lit a torch before walking over to the two newest sarcophagi. He rested his hand on the effigy of his best friend. "Hi Bud," he said trying to stop a tear from falling. "It's me, Scobie. Miss you really bad." He bowed his head and said no more as one tear rolled down his cheek. He then left.

Out on the beach there was amazement among all those present when they saw Heulwyn, never did they see an immortal resurrect after so long. Merlin was delighted, especially when he saw Fafner, he had a special respect for him ever since that first attack when Morgana unleashed her wrath. They listened to Fafner tell Isidra's story and acknowledged the sadness and worry he, Heulwyn and Drayce were suffering. They promised to use their powers to assist in every way possible.

Jacob left the tombs and immediately planned for the wizards and the dragons to make their way to Olympus. He thanked the Titans for their help and issued an invitation for them to visit Olympus at any time.

On arrival in Olympus the wizards created a great buzz among the children of the gods who were amazed at their antiquity. Helena excitedly greeted Drayce and was curious as to who the other dragons were.

Jacob greeted Eala before crossing the hall to sit upon his throne. "It's wonderful," he said to all those in the temple, "how our school for the children of the gods now has the wisdom and guidance of the great wizards. Today they agreed to be your mentor in the ways of magic. So, tonight we celebrate. Tomorrow, while Olympus travels across the cosmos, you'll begin your lessons, and then your training. Enjoy the rest of the day and when the bell tolls for dinner, answer its call."

Chapter 13

Jacob and Eala always enjoyed a good gathering; they knew how to party and always ensured memorable nights for those attending. The best of food and entertainment was provided, and much fun was guaranteed, this night was no exception. Through all the merriment it was noticed that Jacob was distracted, he was straining his ears and seemed restless. "I've a strange feeling," he discretely whispered, after turning to Eala, "I think we're about to receive an unexpected guest. There's a low rumbling."

"It's your imagination," replied Eala, "there's no sound. Look at the dragons, they're not distracted. If there was a rumbling, they'd be first to hear."

Another hour passed and this time Jacob was certain someone was coming. He requested silence and listened intently. He stood from his throne and looked across at Eala while at the same time raising his hands to cover his mouth then his eyes. He paced as the excitement grew then kept repeating, "It can't be, it can't be."

"What is it?" said Eala, gripping his arm. He just kept shaking his head while pacing back and forth. "Jacob," she yelled, "you're frightening me, what is it?" Obelius reached for his sword only to be told to put it away.

Jacob didn't reply, he requested the stewards clear the Great Hall and prepare for the visit of a very important guest. He instructed all present to go to their rooms and return as quickly as possible wearing their imperial dress robes.

"I could kill you at times," said Eala as she and Jacob rushed to their room, "it takes hours for a lady to prepare, and you expect me to be ready in minutes."

"Stop moaning," he snapped. "And don't ask me who's coming. I'm not telling you; I want it to be a huge surprise."

"It's Panya and Odi?" guessed Eala.

"No. It's not!" snapped Jacob again. He refused to budge, "stop trying to guess, you won't wear me down."

"Is that a challenge?" she said while snuggling closer.

"You wish!" he said with a sneer. "Get ready, there's little time, he's very close. I can hear his chariot. Hurry!"

When ready they rushed back to the Great Hall, they were first to arrive. They sat on their thrones and waited. Soon the boys and girls arrived and were placed in a line along both sides of the Hall. Apollo and Chiron stood each side of the statue of Zeus and when the wizards arrived, they stood in a place of honour alongside Jacob. Fafner and Heulwyn sat on two hastily prepared ornate thrones to the right of Eala.

Jacob was thrilled by how everyone looked and acknowledged their efforts. He turned to Apollo. "I remember the last gathering of the gods," he said loud enough for everyone else to hear, "I stood near your statue and watched the greatest ever gathering. Today it's the turn of our children to witness the arrival of a most esteemed deity. The sound of his chariot grows louder."

"Father," said Helena, "I hear nothing."

"Darling," replied Jacob, "trust me. The sound is getting louder, isn't that right Drayce."

"I do hear a loud rumbling," said Drayce meekly, "I thought it was my imagination and yes, it's getting louder."

Jacob got more excited and couldn't sit still. Soon the rumbling got so loud, all heard it. It stopped and they held their breath. The doors opened and a very low, subdued voice was heard to say, "My lord Jacob! May I enter your hallowed halls?"

Jacob was surprised and seemed confused; he made his way to the centre of the hall. "You, my brother," he said still showing confusion. "Of all the gods, I'd expect you to just barge in and make your presence felt. Of course you can enter my halls."

Eala recognised the voice and got emotional, Magni always held a special place in her heart. Her tears gathered as she and Jacob held hands.

Magni looked subdued and slowly walked to greet Jacob. He was not alone; beside him walked two young armed and very powerful looking warriors. On reaching Jacob all three clenched their right fists, placed them over their hearts, and bowed. Jacob thought this odd but accepted their homage. He sensed distress. "It feels strange to see my brother so subdued," he said, "tell me, what troubles you? Why armed guards?"

"Let's walk in the gardens," whispered Magni, "I've much to tell."

Eala reached in to embrace him, and she too felt his grief. "Magni," she said, moving her hand to caress his cheek. "Go with Jacob, I'll look after your guards."

"No," he replied, "I'd like you to join us."

Demetrius was instructed to look after the guards and see to it that they are fed and given a room.

It was as they were walking away when one of the guards said, "Father, we should go with you. Remember our agreement? You're never to be out of our sight."

"Father?" said a shocked Jacob.

"Father! Father?" said an even more shocked Eala.

Magni turned back to reassure his son. "Maximus," he said, "this is the safest place we can be. Trust Olympus, evil cannot enter here." He then turned back to Jacob and Eala, "I've much to tell."

"It seems you have," agreed Jacob, "but about Olympus being the safest place? I'm not so sure about that." Magni furrowed his brow but chose to say nothing.

Demetrius took the two guards to a vacant table near the statue of Ares.

"Hi, I'm Demetrius," he said after they settled, "I'm a son of Jacob and Eala, you are most welcome into my father's domain."

"I'm Maximus," said the first guard as he removed his helmet, "and this is my brother Magnar, we are sons of Magni and the goddess, Medeina. It seems we're cousins."

"Do you know?" said an excited Demetrius, "the first words I ever uttered were Magni, Magni, Magni. He's the greatest."

"He's broken," replied Magnar, "we worry for him, and we fear he's lost his will to live."

"Why?" asked Demetrius.

"It's hard to speak of what happened," said Maximus lowering his head. "We need time, we need to rest."

"Your father sure does look like a broken god, he looks devastated," replied Demetrius not letting the conversation drop. "He looks bad, but you two seem as though your worlds have come to an end. Your pain runs too deep for me to help but my sister can, she's a Goddess of the Light and will have the power."

"Our worlds have come to an end," said Maximus trying to hold back his tears. "Everything we cherished was taken that day. We saw them, the Shadow People; we watched them tear Marduk asunder. Since then, our father's spirit has been broken, and neither of us knew how to go to his aid."

"Father did what he did to protect us," said Magnar stretching across to grip his brother's arm, "we wouldn't be here if it wasn't for what he did."

Demetrius called Helena to join them, and when she crossed the hall so did everyone else; their curiosity had gotten the better of them. For Maximus and Magnar, it was overwhelming, they now had two gods, three wizards, two royal dragons and sixteen pupils, all strange faces, all looking down on them. Obelius greeted them, followed by Victor, "Are you of the northern ice lands?" he asked, "You both look to be of Norse descent. Can I ask; from what house do you come?"

"We are descendants of Asgard, from the house of Magni. He's our father, and the goddess Medeina is our mother. I am Maximus and this is my twin, Magnar."

"But I thought that Magni was...," said Obelius without thinking, he was stopped from making a fool of himself by Helena who stretched in and took their visitors by the hand, "I'm Helena, and I'm delighted to have two new cousins. I for one can't wait to get to know you."

"Helena," said Demetrius, "they need your healing power; they saw Bel Marduk fall to the Shadow People and are still grieving."

Helena sat opposite them and as she was about to speak Drayce interrupted, "Hi," he said, "I'm Drayce of the dragon realm and I too witnessed what Shadow People can do. I saw them take Isidra, my beautiful sister. Before I arrived in Olympus I searched everywhere, I know she still lives, there are times I feel her Light reach out to me. You're safe here, Helena will bring the calmness."

Maximus looked shocked and continued to stare at Drayce. "Isidra," he said, "is she as beautiful as her name? It's the name of someone I know; she's a gift of the Gods and is always in my dreams." He closed his eyes and pressed himself against the chair-back leaving all wondered what he was doing. Just then Drayce felt his sisters Light reach out to him.

"Brother," whispered Magnar, "You are embarrassing yourself. You've never seen girls until today, you don't know any girls."

"She's always in my dreams," he replied, "and she's real, I know she's real."

Helena closed her eyes and used her powers to enter their minds; there she saw what they saw. Tears gathered and began to flow; she was so shocked. "What I've just seen," she said, "is too much for anyone to see let alone by two innocent boys. It's my mother you need. She too is a Goddess of the Light but more importantly, she's also an Earth Mother, a powerful one and she will reach where I can't."

"Our father told us that our mother is also an Earth Mother," said Magnar, "she left us when we were toddlers, saying she would seek us when our need was at its greatest, but she never came."

"You say the Lady Medeina is your mother?" said Apollo, "I knew her well; she's a most powerful Earth Mother and one of my oldest and dearest friends. If she said she will come for you, be assured she will."

In the meantime, Magni was trying to find the words to tell Jacob and Eala about what happened. "I don't know where to start," he said. "I'm so confused. The pain won't go away, and I haven't slept for so long for fear Shadow will take my boys; I've never felt so helpless."

"You must start at the beginning," said Eala leaning in to embrace him. He nodded and began,

"Marduk and I found a most wondrous place, a barren rock bathed by the most amazing spectrum of light, there was nothing there, but we were happy. We used our skills to mould it into a copy of the vast lands of Olympus. We then used our magic to call on the Earth Mothers hoping they'd grant us all what was needed to create beautiful meadows, gentle streams, warm lagoons and snow-capped mountains and they did. For many years there was just the two of us and, as I said, we were so happy." He stopped talking, closed his eyes as though remembering all he lost.

"Go on," said Jacob.

"I met him for the first time during the cosmic wars, and then we lost touch. I met him when Panya, Baldor and Thanases arrived in Palmyra, again I lost touch," he paused, struggling with his tears, before turning to Jacob, "Brother! Remember when he came for me, you were there. He came for me, and we left to travel deep into the universe. I always knew he was the one I'd spend eternity with, I dreamt of him every night, even during the great battle. When Lucifer's soldiers captured me and were torturing me it was the thoughts of him that kept me alive. He was the one who made me laugh even when his jokes were the worst, but I also knew he would be the one to hold me when I was feeling low especially during those times when I thought of the loved ones I'd left behind." He stood and paced before continuing.

"Can you imagine?" he said, his voice getting stronger, "me, a War God, putting away my weapons, using my hands to fashion stone into building blocks and constructing a palace suitable for two gods. He was useless and didn't help but he was brilliant at everything else." Another tear began to flow, he wiped it away then said, "You have no idea of the love and affection that was between us. You've no idea of how much I miss his sensuous and soft lips pressing against mine. He was a Sun God and me a War God, can you imagine? There are no words to describe the passion that was between us especially when we became one."

"Magni," interrupted Jacob, "tell me, what happened?"

"Jacob, stop," said Eala getting annoyed, "he'll tell us in his own time."

"We were living a happy life, no interference from anywhere and time moved so slowly our happiness seemed destined to last forever. There was no time to be bored." He sat again. "About two years after I completed the palace, we heard the sound of a chariot, we looked out into the distance and saw it was being driven by a goddess, I knew immediately it was the goddess Medeina. She reached us and when she stepped from the chariot, we saw she was heavily pregnant, I knew at once that the child was mine, little did I expect to find she was carrying twins? Marduk always knew she and I were lovers but neither he nor I expected there would be consequences. I worried, thinking he would be difficult, but I should have known better, he was brilliant and loved my sons as his own."

He went quiet again, this time with his head in his hands. "Medeina was always very special to me, the thoughts of meeting her again, that time when Rhea sent me in search of the Earth Mothers, made my heart race. She was the only woman who ever stole my heart and that is special. I remember her hair and how it always felt like silk; her eyes always drew me in, the very same way that the waters in the Olympus lagoon draws in the gods. Her touch made me feel lost in love, but I don't understand how it was never enough. Even now I can still feel her power. It, yet again, draws me in and I find the thoughts of her hard to resist. She told me how her feelings for me never left and seeing me again had awoken something she couldn't control. I remember saying to her that those same desires were still with me, and I too couldn't resist, my resolve failed me that night. I leaned forward and gently moved my arms to surround her bringing her even closer. We kissed and then the passion took us, before long we were lying on my cape and as the ecstasy grew, we became one. We were so engrossed we didn't notice the light that shot out across the universe announcing to the cosmos that another god had just been conceived." He left the seat to pace again.

"Brother," said Jacob, "take your time. We can stop now and talk later if that's what you want." Magni nodded then showed his concern.

"I need to check on my sons. I worry for them; they've seen too much for boys so young."

He began walking towards the temple with Jacob and Eala close behind and when they climbed the steps the doors were open, so their return was unnoticed. They reached the first pillar and from behind that pillar they heard Maximus say, "My father was teasing us and didn't notice Marduk had walked a short distance ahead. We'd been tormenting both all morning and were having such fun. It was then we noticed Marduk standing still as though frozen in time. We watched his arm fall to the ground; his cries of pain still ring in my ears."

"You don't have to keep talking," said Helena trying to comfort him.

"Yes you do," insisted Drayce encouraging him to continue. "Keep talking, we're here for you. Trust me, it'll help."

"We were only boys, twelve years of age," continued Maximus, "we'd never seen, or experienced, violence of any kind. We continued watching and next we saw his other arm fall and then it was taken. It was savagery, they chewed on his arm and within seconds it too was gone. Others came, he then fell to the ground, his legs were gone, it was then when we saw them. Shadow People, tall and slimy, they wore cloaks of old sack cloth with hoods covering their heads and faces." He paused before resting his forehead on the table.

"Our father ran to his aid," said Magnar, placing his arm across his brother's shoulders, "but it was too late. They savaged the rest of him until all that was left was his head. His head rolled to face us, and his eyes were still open. He looked at our father and it was then when just one tear trickled down his cheek. Our father has been a broken god ever since." He then moved to sit at the front of the table before continuing.

"It was the shadow of the snow-capped mountains where they hid, our father went to the edge and the shadow continued moving towards him. It touched his feet and then we saw them claw at his toes. The blood that flowed frightened us, we'd never seen so much blood, we started crying and my dad turned to protect us. There were no weapons; there was no need before that time. He grabbed us and carried us towards our palace. How he carried us amazes me, look at the size of us. He lit a circle of fires and kept them burning all night, he kept Shadow away."

Magni then stepped forward. "That day was the day I lost my greatest love; it was also the day I decided my boys would become Warrior Gods of Asgard. I opened a hidden door in the palace and extracted my long-concealed weapons. I also saw the weapons of Marduk, took them, and fashioned another set so that all three of us would be armed. I then began the training of my boys. I was tough on them, determined to make sure that when the time came, they were prepared and ready to take revenge. Today they are before you as the grandsons of Thunder, and warriors of Asgard."

"What of Marduk?" asked a curious Obelius.

"We went back the next morning but there was nothing, not even a drop of blood," Magni was now having great difficulty, "I never saw the white mist rise."

"For four years we held them at bay and as each day passed our skills grew," said Maximus. "We became more independent. Father taught us everything; he was relentless and ruthless, so much so we believe we are now his guardians. Distraction comes easily to him, and his mind never strays too far from his loss. He needs us to watch him for we fear he made us what we are so he alone would leave and seek revenge. We challenged him and made him realise that no matter how brave we were, we'd always need him. That was when Magnar decided we should seek out our family. He hoped Olympus and Asgard would take the pain away."

"And that was the right decision," said Eala moving to comfort him. She was surprised while hugging him; she felt his spirit leave, and for just a few moments she noticed his eyes firmly shut and wondered.

Jacob moved to the centre of the hall; he had already announced they were leaving to rest out among the stars. He raised his hands, closed his eyes, and lowered his head. He used his magic and soon a low rumbling was heard, it was the sound of Olympus making its way out into the cosmos. Magni joined him, "I know of a place; there are four suns. Place Olympus in the centre and with all that sunlight no shadow will form." Jacob agreed and within minutes they arrived.

"Wow," cried Obelius who was close to the main door, "come, you all need to see this."

It was an amazing sight, four suns permanently shining, spreading their light, and warming all they touched. Some of the young gods expressed their concerns, wondering how their parents would find them.

"No need to worry," said Eala hoping to reassure them, "They'll know that if Olympus has moved it will be for a good reason, they'll be happy knowing you are protected by the power of this sanctum." It was then when she noticed how glum Maximus and Magnar were. She joined them and formally welcomed them to her home. "Allow me help," she said while gently placing her hands on their cheeks. "Allow the Light of a goddess take away your pain. Allow an Earth Mother to expel the bad memories." The Light came and illuminated her; it spread into the boys bringing them the calmness. It was then when Magni finally relaxed knowing the light had arrived; his prayers were answered.

Later that night when all had retired Jacob found his sleep interrupted. He woke Eala and said, "Magni! A father! Who would have thought?"

"Go to sleep," she said giving him a thump, "there will be time tomorrow to mull over this news." He couldn't sleep; he left the bed, went out to the gardens, and was surprised to find Apollo sitting there. "Can't sleep either?" he asked.

"I sit here, and I wonder." said Apollo. "I think of the old times, near the creation, do you know what I wonder?"

"No, tell me!" said Jacob.

"I wonder why the Ancient One created us, I wonder why we evolved into being protectors of the universe. I wonder why I'm still here instead of travelling across the cosmos with Zeus and my family. I look out beyond the four suns, and I see a new threat, an insidious and sinister presence and I feel a new battle is looming. I wonder why all this has fallen to you, so young, so brave and yet so alone."

Jacob was troubled by Apollo's comments, he'd never felt alone, and it surprised him Apollo felt he was. He dismissed those thoughts and brought up a far more troubling issue. "Something's bothering me and I need your counsel," he said. "Today I detected an evil presence, it was soon after Magni arrived. It comes from Maximus."

"Need I remind you," said Apollo showing his alarm as he leapt to his feet. "Olympus must be protected at all costs, even if it means destroying all Magni holds dear. You are God of Gods and the guardian of this most holy sanctum, you cannot fail. I will discuss this with Chiron and the wizards."

Chapter 14

Jacob left Apollo and went to sit on the sill of the south facing window. There he wondered about the evidence showing the advance of Shadow and what, or who it might be.

He then made his way into the Great Hall and stood before the statues of Ares and Athena. "I need your counsel," he said, "it's time to awaken."

Dust fell from the statues and within a few moments the Gods of War stepped from their plinths.

"There's a new menace," said Jacob, "and I cannot find as to who or what it is. Some form of evil has entered Olympus, and I need your help in finding it. Out in the meadows you will find the wizards, Apollo, and Chiron. I'll meet you there."

Jacob remained in the Great Hall for a short while longer, he walked among the statues seeking inspiration and when none came, he gave up and left for the meadows. Out there the meeting was held telepathically, ensuring Shadow couldn't hear. When there was no more to be said, and a plan was in place, they returned to the temple where breakfast was now being served. There was amazement when the Olympus Gods of War arrived. Some of the younger War Gods were itching to meet them but thought better of it when they noticed how serious they looked.

Magni on seeing them arrive was surprised he wasn't invited, but he trusted Jacob and surmised it was none of his business. He watched Jacob summon Obelius and have what seemed to be a very serious conversation. He then saw Obelius join Zane and Viktor before all three of them moved to stand next to Magnar. He felt this was odd but didn't get suspicious until Ares and Athena sat each side of him. Then he went on alert. He had the abilities of a master chess player and could see ten moves ahead in all conflict scenarios; this was his greatest strength as a War God. This time he couldn't put his finger on what was bothering him. His suspicions were rising when Jacob moved to the centre of the hall and requested silence.

"Last night for me was a very restless night," he said, "I feel nothing, yet I know all is not right. Magni, Maximus, Magnar, and Drayce have all experienced the march of Shadow. Aria, Hemish and Gaia left their homelands knowing something was wrong, yet no one else feels anything. I find it strange that all twelve Titans have come together, they too sense something but cannot see, they feel it and that's what makes it a concern. I've always believed when a threat is subtle, so subtle that it deceives everyone, is when I should be on guard. When just one person feels its menace is when I know we should prepare. As part of that preparation, I've made some decisions that will help until we've more evidence."

He turned to Fafner and Heulwyn, "I know you plan to leave, but under the present circumstances I believe the right decision is for you to stay and assist me; I need your power and wisdom."

He turned to Drayce knowing he wouldn't be happy. "You must trust me. The search or Isidra will begin when we know what we're dealing with. Remember, your grandmother knows she's alive, we must conclude they're keeping her alive for a reason."

He walked over to Magni. "Brother," he said, "you are the greatest and I know you won't agree with one of my decisions, but I must insist you support me." He then turned to the students.

"It's still my plan for you to learn the ways of the gods. Those lessons will start at once. You will be split into two groups, the War Gods, and the Mystic Gods. The War Gods will be trained in conflict tactics by Ares and Athena and the Mystic Gods will be tutored by the wizards. You will learn of the power of magic and then you will return to be trained by Magni and Fafner. Apollo and Chiron will also be available to you. Within three days you will all become warriors trained to be defenders of the Light."

He looked across at Magni and noticed he was looking down at his feet, seemingly distracted, and when he was sure Magni was, in fact, totally distracted, he discreetly signalled to Athena, instructing her to incapacitate him. He then walked to the centre of the hall and said, "Maximus! How is it 'Shadow' showed itself when you crossed into Olympus? I sensed no malice in your father or Magnar, but you; you reek of an evil I'm unaware of."

Maximus froze, not knowing where to turn. Magni tried to react, but Athena's power held him firm. Magnar was surrounded by Viktor, Zane, and Obelius, each of them holding swords to his neck. "Forgive us cousin," said Obelius trying to reassure him. "Please don't be afraid; you must trust us. I know this is strange, I've never seen my father do anything like this. I promise he will not harm Maximus; he's testing him, I sense it. He has a plan, please, please trust him." Magnar nodded but wasn't happy.

Jacob used his magic to conjure up two swords and when they were fully materialised, he used them to taunt Maximus, casually pointing and then withdrawing the blades until he drew first blood. Maximus kept glancing across at his father but could see he was totally incapacitated and unable to come to his aid. He looked for help from Magnar, but he too was held firm. He tried not to panic but when Jacob went on a full and sustained attack his training kicked in.

Jacob lunged forward at such speed all Maximus could do was bend backwards using only the strength of his knees to keep him parallel with the floor. On composing himself he propelled himself against a nearby pillar before somersaulting over Jacob's head. On his way, he managed to grab one of the swords from Jacob, and when he landed, he turned to go on the attack. He fought like a god possessed, briskly moving forward, and swinging his sword from left to right, at times successfully landing a few impacts on Jacob. Magni still tried to go to his son's aid, but Athena's power was so potent it continued to hold him firm.

Maximus continued fiercely fighting but when it came to fighting Jacob, he was out of his depth; every effort he made to hurt Jacob was pointless as he was by far the strongest and the fastest.

Maximus began struggling, his strength waning, his heart racing, and his breathing erratic. He felt real panic, and, in the end, he called out, "Father, father, help me." There was no relief as he frantically fended off every blow raining down on him. What he didn't realise was just how powerful he really was, and how successful he was at defending himself. Although falling many times he always managed to leap back to his feet before going on an onslaught of sheer power. His father trained him well.

Earlier in the day Jacob noticed Maximus slipping away, closing his eyes, and resting against the nearest wall or pillar, always for just a few seconds. He wondered about that and still wondered because while under the pressure of conflict he continued to do it. He also remembered Eala commenting on him leaving his body while his eyes were closed.

Maximus became more frantic; he rushed to lean against a pillar then closed his eyes again, he knew that a few seconds in Olympus was the same as several minutes wherever Isidra was. His hands slowly moved as though embracing something invisible, they then moved as though creating a magical dome. When he opened his eyes he yelled, "You will not stop, or prevent me, from protecting her. I love her; she needs me."

"Who needs you?" yelled Jacob. "Who are you protecting?"

The wizards became alarmed and immediately moved to stand at three points around the Great Hall. They raised their staffs and called on the Light and when it came it lit up the hall before shooting across to enter Maximus. His screams of pain were heart wrenching, even so, no one went to his aid. He fell to the floor writhing, arching, screaming, and when it was over, he just lay there sobbing and in shock. The Light showed there was no evil in him.

Some few moments had passed when Maximus began to compose himself; he stood and gathered his strength, then lunged at Jacob. He landed a powerful punch, but Jacob never flinched. Maximus was startled when he realized he, not only had assaulted his uncle, but he had also just assaulted the God of Gods. He struggled to think of a way out but all he could think to say was, "It's your fault. I heard them talk of you. I'm her only hope, she needs me, and I need a way to save her. Shadow knows everything and because of you she's now in greater danger. You called me back. Why?"

Magni finally broke free and ran to be with his son. "Tell me. Tell me who is it you are protecting?"

"Father," he replied looking around at all the worried faces, "her name is Isidra, and for two years now I've been protecting her. The Light came to me and showed me a princess whose Light was waning, it was to be our secret. It bestowed on me the ability to be in two places at once. I thought it was my imagination but it's real. Each time you see me leaning against a wall or pillar with my eyes closed, my spirit is with her, helping to strengthen her shield."

He turned to Jacob, "That's why you sensed evil, it must attach itself to my spirit, but I can assure you it will never attach itself to me. When I'm there I'm like a ghost, Isidra sees me, but they can't. They know someone, or something is there but they can't figure out who or what it is. Uncle, I've been with her every day and every night since the Light showed me where to find her. She's lonely and is very scared. She needs me to hold her, protect her, and keep them away. My Light strengthens hers; it cocoons her until I return, but even now my Light diminishes."

He turned back to his father. "Now you know why, over the last two years, you've seen me sleeping so much or walking around with my eyes closed."

He began to get very agitated and ran to stand with his back to the closest pillar, he closed his eyes and all watching saw him stand with his arms embracing something invisible. He opened his eyes.

"She's safe again," he said, "but the shield won't last long."

"Father," he said after rejoining Magni. "You are a most powerful War God; you have to help me find a way. You lost your greatest love, don't let Shadow take mine, help me, help me save her."

"Why now?" asked Magni, "Why didn't you tell me of this before now?"

"Because Shadow is everywhere. It's listening to everything, Isidra warned me. It's probably listening now."

Jacob joined them and without asking he placed his hand on his nephew's cheek, closed his eyes, and entered his head. He very quickly withdrew and called Fafner and Magni to join him.

"Close your eyes," he said to Maximus, "and take us with you."

Maximus did what was asked and immediately, all four arrived in a dank and foreboding cave, where they saw that the cocoon he created was seriously depleted, they also saw sinister cloaked beings had gathered and looked as though they were baying for blood. Maximus quickly enhanced the shield, his light was strong but when Jacob joined him, they together, created a much stronger defence.

Fafner hadn't moved, he just kept staring as though in shock, his hands covering his mouth, and his heart beating rapidly.

"Fafner," asked Magni, "what is it?"

"I didn't realise when Maximus mentioned 'Isidra' that he was talking about my missing granddaughter."

Magni comforted Fafner then turned to Maximus. "How is it you cannot rescue her?"

"While in this place I'm like a ghost," he replied, "you three also appear as ghosts, she's not, she's real. I tried everything and nothing works. I tried to take her with me, but her body remained. The power of evil here is so strong it hides everywhere; it waits and is always ready. It hungers for her flesh and blood."

"We'll find a way," said Jacob. "You'll have the power of Olympus with you until we find a way. We must return to the temple and seek counsel."

"I need to stay a little while longer," pleaded Maximus, "look at her, see how her spirit wanes. Oh, just so you know, while here I have the power to move all kinds of objects. It's possible you too have that power. That's how Shadow is suspicious."

He stepped through the shield and when Isidra saw him, she lit up and ran to embrace him, stopping short on reaching him. They had found a way of embracing that to them felt real. Magni watched his son show a gentle side he hadn't seen in him since before Marduk was murdered. He got emotional watching him softly caress Isidra's hair before moving to gently kiss her lips. To him what he was watching was a young couple deeply in love and in his head, he swore to find a way.

Jacob and Fafner stepped through the shield and when Isidra saw her grandfather, she ran to embrace him but slipped straight through him. She turned to Maximus and asked, "Is this a dream?"

He didn't answer but Fafner did. "It's not a dream, darling; Maximus brought us here, I promise we'll find a way."

Maximus got concerned when he saw his father inch towards nearby Shadow guards, Jacob had already noticed. "Magni," he said, "don't even think about it, this is their domain. Don't alert them to what they are dealing with, wait until we're ready to destroy them." Magni got the message and backed away. He stepped through the shield, and everyone could see he was seething and itching for a fight. "So, you're the one who's stolen my son's heart," he said, after approaching Isidra, "I can see why; you're more beautiful than the goddesses of Olympus."

"We should go," said Jacob. "The shield is very strong and will hold for some time. We need to seek counsel from the wizards. Maximus, from this point on I want you to bring a Goddess of the Light with you, their powers are unmatched. They'll assist you in strengthening the shield on each of your visits."

Maximus woke and all four were back in the temple. Magni immediately moved to speak with the wizards and the War Gods. Jacob as usual paced up and down the Great Hall trying to devise a plan. Magnar ran to his brother and berated him for suffering alone for so long. Fafner joined Heulwyn and Drayce and told them what he found. Drayce was devastated and insisted on going with Maximus on his next visit, but Fafner said, "That's not going to happen, Isidra is safe now that Jacob used his powers to strengthen her shield. You, going there, will only complicate things, you may not be able to control your temper. We must trust Jacob and wait for him to find a way." Drayce wasn't happy.

Chapter 15

Jacob joined Magni, "I hope you understand why I needed to treat Maximus so aggressively," he said, attempting to clear the air, and when he got no reaction he continued, "I really did detect an evil force, and it was coming from Maximus. We now know it did come from him and thankfully it's only a residue of his visits to protect the Princess Isidra. You do know I would never willingly hurt him?"

"I trained you well," said Magni, "I'd have done exactly as you did. I must say, it was wise of you to arrange for me to be subdued. My love for my son blinded me to the evil you detected. There are no hard feelings."

"I need to talk to you about some decisions I've made," said Jacob.

"What decisions?" asked an intrigued Magni.

"I've decided to take your counsel," said Jacob, "but I'm not allowing you to be part of any rescue mission."

"Need I remind you I am a War God," said Magni. "I'm one of the wisest and strongest, a brilliant tactician, and my skills are unmatched."

"I can't trust you," replied Jacob staying firm, "you are the greatest, but your hatred of Shadow has consumed you, it has swallowed you. I saw how distracted you were before I fought Maximus and I know if, during the rescue you meet anyone connected to Shadow, you will react and try to take revenge, you will endanger the plan. I want all gods focused on one thing only and that is the rescue of Isidra. I must trust my instincts and they tell me you are too reckless when you are distracted. It's obvious you're still in deep grief."

Magni was livid, but deep down he knew Jacob was right. He requested his skills be used in putting the plans together. Jacob agreed.

On rejoining those gathered in the Great Hall, Jacob announced that Magni will remain in Olympus to oversee the rescue plans. He also announced his plan to immediately travel to Asgard.

"You're going nowhere," announced Obelius, "you are God of Gods, and your place is here under the protection of this temple."

"Excuse me," said a bemused Jacob, "do I not get a say?"

"No," replied Obelius, "you don't get a say."

Eala said as she wrapped her arms around her husband, "It seems you've yet again met your match. You'd better do what your son says." Jacob was about to speak again when Eala placed her hand across his mouth. "Shut it," she said. "Its best you say no more."

"You did agree for me to take control of all plans," said Magni noting Jacob's bemusement, "until we work out what Shadow is, and what it's after, you must stay in the temple, or only travel with senior gods as escorts. My gut tells me we should prepare for all eventualities; something is wrong and even with our combined powers, none of us can work out what it is we face. I believe training the young gods is key to our success, have you not noted the new powers some of them have, have you not wondered why Magnar insisted we come here. Apollo expressed his surprise at how quickly the young gods arrived after you sent out the call."

Ares informed Magni that he plans to begin the training of the war gods at once, using an intensive form of battle training. He also suggested Magni seek the help of the Earth Mothers. He expressed his concern about how Shadow makes no sense, continuously hides, and seems shielded from the gods.

Athena also offered to help but Magni felt her skills would be better used by her taking control of security. He suggested she check the shield for breaches and close any that's found. He asked her to use her skills to create an impregnable barrier around the temple buildings perimeter. He then rejoined Ares.

"We'll train the war gods together," he said, hoping Ares agreed. "When finished we'll send some to Asgard, others to the Fair Lands, and more in search of the Earth Mothers. We have four days." He then turned to the young Gods,

"Many years ago, us War Gods, used our skills to train eight mortals, some of them are your fathers. After four days we succeeded in creating formidable warriors, who became guardians to the four messengers of the gods. Their training was intense, and at times difficult, but yours will be much more difficult. Trust me when I say, within three days, you will become powerful Warriors of the Light." He looked around at the eighteen ashen faces before continuing, "Many of you are still unknown to me but you are the sons and daughters of those I do know, and that's good enough for me. Who among you are War Gods?"

The first to step forward was Aria, who introduced herself as the Lioness of the Gods and daughter of Mulan and Garuda. She was followed by Lovisa who introduced herself as a warrior goddess of the North and daughter of Thanases and Irina.

Thora was next, "Uncle, I'm fairly sure you know who I am." She was followed by Maximus and Magnar who in unison said, "Father, I take it you know who we are? Surely, we don't need training. Do we?"

"When I trained you," replied Magni, "I was gentle, wait 'til Ares gets his hands on you."

Obelius and Tristan continuously shouldered each other as they moved towards Magni, they weren't taking things seriously. "Uncle," said Tristan, "Obelius and I have been trained by our fathers, your brothers, surely there's nothing left to learn?" Magni wasn't impressed, he folded his arms before responding. "I love all my brothers," he said, "but they are not teachers. You will forget everything they taught you and learn to absorb everything Ares and I will show you." Tristan and Obelius said no more.

Drayce was next to introduce himself, telling Magni that he was a Dragon Lord and the eldest son of King Derwyn and Queen Isabella. He attempted to embellish himself by expressing his desire to learn the ways of the gods.

"Show off," sneered Viktor, "now we know who the teacher's pet is going to be. Prick."

"I heard he beat the crap out of you," laughed Zane who was standing nearby. Viktor then stepped forward and bowed. "My Lord Magni," he said while glancing back at Zane, "the last time we met, I was a two-year-old toddler, look at me now. I too would like to learn the ways of the gods."

"Hypocrite!" yelled Zane while making his way to introduce himself as a god of Africa, one of noble birth, and a son of Oba and Jomo.

Ares was heard whispering to Magni, "I'm pleased, ten young warriors, all fresh and innocent, you and I are going to have so much fun."

Magni joined the wizards, who were with the eight remaining young gods. "You too will learn the ways of the War Gods but not today," he said, "most of your training will be in the classroom. The wizards will be your tutors, and they will teach you the ways of the mystics. Now, tell me who you are."

Sagal stepped forward and introduced herself as a goddess of Africa, and daughter of Jamilah and Jahiri. Hemish was next, and he introduced himself as 'Lord of the Earth' and as one who is destined to be a protector and guardian of the Indus peoples. He was followed by his sister Gaia who introduced herself as the daughter of Manasa and Girish, as well as an Indian Goddess of the Light.

After Gaia, it was Galyna who approached Magni and she introduced herself as the daughter of Mia and the dragon lord, Andras. She spoke of the golden chariot and the great respect to which he is held by her parents.

Magni's face lit up on turning back to see his three nieces and his nephew waiting to greet him. It was Demetrius, Helena, Sofia, and Sunniva. "Ah," he said, "Who would have thought that the nine grandchildren of Thunder would be so split, five war, and four mystics. Remember, just because Jacob, Odi and Modi are your fathers doesn't mean you'll get off lightly.

As he walked away, he saw Maximus, Obelius and Viktor leaving the hall.

"And where are you three going?" he asked.

"We're going to our rooms," said Maximus answering for them all, "tomorrow will be a busy day and we want to be on top form."

"Really?" said Magni looking across at Ares.

Maximus got alarmed; he recognised his father's face as one that was about to explode. "We're fucked," he whispered while gripping Obelius's arm.

Magni kicked Maximus towards the exit, then roughly gripped Obelius and Viktor by their ears, frogmarching them out the door. Through his gritted teeth he said, "Your training starts now." The remaining seven trainee War Gods sheepishly made their way outside and waited for direction from Ares.

Magni returned to the temple and joined the wizards. He looked at the eight scared mystic gods and smiled. "Fear not," he said, "your powers are something I know nothing about. You will start your lessons tomorrow morning, I suggest you have an early night."

Through all this Jacob said nothing, his mind was elsewhere. He only took an interest when he saw Magni roughly handle Obelius towards the door. He knew Magni was the one God capable of teaching Obelius manners.

When the temple emptied Jacob and Magni made their way to the ornamental gardens where Athena and Chiron joined them. They sat watching the young gods gather around Ares.

"Look at them," said Magni, "they're acting as though the next few days will be easy. Little do they know what's coming."

"Go easy on them," said Jacob, "they're so young."

"Will Shadow go easy on them?" asked Magni. "I don't think so."

"Does your skills really tell you war is coming?" asked a troubled looking Jacob. Magni just nodded, then said, "something is coming."

Chiron stood and began pacing. "I'm sensing a calamity," he said, "it's spreading through the centaur lands and bringing terror. I must go to them, guide them and if necessary, fight by their sides."

"Go then," said Magni. "Be with them. Before this is over, we're going to need their swiftness." Chiron then prepared to leave. He continued pacing as though he wanted to say more but, in the end, he said nothing. He transformed from being a tall and striking man, to being a powerful centaur. He cantered into the meadows, then galloped towards the shield before disappearing through a waiting portal.

Jacob and Athena went to speak but both were stopped. Magni had placed his finger over his lips. They all knew to place their hands on each other's heads, allowing them to telepathically communicate.

"It seems Shadow is everywhere," said Magni, "even in Olympus. I looked ten steps ahead and it's not good. I believe we've met this Shadow before, but its face is still hidden, and this concerns me. We mustn't discuss our plans in public so from now on we meet like this."

"What plans have you in mind," asked Jacob.

"The ones I have in mind are similar to the ones I already mentioned. They still involve the young gods being sent to Asgard, the elf and dragon realms, as well as the Fair Lands. Others I'll be sending in search of the Earth Mothers. I intend sending Obelius to Asgard, he should be the one to escort King Odi. Demetrius will be sent to the Fair Lands, Hemish will lead the search for the Earth Mothers, and Tristan will travel to the elf realm. Right now, the rescue of Isidra is my priority, and when she's rescued, I'll arrange for Maximus and Zane to escort the dragons back to their homelands, King Derwyn should be informed of what's coming.

Chapter 16

While Magni, Jacob and Athena were discussing the plans, Ares prepared the training of the War Gods. There was much giggling, albeit nervous giggling. The girls said nothing, but the boys acted overconfident until they realised they were unable to read Ares' face. When the smart comments died down Ares lined his pupils up and then turned to face out across the meadows. He raised his arms, closed his eyes, then used his powers to conjure up a workout circuit that stretched for a least two hundred metres. It had all that was required to target every muscle group, even the ones no one knew about. It began with leather-covered stone pommel horses, then dumbbells to target both the upper and lower body muscles using a total of six different exercises. After them, there was a shooting range, set up for target practice involving three different weapons - bows, sling shots and Javelins. There was also a choice of logs, and they wondered about them. This was followed by a climbing wall with movable grips that seemed to have minds of their own. After that there were the black stallions, strong and powerful, leaving them wondering why horses were needed. Beyond the horses stood two large mahogany trees with ten ropes hanging from their elongated branches. The last section was deceiving; it was set up with a series of parallel bars, both high and low, as well as a choice of pull up bars with push up handles, covered in strange looking holes; there was also a selection of stone loaded training sleds.

To the right was a fifty-metre pool, and this looked very inviting. All this made the young gods feel they had enough fitness to withstand anything Ares threw at them. How wrong they were, they didn't predict the traps set throughout the circuit.

Their arrogance and constant banter soon grated on Ares' nerves, and he called for Magni to join him. When Magni arrived, he was shocked. "You can't be serious," he said looking very concerned, "that's my workout design intended for only the most trained of warriors, it's too severe for these novices."

"For Odin's sake," sneered Maximus, "we've completed circuits like that in the past, it'll be easy. The only thing we can't figure out is. The horses! Why are there horses?"

"Uncle," said Obelius, "you're wasting our time; that circuit is too easy, even if we were to complete it ten times, we wouldn't break a sweat."

The boys continued to belittle the circuit while every now and again hurtling derogatory comments about its level of difficulty. Each boy in turn produced a quip designed to insult Ares and Magni but it was after Maximus brought their great age into the banter when it was noticed Magni folding his arms and rolling his tongue against his cheek.

Magnar backed away, taking Zane and Drayce with him, he had a bad feeling. "Don't say another word," he whispered, "look at my father's face! He's up to something, and if Max and Viktor don't shut up, I fear for them."

Thora noticed how Ares' face had also changed, she said to Lovisa and Aria, "The boys had better stop teasing Ares, whatever he's thinking, I fear it won't end well."

"Hey," yelled Obelius, "old men. For every circuit you do we'll do ten. Let's see who breaks a sweat first."

"I love being challenged," said Ares turning to Magni, "I've been waiting for them to show their arrogance. This is also an opportunity for you to finally beat me at something."

"Ten reps on each station, including the extra's," replied Magni. "Let's see who drops first."

"Ten circuits for every one we complete?" asked Ares, looking up at the boys, with a sinister smirk. "Are you sure you want to challenge us?"

"Deal," replied Obelius, Tristan, Viktor, and Maximus in unison.

"You stupid pricks," whispered Magnar, while shaking his head in disbelief. "You've been set up. Some of those stations have multiple exercises. How many laps are there in one rep in the pool?"

Magni removed the horses to a small paddock located nearby then walked over to rejoin Ares. "No need for the horses yet."

They began their warmups, then started their regime, a total of sixteen reps across the nine stations, and when they completed the first round they waved up at the boys. They then began their second circuit followed by a third, fourth, fifth and sixth. They looked over at the boys who were no longer laughing, they then began their seventh, eighth and ninth leading to their tenth, eleventh and twelfth.

"We haven't broken a sweat," said Ares enjoying the blank expressions on each boy's face. "Keep watching." They then continued and completed eight more.

"Do you want us to stop?" asked Magni.

"Ok," pleaded Zane. "You've proved your point. Yes, please stop."

Drayce could no longer contain himself; he rushed over and grabbed both Viktor and Obelius. "You are some pricks!" he screamed, "that's thousands of reps we must do, thousands. In the pool its ten laps per rep, two hundred laps, and that's before we find out what traps are set. I bet, because of you, we will have to repeat the circuits each day over the next three days, that's thousands upon thousands of reps before they are finished with us, and we still don't know what the horses are for."

He was raging and when Viktor tried to apologise Drayce exploded, landing a power packed punch into Viktor's chest sending him tumbling to the ground. Viktor quickly recovered and ran at Drayce only to be manhandled through the air and send twenty feet out into the pool.

Obelius was caught sniggering which infuriated Drayce even more, he walked over and said, "My fire is itching to be released, you might be an immortal but trust me, if I release my fire there's no coming back. Would you like me to release my fire?" Obelius just raised his hands in submission.

Drayce stormed off and as he mounted the steps into the temple, he brushed by Fafner who wasn't impressed with being ignored. He called Drayce back and got no response. He ran after him and grabbed him by the neck. "You've every right to be angry," he said, "but the way you treated Viktor is unacceptable. Go back, offer him assistance, and apologise."

Drayce was having none of it. "If you want to apologise," he yelled. "Be my guest, but I won't apologise to that prick."

"Really?" replied Fafner while dragging Drayce towards Viktor.

Fafner wasn't prepared for what was to happen next, Viktor landed a dangerously strong punch into Drayce's face, breaking Fafner's grip, and knocking him to the ground. Drayce responded with an equally powerful punch, and so began one of the epic battles between two powerful young gods.

The viciousness in which they fought was unheard in Olympus; the fight lasted for an hour with no interference from those present, even Fafner decided his grandson needed a lesson and backed away.

There were no filters. Hands, arms, knees, legs, and heads were used as weapons. Blow after blow brought forth bruises and trickling blood. When one fell the other took advantage, only to immediately lose that advantage. It soon became obvious they were equal in every way, neither was going to outdo the other. It was then when the fight turned particularly dirty. There was biting, scratching, gouging, and targeting of sensitive areas. A primal violence came into play but still one couldn't best the other.

The fight had now reached the beach and was soon to end up in the shallow waters of the foreshore. The sound of their impacts was muffled by the crashing of the unusually high waves rolling close by. This gave Drayce the opportunity for which he was waiting. He grabbed Viktor's arm and twisted it so mercilessly Viktor retched from the pain.

Drayce moved his mouth close to Viktor's ear. "Viktor," he whispered, "we must keep viciously fighting for a while longer. I needed to drag this fight out into the waves so no one can hear what I have to say, please trust me."

Viktor freed himself and managed to grip Drayce by the neck forcing him under water, he then pulled him above the waves. "What are you talking about?"

They then grabbed each other's heads pulling their foreheads together as though preparing to wrestle.

"Something's wrong," said Drayce. "I might still be a young dragon, so I don't know who or what to trust. My hearing must be very acute, I can hear muffled sounds, I sense an evil presence. The worst is, everywhere I go I smell them, they're all around us, but I can't see them. My grandparents don't seem to detect them, I don't understand."

"What about Galyna," asked Viktor, "does she detect them?"

He then landed a devastating punch into Drayce's head which was met with an equally crushing response, forcing both under water.

When they surfaced, Viktor had Drayce above his head ready to throw him ten feet across the beach. He threw him, and then ran to frantically kick him while he was on the ground. Drayce managed to move his leg and upend Viktor giving him the chance to leap across and pin him down. The sound of the crashing waves was still loud enough to drown out anything being said.

"Stay on guard and keep me informed," whispered Viktor. "I'll find a way to alert the senior gods. We should act as though we hate each other until we figure out what's going on."

Magni and Ares then decided to end the fight and were walking over to the beach when they felt Jacob in their heads. "Leave them," he said, "all is not what it seems." Magni and Ares returned to begin their training of the young gods.

Jacob left the temple and blinked his way to the beach. He was angry and when he was seen waving his arms and pointing his fingers, those watching knew Drayce and Viktor were getting a roasting.

Jacob then gripped both boys, blinked again, taking them out into the universe to one of the biggest and brightest suns he could find. He found an orbiting rock and materialised.

"Why didn't you come to me?" he asked.

"I don't know who to trust," replied Drayce, "it's everywhere and it frightens me."

"Have you forgotten who I am?" said Jacob giving him a clatter across the back of his neck, "I am God of Gods. Don't you realise I too can sense all you can? I too can't figure out what's going on, and that's the worry."

"You and Drayce will work together," he said turning to Viktor, "you will report everything you hear, see, smell and touch. When either of you blink twice in my presence, I'll take it as a signal for me to enter your heads." Jacob prepared to blink them back to Olympus but before he did, he said, "Pretending to hate each other is a nice strategy but I'd prefer if you work together. That fight you had was too vicious, is there something you need to tell me?"

"There's nothing to tell," protested Drayce, "I thought fighting Viktor would allow me to find a way to share my concerns without alerting Shadow. I've the greatest respect for him, and know he feels the same for me. We've become great friends."

"Good," said Jacob. "I'll return you to the meadows and arrange for you to be excused from training until tomorrow. See Apollo, he'll look after your injuries. On arrival, let all see you are friends." Soon they arrived back in Olympus.

Drayce saw Fafner standing nearby. "Grandfather," he said after joining him, hoping we wouldn't be rebuffed. "I'm so sorry. Please forgive me?" Fafner just stared, walked away, saying nothing. This really upset Drayce, and he swore he'd work even harder to prove himself.

Chapter 17

Jacob joined Ares and Magni just as they were preparing to give their final guidance. He suggested the training be deferred until the following morning, considering what happened between Drayce and Victor, and it was agreed.

The following morning was an early start; all ten students were present. Drayce and Victor were still sporting extensive bruising.

There was no standing on ceremony, it was straight down to business. Ares began. "Yesterday," he said while looking at Drayce, "you saw Magni and I work our way through nine stations that between them hold sixteen different exercises, each one with ten reps, that's one hundred and sixty reps per circuit. You saw us complete twenty circuits, that's three thousand two hundred reps. You agreed to do ten times what we did, that's thirty-two thousand reps. You need to get started, but before you do, be aware of the traps, there are many, and they will test your skills. By the time you're finished you will have a new awareness of what's around you; you will learn to anticipate dangers and how to beat them."

"If you spring any traps," said Magni, "you must return to the pommel horses and start that circuit all over again. Oh, just so you know, we don't expect you to complete ten circuits for each one we did, we will be happy with three in total. You'll have noticed the stallions are back in position. Your task is to tame and train them to be War Horses. Difficulties with the horses will not cause you to restart the circuit."

"Off you go," said Ares.

All ten began a ten-minute warmup before mounting the pommel horses to begin a slow and rhythmic movement of their trunks and legs. They built up to a quicker pace using crosses as well as single and double leg circles, all without stopping. Each movement was completed ten times without incident.

They moved on to the weights section where two 3kg dumbbells were laid out for each of them. They were delighted with the light weights and began their program. They started with a ten-rep bicep curl followed by triceps' extensions, shoulder presses, weighted crunches, lunges, and leg squats. Again, no incidents to alarm them.

The weapons training was the one thing they looked forward to, they were all adept in the use of javelins and bows, but sling shots were new to them. They each got a perfect score in javelin throwing and in the use of the bows, but they failed miserably in the use of the slingshots, except for Maximus and Magnar, both of whom were trained in their use several years earlier. They then reached the logs, laid out from light to heavy. They raised them above their heads, held them for ten seconds, then threw them as far as they could. They had no problems with the first to the fifth, but began struggling on the sixth, and had real difficulty by the time they reached the eighth. Zane, Viktor, and Drayce were the exception, they had an almost super-human strength, allowing them to complete the task way ahead of the others.

They moved on to scale the climbing wall, again without difficulty. It was thirty feet high with no safety net. When they completed their ten reps, they used a sturdy zip line to take them to land among the horses. Obelius was now getting suspicious, he thought the circuit was too easy and wondered as to where the traps were set.

The horses were temporarily spooked, it was the scent of a lioness, and this caused a degree of embarrassment for Aria. Her discomfort was noted by Obelius who said, "They sense the lioness in you, let them know you are also a Goddess of the Light, go calm their fears." She approached the stallion allotted to her and used her skills to gain his trust.

They no sooner mounted their horses when the rearing and bucking started, causing five of the gods to painfully hit the ground. The other five had great difficulty, but their ability to balance themselves in such difficult circumstances led them to quickly become Horse-Lords. They began riding towards the woodlands only to be stopped by Magni. "Not today" he said, "the ropes await."

All ten made their way to the ropes and began climbing, they easily completed ten reps, then made their way to the parallel bars, where they also excelled in the various movements designed to tone their core muscles. The training sleds were heavily weighted and created some difficulty, but they soon managed to complete ten reps. After the training sleds they made their way to the pool.

Drayce thought he saw something in the water and was confused when on inspection there was nothing. He was suspicious, wondered if their first trap was about to be sprung. They then dived in, fully clothed and weighted. They swam the required laps with no incidents, and this really unsettled them.

Ares was waiting as they climbed from the pool and said nothing, just pointed towards the Pommel Horses for their second circuit. On the way Thora said to the girls, "Trust me, and don't do any more than ten reps at each station. I fear that's where the first trap will be strung. Look at Obelius and Maximus, they're showing off, and will do more reps than required, just to prove a point. They will pay for their arrogance.

She was right; Obelius and Maximus went into competition against each other and were followed quickly by Viktor and Tristan. When they reached seventeen reps each, a wooden, leather covered fist erupted from the base of the pommel horse and landed between their legs, sending them to the ground in agony. The remaining boys cringed in sympathy, and the girls tried not to laugh.

Magni approached them with his hands resting on his hips, he shook his head, showing no sympathy. "You know the rules," he said with a wide smirk. "Go, start all over again." He then walked away, and while out of view, his smirk turned to a wide grin.

The remaining gods reached the ropes and just as they were about to start climbing, Thora paused. "Give me a minute," she said before closing her eyes. She used her eidetic memory to bring herself back to when Magni had climbed. She noted black spots high up on the ropes, and how Magni always avoided them. "Listen carefully," she whispered, "don't touch the black spots."

All six climbed, and made it to the top then back down, they repeated the exercise ten times and just as they were descending for the last time Aria touched a spot and released a lubricating gel that caused her to slip. She hit the ground and was ushered back to start the circuit all over again.

Thora led the way to the next station, the parallel bars. Drayce, Magnar, and Zane watched her like hawks hoping she'd continue using her powers to prevent them from springing any other traps.

Unfortunately for Zane and Drayce, they weren't watching intently enough, halfway through their reps on the high bars they placed their hands on a marked section. Four spikes shot up and impaled them, causing them excruciating pain. The spikes retracted and both boys rolled about in agony, their blood pouring everywhere. The expletives released by Zane will forever be implanted in all their memories. Ares arrived and tried to calm things. "Why are you yelling?"

"Look at the holes in my hands," screamed Drayce, still rolling on the ground, "look at the blood I've lost. I can't continue, how could you do this to me?"

"What blood?" said Ares looking bewildered. "What holes?" he asked, "have you lost your mind?"

"They're fucking playing with our minds," screamed Drayce, looking across at Zane. "Some of these traps are illusions." Zane tried to continue using the bars but was directed to start the circuit all over again and he wasn't happy, especially when he caught Obelius and Viktor smirking.

Lovisa, Magnar and Thora reached the boulder laden sleds and began pulling. They had difficulty getting started, such was the weight, but they were motivated knowing this was the one station to work their back, shoulder, biceps, and grip muscles, perfect for building their strength and power. There were no incidents, so they made their way to the shallow end of the pool. This time Thora stripped, but before diving in she paused. She wondered about the gentle ripples rolling across the surface. There was no wind, or no tremors, so why were there ripples? She concluded another trap was waiting to be sprung and went on alert. Magnar and Lovisa also stripped and together they all dived in. While under water was when they saw them, piranhas, and there were hundreds, all preparing to attack. There was great relief when they noticed that the piranhas were muzzled except for one whose teeth seemed primed and ready to do its worst.

Thora insisted they swim close to each other while all the time keeping her eye on the unmuzzled fish. It was when they reached the eight lap when Magnar saw the piranha swim towards him, and he began to panic. Thora also noticed, and as it attacked, she managed to land a powerful kick, successfully stunning it, but unfortunately, her punch was the cue for it to split in two. This was Magnar's worst nightmare. He had a fish phobia, a phobia that for years he managed to suppress and hide from everybody, especially his father and brother. Seeing two angry fish heading his way caused him to frantically paddle but he wasn't fast enough. They reached him to feverishly gnaw at his heels, causing him a great deal of pain. Around him the water turned red, and he wondered was this another illusion, but the pain he was in made it feel real. He paddled faster not realising that this was his defence. His frantic kicking was so swift he inadvertently kicked both fish out of the pool ensuring they couldn't multiply. They had just discovered how to beat another trap.

They had now completed their second circuit and prepared to begin their third. They were stopped by Ares who suggested they rest while the other seven gods continued with their efforts.

It was mid-afternoon before all, but Obelius and Maximus had reached the end. They had both failed at the parallel bars and had to start all over again. When they reached the parallel bars for the second time, Maximus had his fingers resting on his forehead, he then whispered something to Obelius. Ares looked across at Magnar and concluded they were telepathically sharing how to beat the traps.

Magni also noticed. "They think they can beat me?" He squinted in annoyance, "we'll see about that."

Obelius and Maximus began their reps and looked strong; they had avoided setting off the traps, which was until they reached their seventh rep. Ares deliberately set off the trap but this time he released all stakes. There were ten, and they penetrated their legs, torso, arms, and neck. Poor

Obelius got one in the groin. Their pain was so intense they retched, then vomited. They were so firmly impaled every attempt at movement caused the intensity of the pain to increase.

Magnar was first to object and made his feeling known. He ran to his brother but was forcefully pushed to the ground by Magni who reminded him that he was partially responsible for what happened. Magni gripped Obelius's and Maximus's hair, lifting their heads so he could look them in the face. "I will not tolerate cheats," he yelled. "Get up and start the circuit all over again."

He flicked his wrist, and the stakes disappeared, so did the blood, bruises, and the pain. All that was left was the vomit. There never were any stakes, there was never any blood or bruises, and their pain was just in their imagination, they will never forget it.

Obelius could take no more, and alongside Maximus, he stormed off towards the temple prompting Magni to say, "Excuse me, where are you going?"

"I've had enough," screamed Obelius, "you've made your point."

He turned to continue his walk only to find his way blocked by Jacob who just circled his finger in mid-air. Obelius stepped aside to pass him, but Jacob just stretched out his arm, indicating he wasn't to pass. Obelius grunted, about turned, and walked towards the starting point with Maximus still briskly walking behind.

"Shit," whispered Maximus, "we really blew that one."

"We?" yelled Obelius, turning to stare at him with contempt, "surely you mean that you and your fucking brother blew it; we were doing Ok until he entered your head."

It was then Obelius went quiet. He disappeared and was gone for no more than two minutes. When he returned Jacob briefly appeared alongside him. Magni then ordered him to the starting point. Maximus was curious but knew not to ask any questions.

Maximus and Obelius began working their way through the circuit. This time they made it all the way to the pool, and without thinking, they just dived in, only to be horrified by the amount of un-muzzled piranhas waiting for them.

Obelius reached across to touch Maximus' forehead, "It's now when someone should enter our heads," he said, showing signs of panic.

They got relief when they heard, "Swim and use your heels to flick them out of the water." It was Thora. "If they're coming at you from all directions use your fists."

Maximus was the one the fish targeted; they must have detected the fear held by his brother, but they were mistaken, he was well able to defend himself. He used his brother's earlier experience and as the fish approached, he used his speed to begin flicking them from the pool. Obelius was also adept at defending himself and he too used the same strategy. They soon reached the end of their ten laps.

Ares gestured for all ten to gather at the start and prepare for their third circuit, but before they begun, they were treated to the sight of Jacob leading over a hundred centurion style warriors, across the meadows. They were curious while watching the centurions disperse to take up positions all around the perimeter of the meadows. When in position they stood as fully armed, seven-foot-tall guardians, not that unlike the regular palace guards, the difference being their height, their off-white armour, and full-length hooded cloaks. When in place they lowered their heads and seemed to freeze in time.

When Jacob was satisfied, he rejoined Magni to watch the final stages of the third circuit, which went very well. The young gods worked hard and successfully completed their task without setting off the traps, but there were close shaves. When it was completed he joined Obelius. "Earlier, when you stormed off was unacceptable, and I hope you learned a lesson? I love you, but sometimes your arrogance really annoys me. As a matter of interest, where did you disappear to, that two minutes when you left your training?"

"I saw you going beneath the temple and was curious," replied Obelius. "You are never to be alone; you know that. I'm your guardian and felt something was wrong. I watched you for a few moments and soon satisfied myself there was no danger."

Jacob slowly nodded his head; he was so proud of his son at that moment. "It was the right thing for a guardian of Olympus to do," he said. "Now, go and rest, tomorrow will be just as difficult." He leaned in to kiss his son's forehead.

The following day it was horse training, and it went on all morning. They then spent the afternoon tasked with completing three more circuits. There were many setbacks caused by springing traps, but in the end, the three circuits were completed.

Day three began with a visit from the wizards who spent the morning tutoring them about what can be garnered by using the power of the Mystics. They spoke of Earth, Air, Fire, and Water, and how those elements will help them during times of great need. They spoke of the power of magic, and how seers, sorcerers, wizards, and shamans harness it for all that is good. They warned them about the dangers of dark magic, and how they should never fight it without the help of the Mystic Gods.

After lunch, the young gods began their third session of circuit training which was more intense than the previous days. There were far more traps and as a result they had difficulty coping. The traps were now set on every station and were getting more difficult to predict, but by the end of the day they became masters of the circuit without having to restart. The pool was their biggest challenge because all piranhas were now unmuzzled and this was set to be their most challenging task until Obelius said, "Maths is not my strongest, so someone help me. If five of us guard and five swim, how many laps would we need to do in total?"

"We still do ten laps," said Aria, "five swim unbroken the other five guard and protect, then the guards swim unbroken while the first five guard them."

That's exactly what happened, the first five guards successfully removed over half the fish from the pool leaving the remaining few to be expelled later. The young gods felt proud and in control. They were now working as a cohesive unit, working as though they were controlled by one brain instead of ten. Their abdominals were sculptured to perfection, their biceps were the size of their heads, and their triceps lean and strong. Their shoulder muscles were rounded and protruding making them look like masterpieces of creation. Their grip strength was so acute they could move across any obstacle rapidly, or at a snail's pace, without losing control. In the pool, they swam with a form of fluidity and a precision that looked almost robotic, stroke after stroke they took was so synchronised it was perfection. They had now become Gods of War; some might say, 'less gods and more like weapons with legs.'

Chapter 18

On day one of the War God's training, the Mystic Gods also began their lessons. That morning, they had gathered at an annex that was built on the left-hand side of the temple, where they waited for the arrival of the Wizards. There were two round tables, each set up to sit four pupils. Demetrius sat with Gaia, Sagal, and Galyna, while Hemish sat with Sofia, Sunniva, and Helena.

Mygon was first to arrive, and he took his place at the top of the room, he said nothing, and this unsettled his pupils. Apollonius was next to arrive, followed by Merlin, they too remained quiet as though waiting for inspiration.

"I look at your concerned and fearful faces," said Merlin while looking around enjoying his power over them, "and I wonder why you are so troubled. You are the Seers, the Mystics, the Guardians of the old ways. You are the ones who will be trained to save the spoken word and create the books of knowledge. No Mage will ever learn to stand against you. By the time three days have passed, you will have learned to harness unlimited knowledge. You will be the teachers tasked with bringing balance back between the natural and the supernatural worlds."

"Fear not young gods," said Apollonius after walking to the centre of the room, "you've been blessed by the Ancient One to be harnessers of the Light. Always remember that same Light is the fastest thing in the universe, and you will learn to control its intensity, and its brightness. You will learn to summon it, bend it, direct it, and to use its healing powers. Wherever you walk, no evil will triumph, because nothing can defeat the power of the Light, especially with you as its master."

"Your immortality," continued Merlin, "is the gift that has given you an enhanced sense of awareness, allowing your minds to use energies and powers unheard of, powers to defy physics such as conjuring, invisibility, and illusion. What seems impossible travel will be yours, but most especially you will garner an ability to travel through time."

"Today," said Mygon, after joining Merlin, "we start with Elemental teachings followed by learning to control your mind and body powers. Tomorrow, we study the sciences and then you will be taken through war tactics under the guidance of Athena. On the third day you learn of magic and especially of what is forbidden.

Galyna raised her hand. "I am a lady of the Dragon Realm," she nervously said, "I was born to a powerful War Lord, why am I here?"

"Yes, young dragon," replied Merlin, "you are a daughter of Andras, but you are also a daughter of Mia, a Goddess of the Light. Her aura surrounds you, showing us how you will become a Mystic Goddess and a Warrior Queen of the Dragon Realm, your future lies in the royal house."

Merlin and Mygon then left the room leaving Apollonius to take charge of the first lesson; he placed a cauldron of water, a candle, and a tray of soil before each pupil. He moved his hand from left to right, at first slowly, then rapidly, causing a rush of wind to develop. He had now produced all four elements - Earth, Air, Fire, and Water.

He requested everyone to place their fingers into the soil, close their eyes, and wait for something to happen. Almost immediately Demetrius and Gaia noticed movement, they felt tremors and as they moved their fingers, they found they were communicating with the Earth Mothers. Hemish and Sagal sensed the components and just using their minds they separated the precious metals and the aggregate of rock and stone particles. The other four had difficulty sensing anything and began to feel like failures.

Apollonius then raised a candle; he placed his fingers above the flame and using the power of his mind he caused it to shimmer and sway. He requested the pupils try the same thing; this time Sunniva and Helena took control of its light. They drew the flame higher causing it to send flickering shapes into the roof space. They were able to manipulate its light, creating shadows. The other six had difficulty with this task but their persistence paid off, they practiced until they too became its master.

Water was next to be used and all eight had no problems with this task, each one dipped their fingers into their cauldron and after extracting their fingers, a narrow string of water followed, they stepped away from their desks and used the strings to create rope like shapes. This was when they became artistic; their various strings were intertwining and creating the most amazing water formed images.

The next task to come to terms with was manipulating air, even a foul smelling one, and this was when they began to have fun. Demetrius had a reputation for flatulence and never failed to oblige, but he should have known better. Helena was disgusted and sent a beam of light towards him that ignited his next flatus, burning his back side. He was not impressed and his dancing around the room showed how painful the burning experience was. He had to stand for the rest of the class.

Apollonius had difficulty containing himself, but he managed, and then produced a miniature whirlwind before showing the young gods how he controlled it. Within minutes all eight pupils had mini tornadoes swirling around the room.

Demetrius saw his opportunity for revenge on Helena; he manipulated his whirlwind to rise above her head to release its hailstones. She was not happy, and her screams could be heard throughout the temple. Demetrius knew he was in trouble and ran towards the door only for Apollonius to create a barrier preventing him from leaving. Helena was also prevented from carrying out her retribution by that same barrier.

When calm was restored, Apollonius encouraged the eight pupils to move out into the meadows where for the next two hours they practiced until they had complete control of all four elementals. They were able to produce mile high tornadoes, as well as create amazing water features. They learned to command the waves in the lagoon by raising them to forty feet in height. From the sun they called on its fire, giving them the power to produce balls of molten rocks. They learned to control the speed and direction of the rocks just by using the power of their mind. They then broke for lunch and returned to the temple.

After lunch they made their way back to the annex where they found Mygon resting three feet above the floor, with no supports. They were amazed at how relaxed he looked and sat in awe of him. Without opening his eyes he said, "By this evening you will have the power to levitate just by thinking about it, the power of 'mind over body' is unmatched in the universe and it is the one power that always disarms an enemy."

He asked them to take the lotus position which they duly did. "For you to learn control of your mind, you must understand your body," he said while walking amongst them. "You are gods, but only have five senses; the sixth is still hidden from you. Right now, all you have is sight, hearing, taste, smell, and touch; you need to enhance all of them before your mind can be controlled." He then brought them to the window and asked, "On the horizon, tell me what you see."

"I see different shades of green," said Hemish, "a tree line."

"I see the white horses," said Sagal, "they graze before the trees; I cannot see their heads. I just know what I see has to be the horses." Mygon said nothing.

"Between the two tallest trees I see a faint light," said Sunniva, moving her head from left to right, "it's bright and calls to me, it's a sun, shining far out in the cosmos. My mind tells me I'm destined to go there with..." She looked at the floor and said nothing more.

"I too see that light," said Helena reaching in to hug Sunniva, "It's waiting for you, but not just yet. I also see what you've chosen not to speak of."

"I've no idea of what any of you are talking about," said Demetrius, "I see nothing."

Sofia raised her hand to shade her eyes. "I thought it was my imagination," she said, "right now, but I'm not certain. Below the light, I see a small bird, it's being chased, oh, it's just been caught."

"Impressive," said Mygon.

"I have the eyesight of a dragon," said Galyna, "It's so acute I can see the spines hidden in the leaves even as they shake in the soft winds. I also see something else."

Gaia interrupted, then placed her hand on Demetrius. "Why are you lying?" she asked. "Like Galyna, I too see something else. We both saw what you saw and if both of us saw it, we must report it."

"What did you see?" asked Mygon.

"I saw SHADOW," replied Demetrius, looking very worried.

Mygon got alarmed and left at once to speak with Jacob who, on hearing this news, disappeared to reappear near the shield. Demetrius was watching and wasn't impressed to see his father appear alone at the tree line. He used his powers to reach Obelius, alerting him to what was happening. Obelius was furious, he grabbed a sword, javelin, and bow, and without acknowledging either Ares or Magni he blinked to materialise alongside Jacob.

"Father," he yelled, "What the fuck? You're an idiot. You are never to travel without a guardian, you know that."

"Well," said Jacob, ignoring the insult. "You're here now. Can you smell it? They were here, I think they're gone. If Demetrius, Gaia, and Galyna saw Shadow, I believe them. This is another breach of the temple grounds."

"You THINK they're gone?" said a still angry Obelius, raising his voice, "That's not good enough."

"Don't be so incredulous," replied Jacob. "The amazing eyesight of the mystic gods has given us another advantage. Return to your training, I'll clear your absence with Magni."

"Clearing my absence is all you're worried about?" yelled Obelius, "I'll never understand you."

"Relax," said Jacob, trying to reassure his son. "Plans are already forming in my mind. Within minutes more guards will be deployed, remember son, their sole purpose is to defend the temple by any means necessary."

On returning to the temple grounds, they were greeted by Magni who wasn't happy with Obelius disappearing for the second time. Seeing Magni's face, Obelius knew it would be wise to swiftly make his way back to rejoin Maximus.

"Brother," said Jacob, "trust me, he did the right thing. Don't be too hard on him. Oh, by the way, he called me an idiot."

"Like father, like son????" said Magni with a smile. He then got serious, "have we something to worry about?"

Jacob slowly nodded, then said, "I'm close to awakening another force, far more lethal guards, ones who were created by Zeus, they are ancient and have been asleep for thousands of years. You will have seen me bring the seven-foot palace guards into the meadows, wait until you see these ancient ones."

Jacob left Magni and made his way to the annex. On arrival he acknowledged the growing powers of the mystic gods and remained there for a short while to watch them demonstrate their new skills. As he was about to leave Sunniva said, "Uncle, our new powers allowed us hear you approach from a mile away, we could even hear you breathe."

Galyna interrupted, "When you were at the shield we also smelt the same stench you detected. How is that possible, from that distance?"

"Father," said Demetrius, "never mind what they say, you were four miles away and all of us heard Obelius call you an idiot, how is he still alive?"

Jacob didn't respond, he chose to leave, and while passing a trellis table he grabbed some empty cups and fired them at the young gods. In all cases their reflexes were so acute they successfully caught each cup without any breakages. "I'm impressed," he said, "your hearing is enhanced, your reflexes are amazing, you can smell decay from a great distance, and your sight? Is it as good as I suspect?"

He went to the window and looked towards the tree line. "I see a spider," he said while pointing into the distance, "It's on a leaf to the left of the tallest tree, tell me its colour, and when you find the spider, tell me what's on the next leaf."

All eight gathered at the window and within seconds, each wrote down the colour they saw, all got it right. They then wrote down the insect feeding on the next leaf, again they all got it right. "Now tell me what they are doing," said Jacob with a wry smile.

"Wey Hey, insect porn," said a giggling Hemish without thinking. Jacob threw his eyes to the heavens and left the room.

Mygon called the young gods back to their desks. He congratulated them on their enhanced senses and encouraged them to move on to their next challenge. Each was blindfolded, given a piece of masonry, and a large metal nugget. They were asked to identify the components of both the masonry and the nugget.

Their sense of touch kicked in and as the minutes passed, they began to accurately name the components. They were not allowed to speak but had to individually remove their blindfolds and write down the answers. All but Hemish and Sunniva correctly named copper, gold, tin, mercury, titanium, and uranium as the components of the metal nugget; they also identified marble, granite, limestone, flowstone and cast stone as the components of the masonry. It took Hemish and Sunniva some time, but they too eventually completed the task.

There was still two hours to go before their lessons were due to end and during this time they were again blindfolded. "Empty your minds," said Mygon. "Allow your hearing filter out all sound so that my voice is all you'll hear. When my voice fades allow your minds take you to the farthest reaches of the universe where you will learn to use your powers to control all that is natural."

Two hours passed and they all began to awaken; when they did, they felt confused. Mygon was still in deep meditation.

"I feel no different," said Hemish who was first to speak.

"I feel sick," said Helena, looking a bit shaken. "Where did we go?" she asked.

"My legs are stuck," said Demetrius trying to stand. "What the fuck?"

"There's no difference," said Sofia.

"I don't think all is what it seems," said a confused Galyna.

"I feel a strange power has taken me." said Gaia looking at her hands.

"Something has changed but I can't put my finger on it," said Sagal.

Sunniva said nothing.

Mygon was still levitating. He eventually awoke and stood before Demetrius who still couldn't move. "You say your legs are stuck," he said, "why not think about sitting on the windowsill and let's see what happens." Demetrius thought and then suddenly, within a nano-second, he was no longer stuck, he was sitting on the sill.

Mygon then stood Sagal and Helena ten feet apart. "Without moving any closer," he said, "think about trying to reach out to each other." Suddenly their arms elongated, and they were touching each other.

"Create a fireball," he suggested to Helena, "and send it towards Gaia, send it at the speed of light." Helena raised her arms, and a fireball formed above her palm, it was immediately extinguished, Gaia had gotten a power that allows her to negate any threat, even if it came from a friendly source.

"Today," said Mygon, sitting them down to explain what happened, "Today you learned to enhance normal senses, and during the last two hours you've gained supernatural abilities. Abilities not available to the War Gods. We finish now and tomorrow you begin your science training."

The following morning, after a hearty breakfast, the young gods had some free time before going to the meadows for a light workout. They then made their way to the annex where Apollonius was waiting. When they settled he welcomed them to day two of their lessons.

He began by saying, "For the next five hours you will learn how the laws of the universe control everything. You will also learn how the laws of chemical periodicity, and conservation of mass, will enhance the many powers you already have. It's possible that, with your amazing eyesight, an ability has developed allowing you to see electrons, neutrons, and protons, but none of this will happen without you understanding atomic structure and the reason why all the known elements sit where they do on the periodic table." He then ushered the gods over to an area where test tubes, burners, hot plates, and other experimentation equipment was set up. He then guided them through several chemistry experiments.

After another few hours had passed Apollonius called the gods back to their seats to discuss physics. He helped them to understand classical mechanics and the laws of motion. He taught them about electromagnetism and the effect of charged particles, as well as how visible light is a feature of electromagnetic radiation. He spoke about the theory of relativity and how it will become clear to them when they grasp how the faster you move the slower time passes.

He paused many times allowing them a few moments to absorb all he said, then told them how physics is the master of every minutia of the known universe, how it alone explains all the natural happenings they will encounter in the physical world. He spent the next few hours helping them understand the most important laws of physics, and how they will be needed in the future. He then told them of how physics doesn't explain the power of the gods.

When the classes ended, they moved out onto the meadows to be met by Athena who took them through the basics of swordsmanship, the uses of their staffs and most importantly, war tactics.

The third day began with a light workout in the meadows, followed by a wholesome breakfast. The gods then made their way to the annex where Merlin was waiting. He looked stern and profoundly serious, and the young gods understood why, this was the day they were to learn about what makes them gods, they knew that by the end of the day they would become masters of High Magic, and vanquishers of all that's Dark.

When they settled Merlin presented each one with a well carved staff that had in its head, a large crystal. He waited for them to finish examining their staffs before saying, "The strange thing is, you don't really need a staff, but they do have their uses. They can simply be used as support especially while climbing steep hills, they can also be used as a weapon. Through the crystal, your staff will be a conduit for the arrival of the Light. Always remember that you too are conduits of the Light."

Like previous lessons he allowed them to absorb what he said before continuing, "Since the beginning of time each new invention looked like magic, especially to the weak and less evolved of early man. When the first wheel rolled, it was used to improve life, to move heavy weights and transport food, then those living in darkness discovered it can be used for war. Real magic is the same; its intention was always to help, but just like evolution it too has a dark side. Those who practice dark magic revel in abusing for pleasure then causing pain and death. They start by bringing fear and trepidation before using its power to take control. Those who practice high magic strive to support balance throughout the natural world. Your task is to use your high magic to counter the advance of those who walk in darkness, those who walk in Shadow."

He walked among them and as he walked the tapping of his staff impacting the tiles, it echoed through the room. "Magic," he continued, "can be used for many things; its power when used in the right way is infinite.

Apollonius, Mygon and I were once mere men who became wizards, our power is not infinite. You, as children of the gods are different, you were not born as human, you were born as gods and when you learn of magic, you will become most powerful. High magic will allow you travel through solid walls without harming yourself, it will allow you use your mind to look back into the past as well as see into the future, it will allow you manipulate time, but always remember you cannot change the past, for time always finds a way and will bring your changes back into balance. Those who try to manipulate time will not like the result. You will learn by using what's available to you in the natural world, for example, its herbs and potions that will allow you to shape-shift, call for inspiration, create portals, and among other things you will learn to reach into the minds of others, and communicate telepathically."

He walked back to the head of the class and turned to face his pupils. "Dark magic," he said, "is forbidden, use it once and you open the door for The Darkness, beware its power. Never conjure up spirits, never bring back those who have died, never enter the mind of another with the sole purpose of occupying or controlling them. You must never try to enter the minds of those unable to defend themselves, never use your powers to abuse them, cause them illness, or worse, kill them. Always remember how dark magic never rests, it travels using the negative forces of the universe. It only feeds on jealousy, envy, suffering, and pain. I say again, it never rests."

Galyna raised her hand and asked, "You say we should never bring back those who have died. How is it the Emperor Fafner and the Empress Heulwyn came back to life?"

"A very good question," replied Merlin. "They were immortals, not human. They were still intact, no decapitation, there was no decay. They are blessed by, and favourites of the Ancient One."

For the next few hours, they spent their time practicing using their newfound powers, they begun by creating illusions, merging two objects to become one, they learned to walk through each other, they turned themselves into pillars, tables, books, vermin, and the most difficult of all, aerated liquid. They played with each other's minds by erasing memories and fostering false ones, they magically moved objects around the room with no resistance; they entered and left the minds of the War Gods, causing great confusion out in the meadows. Their powers were now almost complete.

Helena looked distressed and Merlin noticed. "Tell me, princess of Olympus," he asked, "what troubles you?"

"I listened carefully to what you said to Galyna," she replied, "but still I don't feel assuaged. Drayce is important to me, and after listening to your lesson on dark magic I fear for him. What happens if he sings the 'Song of the Dragons' again, and inadvertently opens a portal for The Darkness to enter our realm?"

"Drayce broke no laws," said Merlin trying to allay her fears," he alone has the power to use the song to raise a dead immortal. He can only do this with the help of the Ancient One. The rules against the use of Dark Magic refer to being used on mortals and mortals only."

Apollonius and Mygon rejoined the class, and with Merlin they used their staffs to open a portal through which they all passed. They entered a long galley style room with arches running along both sides. Under each arch were the engraved images of the twelve primary Olympians and the twelve Titans. Towards the end of the hall stood two colossus statues of the first ones, Father Sky and Mother Earth - Uranus, and Gaia.

The young gods were in awe of what was before them, under every arch were smaller alcoves storing thousands of books, scrolls, and codices. Never had they seen such a wealth of knowledge held in just one place.

They made their way to where the statues of Uranus and Gaia stood. Between the statues they found a large ornate water font, wafting a gaseous, constant mist that shielded what was behind. They walked through the mist to find a four stepped pedestal holding eleven antiquated books. Each book was upright, showing its title and facing outwards for all to see. Each cover was made from a brown coloured leather, and inlayed with peeling gold lettering. The leather was cracking, dry from what was obviously the result of a great age. There was a fear of touching the books; they looked like their stitching was barely holding them together, and the merest touch would cause them to turn to dust.

"Look upon all the knowledge of the universe," gasped Merlin. "They're waiting to unleash their words. Here they have rested, hidden, and protected, as the years turned to centuries and centuries turned to millennia. During the great battle, when Jacob was preparing to fight Lucifer, we searched everywhere and never found them. Through all that time, they were here, under our noses, under the protection of Olympus. Now they've shown themselves, and we wonder what calamity approached."

Sagal approached, and slowly moved her hand towards the nearest book, the 'Book of Wisdom'. She nervously gripped then raised it, shocked at how old and heavy it was. Suddenly the Light came, and the book became pristine, the leather softened and there were no cracks. The gold lettering was restored and became as new.

Demetrius stepped closer and read each title aloud. "Book of Stars, Book of Darkness, Book of Creation, Book of the Dead, Book of Gods, Book of Names, Book of Magic, Book of Memories, Book of Languages, Book of Maps."

"Something's not right," he said turning to Helena, "there's no room for another book, yet I sense there should be a twelfth." He looked at Merlin quizzingly, "Am I right?"

"Yes," replied Merlin, "you are right. The long-gone wizards always spoke of twelve books but never claimed to have seen them. They've always been hidden, and no one understands as to why. This is our first time to see them and for that alone, we feel honoured to be guided towards this most holy of sanctums. It would seem the eleven of us are to become the guardians of all knowledge."

Hemish cautiously raised the next book, the Book of Stars, he opened it and the light that shot out illuminated the whole temple. He closed the book and handed it to Sagal, then picked up the next one, the Book of Darkness. No one noticed that the first two books had melded together until Hemish placed the third book into Sagals hand, it too melded, leaving Sagal still holding a single book.

Galyna reached in and picked the next book, the Book of the Creation. She placed it in Sagal's hand, and this book also melded into the others. She continued until all books had melded, and then two magical things happened. All eleven books were replaced by exact copies, and the eleven melded books in Sagal's hands began to glow. The cover changed and the writing became more pronounced. Sunniva read the new title aloud, "The Book of Life."

"Is this what attracts Shadow to Olympus?" asked Helena, placing her hand over her mouth, "is this what Shadow seeks?"

"We must tell Jacob of our suspicions," said Sagal while rushing towards the door, "he'll know what to do." Helena joined her, only to be taken aback when the book faded, then disappeared, just as they walked through the door. It seems the book can never leave the sanctum.

"It's no coincidence," said Demetrius. "There are eleven of us, there's also eleven books. Why don't we take a book each and study its writings? If I'm right we will, between us, soon hold all the secrets of the universe. Earlier we learned how to meld together, allowing us to share our thoughts. Let us become repositories of all knowledge." The wizards were impressed with the suggestion and made the arrangements to share out the books.

They studied the texts while all the time absorbing every iota of information. They were so engrossed they didn't notice the tolling bells announcing, at first dinner, and then breakfast.

It was the following evening after the bell again tolled for dinner when they finally finished and made their way to the Great Hall. The War Gods had already arrived and were sitting enjoying their meal. They were, as usual, boisterous, and loud, but when they saw the Mystic Gods arrive, they ran to greet them only to be interrupted by an anxious Jacob, "I wondered how long it would take you to work out its secret."

"Father," replied Helena reaching across to hug him, "even after all these years, Olympus still has places that are as yet undiscovered, today we found the books of knowledge, there are eleven."

"Tell me darling," he said, "did you find the twelfth?"

"The twelfth is when all eleven come together," she replied.

"You knew?" asked Merlin, furrowing his brow.

"I've known since soon after the great battle," said Jacob. "That night I was restless; I found myself being guided through the corridors of Olympus. I reached the rear of the library, and a secret door magically opened to show me what lay behind. For almost sixteen years I've read my way through all eleven books, have you noticed how as the hours pass the back pages continue to gather more writings?"

"But why say nothing?" asked Demetrius.

"Something inside cautioned me to remain quiet," replied Jacob.

He stood and called all the young gods into his presence. "Eighteen young innocents entered this temple as Children of the Gods," he said, "and, although not quite there yet, you are certainly on the path to be the gods you were destined to be. You've worked hard for three arduous days and deserve a break. Tomorrow, you should go out into the vastness of our realm and have some fun."

"Father," said an already scheming Obelius, "you're right, we did work hard, but there's no time like the present to play hard. We're not going tomorrow; we're going now." There was a huge cheer and all eighteen quickly put their plans together, arranged for provisions and when ready, left the temple to make their way towards the mountains.

When they were gone, and after two minutes had passed, Jacob remarked to those remaining, "Can any of you hear it?"

"Oh yes," said Athena, "the silence, no pesky teenagers, just peace."

"Peace is all very fine, if you can trust it," said a serious Merlin, "Helena fears the Book of Life is the reason Shadow is probing at the gates of Olympus."

"She may be right," replied Jacob. "Doesn't it bother any of you as to who Shadow is? No hand has been shown; no hint has been given; does this not make you wonder? It sure does bother me."

"Let's not worry about Shadow tonight," said Magni. "Let's rest in the knowledge that the Book of Life is now protected in three places - the sacred sanctum, in the minds of the wizards and the Mystic Gods, and most importantly, inside you brother, the God of Gods."

"I find it very difficult not to worry," said Jacob, "Out here among the four suns I thought we were safe, and free of Shadow. Today I sensed its evil presence. Demetrius, Gaia, and Galyna saw something out near our perimeter, they identified it as a shadow, it seems this Shadow is everywhere and as a result I've decided to take Olympus back to earth. All other pantheons will then know where we are; we need to be always available to them. Shadow is targeting Olympus with this constant probing; imagine what they could do to the peaceful pantheons if we are not there to help? We leave in the next few minutes."

Chapter 19

Jacob moved to the centre of the Hall and raised his arms towards the heavens. Within seconds there was a low rumbling, not that unlike a mild tremor. At first the four suns brightened, then faded. It suddenly darkened; the only light being that of millions of stars streaking by. They were travelling faster than the speed of light.

Out in the meadows the young gods felt the tremor and weren't concerned. Even when it darkened they cared less, they were fascinated while watching the streaks of passing star light racing by. At times, the heat of the brightest suns was oppressive, but it was quickly replaced when more streaks of light appeared. Demetrius, because of seeing Shadow earlier was still concerned, he raised his fingers to his forehead and telepathically reached Jacob. "Father," he said, "is there something wrong? What's happening?"

"Nothing to worry about, son," replied Jacob, "I'm moving Olympus back to earth, we should arrive in a few moments. Enjoy yourselves."

Throughout the Middle East people noticed a series of flickering lights high in the sky, they weren't alarmed. They were always aware of strange happenings and felt what they saw was the gods watching over them.

With great precision, the stewards slowly guided Olympus into a safe location in the Sinai Desert, close to a rarely visited small oasis that was home to around two hundred villagers. Time as usual was playing tricks, when Olympus left the four suns, it was late evening. When it arrived on earth, it was morning, giving the young gods an extra day for fun.

When all was settled, the young gods continued with their journey, determined to enjoy their adventure. They agreed among themselves not to use their powers unless it was absolutely necessary. They then broke up into three smaller groups, planning to come back together at the end of the day.

The boys chose to head further into the mountains and climb the highest peaks, while Lovisa, Thora and Aria opted to go horse riding, the remaining girls went swimming. Overall, it was an uneventful day but when they all came back together, the real fun started. Obelius opened his satchel and said while extracting eighteen glasses. "You didn't think I'd go on an adventure without bringing a few home comforts, the one thing I'm certain of is we can't have a party without a barrel of beer." He then produced the beer to great excitement.

Sunniva, as she extracted a cask from her satchel said, "I think a really fine wine is more becoming for a night like tonight, a touch of class that's more suitable for such esteemed gods and goddesses."

"And just to complete the feast," said Helena with a smile travelling from ear to ear, "look what I managed to secure." She extracted from her satchel a wide variety of foods that was prepared earlier for that evening's dinner, "I'd love to be a fly on the wall of the kitchen when the cooks arrive to find half that evening's food missing."

Viktor, Drayce, Zane, and Tristan gathered enough wood to keep a fire going all night.

Everything was now in place for a wild and boisterous night. In fact, it was so noisy it kept the gods in the temple awake, even thought they were four miles away. Jacob, Fafner, and Magni were on the terrace, feeling a bit envious. They could see the fire, and hear the amazing singing voices of Drayce, Gaia, Tristan, and Sunniva, they were tempted to join them but thought better of it. When Maximus tried to sing, Magni cringed, he threw his eyes to the heavens. "He drove me mad when he was a child," he said still cringing, placing his hands over his ears, "I've never recovered from his incessant attempts at singing, and even now he still hasn't a note in his head."

"You think that's bad," laughed Jacob, "I pray Obelius doesn't start, he hasn't a clue." His prayers weren't answered. He placed his head into his hands, "Please stop, the pain, I can't take it." They all laughed.

"Oops," said Fafner, moving to stand before Jacob.

"What did you see?" asked Jacob.

"Nothing," replied Fafner, taking a deep breath.

Jacob got suspicious especially when Magni moved behind him to firmly grip him. "Just like the dragons," he said, tightening his grip, "I have powerful night vision, and I too saw what Fafner saw. We both value Drayce's life and now that he has just kissed Helena, you can't be trusted. They've moved away from the group, and we can't have you spoiling their fun."

"Spoil their fun?" laughed Jacob as he broke free, "I wouldn't dare, Eala has being threatened me for weeks. She warned that if I interfere, I'll never have any fun again."

"Sunniva and Hemish are getting very close," said Fafner, "also, Demetrius and Gaia seem to be spending more and more time together."

"It's good to see them pairing up," said Magni, "but the animosity between Viktor and Thora is not abating. It worries me but, at the same time, it pleases me how they have been able to put it aside to work and train together as War Gods."

"You know?" said Jacob, getting serious. "I'm immensely proud of them, it's good to see them having so much fun and being so close. They will always be friends just like we were. It hurts me to see what lies ahead. For them I see battles; some of which will be against terrible odds. They're well trained, but they are not quite gods yet. We'll need to be on our guard, and ready to go to their aid when the time comes."

Magni said while getting up to leave, "That was three days of hard training, I too am very proud of them. I'm calling it a night." He then left.

"Old friend!" said Fafner as he too was about to leave, "would you like me to stay?"

"Yes," said a delighted Jacob, "please do. I need to bounce my thoughts off somebody, and who better than you? I can't get my head around the strategy of this Shadow; its constant probing is troubling me."

"Remember how we fought the greatest battle of all time," said Fafner reaching across to reassuringly grip Jacob's arm, "worry not, old friend, we can deal with this, we just need to figure out who it is we're fighting." Jacob just nodded, he placed his hand on Fafner's, telepathically linking them, allowing them to discuss what evidence they had, and what plans should be put in place.

In the meantime, the party got wilder and even more boisterous, with the singing and dancing going on until near dawn. By sunrise they were all comatose.

They were no more than two hours asleep when they were awoken by the sound of panic and despair. They didn't realise how close they were to the shield.

Galyna agreed to investigate, but she had great difficulty standing and when she did, she bent forward and retched, her hangover was the worst pain she had ever experienced. Her pain dissipated as the screams from beyond the shield grew louder. When she reached the shield, she was horrified to see a company of around sixty riders attacking, pillaging, and raping their way through the nearby peaceful village. She quickly sobered and called for help. The young gods soon joined her and when they saw the savagery, they too quickly sobered up.

Obelius was about to attempt a rescue but was stopped by Viktor and Drayce. "You know the rules," they said, "we cannot interfere." They held his arms tightly, ensuring he couldn't react, even though they too were horrified by what was happening to the women and children. The abuse being meted out on the men was so savage, all three had difficulty controlling their tempers.

Worse was to come when the pregnant women were being beaten into a hastily built corral, but it was the treatment of one woman, who was in the late stages of labour, which for them was the most shocking. Thora and Helena were tempted to use their powers, but they too were stopped by the intervention of Demetrius.

The baby's head was crowning when one of the riders bent forward and forcefully yanked the baby into the world; he then punched the mother with such force she was left unconscious. The baby hadn't even taken his first breath when the horseman raised him above his head and used a dagger to cut his throat.

No sooner had the baby's blood started flowing when an arrow arrived out of nowhere, it penetrated the rider's skull, killing him instantly. Time seemed to slow down when the baby began falling towards the ground, and this was too much for Obelius to watch. He used his powers, blinked, and raced across to grab the baby before it hit the ground. He didn't waste any time; he blinked again and reappeared on the steps of the temple. After running past Jacob and Fafner, he entered the Great Hall, screaming for Apollo. He was frantic when Apollo arrived, "You've got to save him, use your magic, please Apollo; he hasn't even taken his first breath."

"Fear not young god," said Apollo while taking the baby into his arms, "he's now in my care."

Back in the village the carnage continued, but this time it was the riders who were suffering. What surprised the gods was the speed and volume of arrows that were been used, and they were coming out of nowhere. They searched but failed to identify the source.

In the temple, Obelius anxiously paced the length of the hall, he was acting like an expectant father. He couldn't relax and became very agitated, that was until he heard the first cries. He reached Apollo just as the last of the baby's sliced skin knitted back together, leaving no marks. Apollo then administered a dark coloured potion to encourage the baby's body to produce enough blood to replace all he lost.

A few moments later the baby cried louder, and without thinking Obelius reached in and took him from Apollo. He cradled him, then kissed his forehead, and almost immediately the baby stopped crying. To the surprise of the gods the baby raised his hand to rest it on Obelius's cheek, bonding them together forever. Obelius kissed him again and was heard to say, "Hi little man, I'm Obelius, you're going to be fine, and just so you know, I've risked everything for you, you've no idea the trouble you've got me into."

Jacob approached, his face showing how pained he was, he never looked at the baby, just kept staring at his son. "How could you?" he finally said, "you've broken one of our most sacred laws, what were you thinking? From this day you will be banished from the realm of the gods. You will also lose most of your powers. Leave Olympus, there's nothing I can do."

Obelius was having none of it. "Father," he said while stepping in front of him. "Father," he repeated, "take him and look upon his beautiful and handsome face then tell me I did something wrong." Jacob stepped aside to continue walking away, "Father, look, don't turn your head. You'd have done the same." Jacob's heart was breaking, especially when he looked up at a distraught Eala. Obelius was now getting angry. "Father," he yelled, "don't you dare turn your back on me. You know I did the right thing." Jacob stopped but before he had a chance to say anything Obelius continued, "I knew exactly what I was doing. His mother, and the rider were both on the ground. The rider was dead, and I used his body to conceal myself. I blinked and materialised just in time to catch the baby, it was so fast, only the gods, and the bowman, could have seen me. The strange thing was, the arrow came out of nowhere, but it was travelling in the Light. Father, I didn't break the law, the baby wasn't given a chance to breathe. I heard a faint heartbeat and as a god, I decided he had a right to life."

Back at the Oasis, the bowman was ruthlessly eliminating the remaining riders which he successfully completed, but not before the gods began to track him. Sofia was the first to see him. "He's tiny," she said, "no bigger than a dragon fly. He's fast, see how he speedily flies from boulder to boulder and branch to branch."

"I know of them," said Drayce after catching a glimpse, "he's of the Little People, the Fairy Folk. Their domain is next to the Dragon Realm. Why is he so far from home?"

The gods noticed how each time the bowman was about to release an arrow he hid behind a boulder, or a fallen tree, before taking his human form. They also noticed how he looked surprised when his arrows failed to strike three of the riders. They had difficulty keeping up with him, he never stayed in one place any more than three seconds. It was only when he landed beside the shield, when they got their first real glimpse of him. The goddesses were in awe of a how handsome he was and couldn't take their eyes from his long and toned, yet thin body, a body that was perfect in every way. They admired his neck length brown hair as it lightened under the captured rays of the morning sun. They felt his pain when they looked into his deep brown eyes.

The bowman remained close to the shield and used a large crack in the boulder to watch the villagers capture the three remaining riders. He particularly watched the mother of the now missing baby slowly recover from the punch she received. He, like the gods, watched the mother frantically search for her baby, then go into hysterics when she realized her baby was gone.

It was then when the opportunity for the gods to act presented itself. Hemish moved first, he used his powers to negate the bowman's abilities. Galyna and Helena elongated their arms enough to stretch through the shield and pull him back into Olympus. Viktor and Drayce were waiting; they totally incapacitated him. Every effort he made to escape was completely suppressed by the power of the mystic gods. Tristan then ripped part of his skirt to be used as a blindfold.

"How could you?" yelled Demetrius grabbing him by the neck, "you have the powers of a god, and you've used them so ruthlessly. It's forbidden to interfere in the affairs of man and yet you killed almost sixty of them, what gives you the right to break our most sacred law?"

"I've every right," said the bowman, "they don't walk in the Light. Release me, release me now."

"Are you for real?" sneered Demetrius. "No! I won't release you. You are our prisoner and will come with us."

They frogmarched him towards the temple and when they reached the steps Maximus ran ahead to tell Jacob of what had happened. Viktor and Drayce were close behind and when they reached Jacob they forced their prisoner to kneel before him. The bowman fought the humiliation, insisting he would kneel before no one. "

He has the powers of the Little People," said Drayce, "I suspect he's from the Fair Lands."

"Remove his blindfold," said Jacob. Magni, Ares, and Athena moved closer in case of danger. The Mystic Gods continued suppressing his powers.

"Who are you?" Asked Jacob. "And from where did you get your powers?"

The bowman looked around the temple, taking in all the statues, ignoring Jacob, who then said, "You can choose to ignore me, or you can suffer the indignity of having me enter your head and seek out all your secrets: Would you like me to do that?"

The Bowman kept looking around and on seeing Obelius. "You saved him," he said as his face lit up, "how you hid yourself from the villagers amazed me. Tell me, is he going to be OK?"

"I think you'd be better answering my father's questions," said Obelius while walking over to show him the baby, "the baby is in the care of Olympus and will be fine."

"I answer to no one," the bowman said when he turned back to face Jacob. "Release me."

"What you did has broken the most sacred law of all immortals," said Jacob, "not only that, but you also caused my son to break that same law. He will now be banished, losing most of his powers, why do you still defy me?"

"Your son and I didn't break any law; my arrows are laced in the magic of the Fair Lands and crafted by the hand of Lugh," said the bowman raising his voice. "The Light will only allow my weapons kill those born out of absolute evil, which is why the three remaining horsemen didn't die; they are human, although now possessed by an evil force. They're protected from my wrath. The others were all Shadow Riders, and my arrows are the only weapon capable of destroying them. I've been trailing them, following the havoc they're wreaking upon village after village, they've shown no mercy. They reek of pure evil and seem to come out of the shadows. They have the potential to take over earth and I will not allow that happen. The villagers had no hope until I arrived." Jacob's face showed great relief now that his son's story has been confirmed.

It was then when the wizards arrived. "Master Finn," said a surprised Mygon, "I wondered how long it would be before you'd show your face, little did I expect for it to be in Olympus."

"Teacher," said Finn, turning to face his former mentor, "how long must I suffer?"

He thought for a moment and looked a bit startled. He looked back at Jacob, then looked again at the statues, it was slowly dawning on him that he was before the God of Gods. He fell to his knees and bowed. "Please forgive me," he said reaching across to grip Jacob's tunic, "I didn't know, I never met you, I only ever heard of you from my parents."

"Let us try again," said Jacob, releasing him from his binds.

"I am Finn," he began, "I'm a banished prince of the Fair Lands, the eldest son of the Lady Danu and Lord Faer. I've been exiled by my father for constantly challenging his authority. I sensed the probing of our shield and when I investigated, I saw Shadow, yet no one believes me. I then endangered my younger brothers, and that was the last straw for my father. I'm tired of hiding and now seek forgiveness, I want to see my family again. "

"You know of Shadow?" asked Jacob.

"Yes," he replied, "I know of Shadow, I've been fighting them for months. I've trailed and harassed them but can't find their source. I fear a powerful foe is about to show himself."

"You said 'himself'," said an intrigued Magni, "is Shadow a man?"

"I'm unsure," replied Finn, "two days ago, in a small village on the edge of the desert I slaughtered many Shadows Riders and when I thought I was finished I saw 'Him', at least I think it was a man. He appeared in the form of a mist, a very dark mist. I saw him feed on the spirits of the villagers, sucking their white mist from their mouths. His Shadow Riders then devoured the bodies and when finished they turned into a shadow and entered his mouth. It's as though he needs flesh and bone, when finished he looked stronger."

"Your knowledge will be of assistance to us," interrupted Athena, "allow us enter into the furthest recesses of your mind."

Finn agreed and bowed. Jacob, Magni, and Athena placed their hands on his head and travelled through his memories. They gathered as much information as was available and when finished Jacob said, "Your assistance has been invaluable, and I see what you mean about how Shadow hides its source." He placed his arm across Finn's shoulder and continued, "I see how restless you are, stay with us, allow the calmness of Olympus help you recover from all you've seen. I also see how you miss the Fair Lands. I promise to speak to your father, I'll ask him to reach out to you."

"Your offer is very kind," replied Finn, "but I must decline. My destiny is fighting Shadow, and I fear it's making its way towards the Fair Lands. I plan to harry and delay, until I find out who I'm dealing with." Jacob acknowledged his decision with a slight bow.

Finn joined Obelius and asked to hold the baby. He moved to the centre of the Hall, and while gently cradling the baby he reached in to kiss his cheek. Just then, the Light came and illuminated both. His wings appeared, glowing brightly in fluorescent white light. He whispered 'go gcosnóidh cumhacht na nDaoine Beaga tú.'

"What did he say?" asked Demetrius.

"He said, 'May the power of the Little People protect you.' It's an Irish blessing," explained Mygon.

"We should take him back to his parents," said Finn gesturing for Obelius to join him, "before too much time has passed."

"No," replied Obelius, "not yet." He turned to Jacob, "Father, allow me also bestow on him the protection of a god?"

"If you weren't going to do it," replied Jacob, "I was."

Obelius was still in the centre of the hall with Finn when he took the baby back and raised him above his head for all gods to see. "Let it be known," he said while turning in all directions, "this boy is under my protection. I am Obelius, God of Olympus."

Jacob and Eala were enormously proud; they'd never seen this softer side of their son. They could see he had bonded with the baby and would never allow anything bad happen to him. Finn and Obelius then left and made their way to the rim of Olympus. On their way they worked out a plan to return the baby to his parents. It was agreed Obelius would do it, using his powers to blink from beside the shield to conceal himself behind a nearby tree. He used magic to change from Olympian to modern earth clothes before revealing himself, he made his way to the distraught mother and father who were both dumb founded. "How did you save him?" asked the startled father, "I saw the knife, I saw the blood, I saw him fall. When I was freed, I rushed across and found him gone."

"I was behind that tree," said Obelius trying to hide his devastation, "and when I saw him fall, I crawled across, out of sight, and grabbed him. I healed him using the last of the herbs from my homeland. Now be happy, he's safe back in your arms. The gods were looking down on him this day."

He reached in to gently caress the baby's cheek before backing away. When out of sight he blinked and rejoined Finn. "That was very hard to do," he said, "In the short time he was in Olympus I bonded with him."

"You've restored my fate in the gods," said Finn, taking Obelius' hand, "in another life, you and I would have been good friends." He bowed as he made his way through the shield.

"Never mind another life," said Obelius, waving goodbye, "in this one, I know I've made a new friend. We're destined to meet again, and I look forward to it." Finn disappeared.

Obelius slowly made his way back to the temple, he was seriously missing the baby. He reached the ornamental gardens where he sat on the bench blankly staring at the statue of David. He was joined by his mother who said while reaching in to hug him, "Now you know what it's like. They're the same feelings your father and I have for you. They never go away."

"I don't even know his name," said Obelius, "his eyes, I still see them. They reached deep into my heart."

"Son," said Eala, pulling him closer, "it doesn't matter about his name. Thanks to you and Finn, he's safely back with his parents. He's where he should be, he will always be in your heart."

"Just thinking," said Obelius, "would father really have expelled me?"

"Yes," said Eala, "Only for Finn confirming your story, I'd have lost you."

They went quiet for a while and just seemed to enjoy comforting each other, then Obelius, while staring at the statue wondered aloud. "Mother," he said, "how could Uncle Odi model for that statue, his bits and everything are on full view; it's embarrassing."

"You Uncle Odi is an Asgard God," laughed Eala, "and one thing they care about is their appearance and showing it off. When I sit here, I don't see Odi naked I see your father, after all they are identical twins, identical in every way."

"Mother," responded a disgusted Obelius. "For fucks sake, too much information: Go away." Eala stood then walked away, having great difficulty containing herself. She managed to make it to the temple before falling into a fit of the giggles.

Obelius remained sitting on the bench and was soon joined by Aria. "That was a nice thing for you to do," she said, "I'm so proud of you." She moved her hand to gently rest on his.

"You're not going to believe the conversation I just had with my mother," he said still trying to recover. "She remarked on that statue and how she doesn't see Uncle Odi, she sees my father, just because they are identical twins, I was mortified."

Aria looked at the statue, stood up and as she was walking away said, "I come in here to look at that statue and I don't see either King Odi or your father."

"Who do you see?" he asked.

"Is it not obvious," she said with a wide smile, "it's you. You may not be as broad as your father, but you certainly are identical in every other way. We girls enjoy watching you swim in the lagoon: Your muscular, toned, and smooth naked body always looks good. Viktor, your Asgard cousins, they may love themselves, always flexing and preening. They are handsome, but they don't have a patch on you. Look on the face of that statue, I see the face of a Greek god, it's you. I look on his body and see a Greek god, it's you. You have something special, and that statue captures it." She walked away.

Obelius remained in the garden for a while longer, still seriously missing the baby, and the feeling of loss wouldn't leave him. The bell for lunch tolled but he didn't respond, he snuck in the back door and made his way to his room where he fell asleep.

Chapter 20

The following morning the young gods were waiting anxiously for the arrival of Magni, and when he arrived he very quickly got down to business.

"Over the next few days," he began, while at the same time creating a cocoon, preventing Shadow from hearing his plans, "many of you will travel to various realms, your sole purpose is to warn them of what hides in shadow. I need you to ask them to prepare, their help might be needed. The first group to leave will travel to Asgard and after delivering the warning, they will also be tasked with escorting King Odi to Olympus. I've chosen Obelius, Magnar, Viktor, and Thora for this task, it makes sense to send gods who are of Asgardian descent, so go and prepare. The rest of you meet back here tomorrow afternoon and we'll discuss the next trip."

The four gods went to their rooms and when they returned, they were wearing their imperial robes and armour. Viktor, Thora, and Magnar were wearing the robes of the Asgard realm, and Obelius, the robes of an Olympus god. They were briefed again on their task and when all was ready, they mounted two chariots and quickly left towards a waiting portal.

Obelius, although still a bit subdued, had earlier allowed his mischievous side to show. He had deliberately arranged for Viktor and Thora to share the first chariot, suggesting they both knew the way.

"We're going to have so much fun," he whispered to Magnar. "Look at Viktor's face, he looks sick. He acts as though he hates Thora and won't admit he's besotted by her."

"Look at Thora's scheming face," said Magnar, "she's going to make his trip a nightmare."

"Viktor's right," said Obelius, rubbing his hands together, "she is a bitch, see how she's enjoying every minute of his discomfort. This is priceless."

The portal closed behind them, and after turning north towards Asgard, they flicked their reigns to begin their journey out into space.

"My father warned me about gods like you," said Magnar, "and he's right, you are a bollocks. You did that deliberately. They've already started bickering. Do they not realise we too are gods and can hear everything?"

"I know," sniggered Obelius, still rubbing his hands together, "isn't it great."

Viktor held the reigns firmly as the snide remarks began. He refused to look at, or even talk to Thora and anytime she tried to speak he cut her short, telling her to shut up. She wasn't fazed; she was relishing the teasing, and then upped her game a notch. She moved her hand across to firmly grip his muscular back side and waited for a reaction and when it came it was one of utter contempt. "Piss off," he yelled, "bitch."

She didn't care, she knew he didn't really mean it. She got more adventurous by gently rubbing her hand up and down his back and when that failed she targeted his inner thighs. He still didn't react.

"Tell me Vicky, why do you hate me so?" she coyly asked.

"Firstly," he said through gritted teeth, "my name is Viktor, not Vicky, and secondly, you're a bitch, and a bully. You've treated me like dirt for as long as I can remember. For years you found ways to humiliate me, embarrassing me on front of my family and friends; I hate you!"

She wasn't giving up; she knew he wouldn't loosen the reigns while travelling at such speed, so she moved to stand behind him, wrapping her arms around his waist. Within seconds she had her hand under his tunic, caressing his chest. "Wow," she said, increasing her efforts, "the body of a god, why hide it from me?" He didn't answer; he was doing all in his power to block her from his mind, he was also tightly securing the reigns to a hook, centred on the main chariot shield.

She continued her teasing by removing his cape, then opening his tunic, before working on his breeches. She undid his belt causing his breeches to slip. His resistance was weakening but he refused to lower his guard. "Your efforts at seduction will fail, I still hate you; piss off."

She nudged closer, sliding seductively up and down against his now bare chest. "There's no way you hate me," she said, "there's a stirring, and it tells me something very different." She reached up to kiss him, but he pulled back.

"There's no point in pulling away," she continued, "you're trapped, stuck with me, and by the time I'm finished you'll be putty in my hands."

"Really?" he sneered, "trust me, you wouldn't be able for me!"

"Is that a challenge?" she said, moving her hands to lower his breeches even further. She stood back to stare at his almost naked body. "Truly you are a god of Asgard," she said, "there's no other who compares to you."

Obelius caught Magnar looking at Viktor's now naked body. "Do you think if we were naked," he said, "would we look as good as him?"

"Apparently, as a god of Asgard," said Magnar. "I too should look like that, but I don't think so. And just for the record, if I were naked, it certainly wouldn't be with you."

"Cheek," said Obelius, "There's nothing wrong with my body, we Greek Gods might be slimmer, but trust me, we do have the physical strength. Even so, I wouldn't mind looking that good. Maybe if I had a body like his I might have a bit more luck."

"Shit, they're kissing," said Magnar, "I can hear their shaky breathlessness and their quickening heartbeats. I'm beginning to feel their full-on passion, and I wish we weren't this close."

"Never mind the kissing," said Obelius, "they're starting to do everything else. He's removing her clothes. Can you sing? Start singing loudly, I don't want to hear what's coming next."

"What's coming next?" asked Magnar, "I'm innocent, I never met girls until I came to Olympus, but if it's what I think it is, there's no way I'm going to sing. Viktor will kill both of us if our singing ruins his moment of passion."

"It's too late," said Obelius, "His breathing is out of control, they're both naked and will soon be on the floor. I wish this chariot would stop vibrating."

Beads of sweat gathered across Magnar's forehead; he was also feeling the effects of the vibrating chariot. "How long will this go on for?" he asked.

"How the fuck would I know," snarled Obelius, "I've never been lucky enough to be with a girl. This is terrible; it feels like it's going on forever."

Thora and Viktor were now out of sight, but their passion was so potent, every sound, every movement, every released gasp of sheer ecstasy gave them a pleasure they never experienced before. As their passion grew, they became one and it was so intense they didn't realise a powerful Light shot out across the universe.

"What the fuck was that?" asked a shocked Magnar.

"Oh shite," replied an equally shocked Obelius, "If I'm right, Thora and Viktor have just conceived a baby. Uncle Odi will kill him."

Magnar looked across and could see that Viktor and Thora were oblivious to the Light and were now standing in an embrace showing they were still enjoying the ecstasy. He tugged on Obelius, "They're still naked; Thora has her back to us."

Obelius looked across, just as Viktor raised his head. Viktor smirked and then stuck out his tongue, and knowing he was being watched, he suggestively moved his hands up and down Thora's back, then moved them out of view.

"He's doing that deliberately; trying to make us jealous," said Magnar. "The lucky bastard."

Viktor, still aware he was being watched, then gave them a well-known single finger gesture.

"He can stick out anything he likes," said Obelius, whispering under his breath, "trust me, he'll have a lot more painful things stuck up places he never thought they'd fit when our uncle Odi gets his hands on him."

Viktor leaned down and kissed a very contented Thora. "The boys are sick," he said, "I feel their envy. We best get dressed, I mustn't have tightened the reigns enough, they've loosened, Asgard is in view."

"I was so engrossed by wearing you down," she replied as she quickly dressed, "I forgot we had an audience. No matter, you've no idea how long I've waited for you,"

"I thought you hated me," he said, acting surprised. "I told everybody I hated you just to protect myself from being hurt."

"Well now you know," she said, holding him closer. "I'm sorry, I should never have treated you so cruelly. When you stopped pestering me I began to miss you, only then did I realise it was always you I wanted. I knew you felt the same way when I was told you were always spying on me. When you were watching me in the lagoon, I knew you were there, I used my power as the daughter of a time traveller to move back and forth between the water and the sand dunes without you noticing. I saw your fight with Drayce; you were so cruel."

As they approached Asgard, King Odi was informed. He quickly made his way towards the main gates, next to the Bifrost Bridge, where he anxiously waited. From there he watched Heimdallr, the guardian of Asgard, open the gates at the far side. While waiting, he was joined by Panya, Modi, Eris, Baldor, Thanases and Irina.

The chariots arrived and Heimdallr greeted the visitors. "My Lady Thora, back so soon?" he said before turning to Viktor, "my lord, you look quite flustered, is everything in order?" Viktor was still on a high and just nodded. Behind them was Magnar and Obelius, they stepped forward and bowed. They were wearing their helmets and kept their heads lowered.

"My lords Jacob and Magni, you are once again most welcome," he paused, and looking confused, he went on alert. "Something's wrong," he said, "you are not Lord Magni." He raised his staff and prepared to attack, only to be interrupted by Thora, "Fear not, Guardian of Asgard, he's my cousin, a son of Lord Magni. He seeks audience with my father."

"And the other one," enquired Heimdallr.

"Obelius," replied Viktor. "He is a God of Olympus and son of Jacob."

Although unsure, he felt no threat, he relaxed and said, "Welcome, sons of the Gods; welcome to Asgard."

Odi watched his daughter cross the bridge, and his excitement continued to build as she got closer. While watching he flinched when he saw her hand move across and gently caress Viktor's, when he saw Viktor grip her hand, he felt his anger grow.

"Don't even think about it," said Panya, noticing his face tensing. "If you dare, I'll make you pay in ways you won't like. It's about time they discovered each other."

"If he's laid his hands on my daughter," replied Odi, "he will regret the day he was born."

"I'm warning you," responded Panya, squeezing his hand, "if you touch him, it's you who will regret the day you were born." She then said, "I can't believe Jacob is visiting unannounced, and when did Magni get back?"

"That's not Jacob," said Odi, "it must be Obelius. The other one is definitely not Magni; he doesn't have the swagger. I don't know who he is."

"Are you sure?" asked Panya, looking confused. "If they're not, they are clones."

Thora and Viktor were first to arrive at the steps. They bowed, but Odi ignored convention and ran to hug his daughter, on his way he managed a very subtle but forceful dig of his elbow onto Viktor's ribs prompting Obelius to say to Magnar, "Told you, he's going to make Viktor's life Hell, and this is before he finds out she's pregnant."

"Darling," asked Odi, "why have you returned so soon? Did my brother throw you out?"

"No father," she replied, showing concern. "Jacob needs you; there's something wrong. He's preparing for war."

"Why didn't he blink," asked Odi, "he knows I'll always answer."

"Magni wouldn't allow him leave Olympus," said Viktor, still nursing his ribs, "he insisted on training us as War Gods, believing us capable of escorting you back to Olympus. Shadow has attacked the dragon realm, it has made its way into Olympus, it's been sighted in the eastern and Indus realms" He lowered his head and looked back at Magnar. "Out in the universe, it killed Bel Marduk." Odi's face drained, such was his shock.

"Obelius," said Odi, reaching over to hug his nephew. "How you've grown, you are your fathers' image,"

"Uncle" said Obelius, "Father needs you; this Shadow is immensely powerful. It has taken Princess Isidra of the dragon realm and holds her in its lair. She's protected by the spirit of Maximus, and my father believes you and he together, have the power to rescue her,"

"Maximus?" said a perplexed Odi, looking across at Modi. "We've heard that name before, who is Maximus?"

"Maximus is my brother," said Magnar removing his helmet, "I am Magnar, we are the twin sons of your brother, Magni of Asgard." He bowed as he stepped forward, "Our mother is a Goddess of the Earth, her name is, or was, Medeina. We don't know if Shadow has taken her." Foe Odi, the shocks just kept coming, he looked across at Modi who had his mouth covered and was getting very emotional.

"We were twelve-year-old boys," continued Magnar, "when we watched the Shadow people savage Bel Marduk. My father is a broken god, but since his return to Olympus he has taken control of Jacob's security. He sent us to escort you."

"I'm not happy with this," said Modi, "you should take Asgard escorts."

"Uncle," said Magnar, turning to Modi. "When my father speaks, you would do well to listen. He is a master, when a butterfly flaps its wings, he knows that somewhere in a distant land, a hurricane will not be too far behind, and exactly what land will suffer. He has chosen us to escort King Odi and expects us to do our duty."

Modi wasn't happy and insisted he travel as well; he also suggested Odi call an emergency council of Asgard.

In the meantime, Panya continued to embrace Thora. "I've waited so long for this day," she said, "I'm so happy you and Viktor have finally realised how you feel about each other. I can now look forward to the birth of my granddaughter."

"Mother," said a shocked Thora, "I'm not pregnant,"

"Yes darling," replied Panya with a wide smile, "you are."

Viktor went into shock and began to panic. He saw Odi's face change and knew he should run and hide. Obelius noticed his distress and turned to Magnar.

"I think we should move to protect Viktor," he said, trying to devise a plan, "Uncle Odi is about to explode, he was in Panya's head when she announced Thora's pregnancy."

His suggestion hadn't time to be implemented, Odi did explode and using his godly powers he roughly grabbed Viktor and took him far out into the universe. Thora went into hysterics. Panya was disgusted Odi totally ignored her, and Modi couldn't believe he would kill the son of one of his closest friends. Odi had no intentions of killing Viktor, he took him to a place he knew was safe from Shadow.

"Viktor," he said, trying to reassure him, "I've known for some time that you were to be the father of my grandchild and I'm really happy for you both. I could never figure out why I needed to know this, but I feel it's something to do with this Shadow. I have a plan, and you are part of it. When I return to Asgard, it must look like you and I have beaten the living daylights out of each other, and I've left you for dead. I will open a portal to allow Asgard see us fight. In the end they must see you fall, and my sword penetrate your armour. Start the fight by punching me full force in the face and do it when I am least expecting it."

"Why are you telling me this?" replied Viktor. "I know nothing of Shadow and right now all I want is to get back to be with Thora and make plans for our future."

"Thora will be well looked after," said Odi, "she will be protected by the power of both Asgard and Olympus." He barely had the words out of his mouth when he was floored by three unexpected punches, one to each side of his face and the third into his chest. He was seriously winded and struggled to recover. Blood oozed from his nose and is right eye socket.

"When I said, 'do it when I least expected'," he yelled, "I didn't mean you should try kill me."

"Sorry," responded a panicking Viktor, "sorry, sometimes I don't know my own strength."

"Ok, ok. We don't have much time," said Odi, pausing to take a breath in the hope of lessening the pain, "a portal will soon open, and we must let the gods see us fight. We'll transport to earth and become visible. Our battle will be broadcast everywhere, and you will succumb to my beating, then plead for mercy. Remember, I will pierce your armour and leave you to die. Humans will rescue you, and they will nurse you back to health. Your task during that time is to allow agents of Shadow approach, but you must play hard to get. You must betray the gods to quickly gain their confidence, but always be aware of the power of evil. Do not allow it to turn you. Learn of their ways and their plans, be a warrior of Asgard and report back to me everything you discover."

"What are you going to tell my parents?" asked Viktor, "what are you going to tell Thora?"

He never got an answer; he was beaten and kicked through a portal taking him close to the mall in London. As planned, a second portal opened, showing the gods a vicious fight where Viktor was giving as good as he got, until Odi lost control and used his sword. They saw Odi stab Viktor and then leap through the portal.

When he arrived, he showed no compassion or remorse, he just barged his way through the waiting gods but was stopped by Thora who pounded her fists off his chest. Thanases and Irina were distraught, and the tension was palpable, especially when Thanases lunged forward to attack Odi, only to be stopped by the spears of the palace guards.

Modi took Odi's arm and whisked him away. "Have you lost your mind?" he yelled, "Thanases is one of Jacob's closest friends, and you left his son to die just because you can't handle the idea of your daughter being with him. How can a God of Asgard act in such a way?"

Odi was hurting and his blood was still flowing, he stared at Modi and said nothing, but Modi noticed a twitch in his cheek and then knew it was a signal. All was not what it seemed.

"Leave Thanases to me," said Modi, "I'll take him away; it will be difficult for him to control his temper and his newfound hatred of you."

On his way back to the gates Modi met his nephews and could see they were still in shock.

"Uncle Modi," said Magnar, "such savagery, even the forces of Shadow would never treat one of their own like the way King Odi treated my friend."

"Uncle Modi," said a devastated Obelius, "what the Hell? Viktor is my best friend, why would he leave him for dead? Where did he leave him?"

Modi ignored them and walked over to grip Thanases by the arm. "Come," he said, "we'll search for Viktor and bring him to Olympus."

Irina joined them, "Please find my baby," she pleaded, showing deep grief.

Together Modi and Thanases mounted a chariot and crossed the Bifrost Bridge. When they left Asgard they headed out into the universe, instead of heading to where they believed Viktor was left. Modi found a distant sun, one that was emitting loud erupting flares, he used the noise to drown out what he wanted to say. When they were close enough, and confident Shadow wasn't about, Modi stopped the chariot. "Odi sent me a signal," he said while still checking it was safe. "All we witnessed is a ruse. Odi is up to something, and Viktor is part of his plan. We need to spend a few days out here and then make our way to Olympus."

"Are you sure?" asked a still devastated Thanases. "All I saw was my son being beaten to a pulp."

"Thanases," replied Modi. "You do realize your son is a trained War God? A few punches, and a single stabbing will not even faze him. He's an immortal and very powerful. Think about all the things that happen to us gods, no matter how bad, the following day we just move on as though nothing happened. Have you never noticed that?"

"I've always noticed it," replied Thanases, "especially when Fafner died. The next morning, it was as though he never existed. It doesn't take away from the fact that Viktor is my son, and it really hurt to watch him being treated so cruelly."

Meanwhile, back in Asgard, Odi met with the council. He appointed Prudr, and his uncles, as guardians of the realm.

Chapter 21

After the council Odi left and made his way to where three chariots were waiting. He mounted the first and was joined by Baldor. Panya refused to travel with him choosing to travel with Thora and Irina on the second chariot instead. Eris, Obelius and Magnar travelled on the third one. When Asgard was left far behind Odi finally spoke.

"My friend," he said, "I need you on my side."

"You're putting me in a very awkward position," replied Baldor. "Thanases and Irina are my closest friends. You've half beaten their son to death and left him to suffer alone."

"Raise your staff and send out your light," instructed Odi.

Baldor did as was asked, and when the light came its power prevented any Shadow from forming.

"Viktor is working for me," began Odi, "he's on a mission of deceit and will report back his findings. He's a Warrior and has been well trained by the War Gods, he has more powers than he realizes, and they will come to his aid when he needs them the most." Baldor was relieved.

Odi looked back at Panya and could see she now held him in total contempt. "Looks like I'll be sleeping alone for a very long time," he said, "I think they all hate me."

"I'm sure Jacob will find a room for you," said Baldor trying to prevent a smile. "If that fails, sure the stables will be warm." Odi showed a nervous smile.

They soon arrived at the portal leading them into the realm of Olympus where they were met and greeted by an excited Jacob and Eala. The tension almost immediately showed itself, Obelius ignored his father and just walked into the temple. Eala sensed the distress in Panya and noted smudged makeup around Irina and Thora's eyes. Jacob also noticed and could see Odi was hiding something. He entered his head and at once saw everything that had happened. "That was some ruthless action you took," he said, trying not to react. "But I understand why you did what you did and will stand by your decision."

Irina was devastated hearing Jacob endorse Odi's actions; she ran up the steps into the temple. Odi gestured for Baldor to follow her, which he did and when he reached her, he held her tightly. "I am no good in situations like these," he said, "but do you not think it odd that Modi took Thanases with him? That Jacob so quickly agreed with Odi's actions?" He moved closer, and whispered, "You do realise Shadow is everywhere? Trust Odi, I do."

Irina looked into his eyes, saw his sincerity, and began to relax. He then said, "You must keep showing your tears, they will help." She again understood his meaning and sobbed while accepting his caring embrace.

Some hours later it was noticed Obelius was nowhere to be found, Jacob went searching and found him sitting alone out in the meadows. He joined him, said nothing for a while knowing how upset he was. When he eventually did speak, he said, "Getting older and taking responsibility isn't easy, is it?"

"A portal opened," said Obelius, "and we all saw that prick beat the crap out of Viktor, he really treated him like dirt, it was terrible to watch. Viktor is my best friend, and I didn't know what to do. Uncle Odi is a bollocks. He stabbed him, he actually pierced him with his sabre, all this because he got Thora pregnant."

"Wow, I didn't know he got Thora pregnant!" said Jacob.

Jacob stood and raised his right arm; he closed his eyes and called on the Light. When it arrived, he turned a full circle and the Light followed, it formed an impregnable wall around the folly. He knelt beside Obelius and said, "The Light will keep Shadow away." He then said, "a portal opened?????"

"Yes father, a large portal opened, we all saw the beat..." He paused and said, "Why would a portal open just to show us...? Father, all is not what it seems, is it?" Jacob placed his hand on Obelius's shoulder, smiled and walked away.

Obelius sought out Thora and asked if she would walk with him, she was still very distressed, crying continuously. "They say a good long walk always helps," he said, taking her by the arm, "let's walk beside the lagoon."

They walked for several miles and when he placed his arm across her shoulder, she moved her arm around his hips. "Cousin," he said, "who would have thought that you and Viktor would get together? Considering you liked to kill each other."

He bent down and wrote 'All' in the wet sand, he made sure she saw it before it was erased by the rippling waves.

They walked on and Thora said, "When we were toddlers, we fought all the time. As he got older, he became a pain in the backside, and was like a lapdog, always running behind me. I was only interested in him as a friend, not a boyfriend, he seemed to be everywhere; I felt stifled. I did all those terrible things just to make him go away and when he did, I soon realised it was him I was attracted to, I missed him and then it was too late. When you arranged for us to share the chariot I decided to try and fix what I had done and the only way I felt a War God would react was to seduce him. I did and he responded. It was amazing and my real feelings showed. His feelings for me came back and we became one."

"I know," said Obelius, letting out a hearty laugh, "I was there, remember gods not only have amazing sight, but we also have acute hearing. Magnar and I saw and heard everything." She got flustered.

"I can't believe you and Magnar saw and heard everything?"

"Let's just say," he sniggered, "even a dumb ass like me learned a few lessons while listening and watching." He bent down again and wrote 'is' in the sand and again when he was sure she saw it, he quickly erased it. He placed his finger across her lips.

"Viktor's my best friend and I already miss him," said Obelius, "my powers tell me our paths will cross again."

"I don't feel pregnant," she said.

"Thrust me, you are," sniggered Obelius. "Magnar and I saw the birth Light shoot across the cosmos; it clearly announced a new god had just been conceived."

"Can you imagine me," said Thora, "a Goddess of War; weapons and armour and a big bump."

"No," replied Obelius. "I can't, but can you imagine the girls, there will be nothing but baby talk for the next few months, it'll drive us boys mad." He bent down again and wrote 'not' and again quickly erased it.

Thora thought to herself, 'What's he trying to tell me? - 'all is not'" She moved her head to rest on his shoulder, "This is nice, but I should be doing this with Viktor."

"It is nice," he replied, "I've never had a girl walk with me, hold me, or rest her head on my shoulder, it stirs something nice inside."

"Hey big boy," she said, jokingly pushing him away, "get those stirrings under control, I'm your cousin."

"I wasn't thinking of you," he said, horrified, and whipping his arm away, "I was thinking of..." He wouldn't say, and Thora began to tease him. He bent down again and wrote 'what' in the sand and then erased it. They continued their walk and soon he again bent down and wrote 'it' in the sand, erased it, and moved on. Thora thought, 'all is not what it'.

"Come on, my curiosity is killing me," she said, "who is she?"

"I'm not telling you!" he said. "You'll have it all over the temple, scaring her away."

"It can't be your cousins," she said, trying to work it out, "so she has to be either Lovisa, Aria, Gaia, Galyna or Sagal. I'm going to eliminate Sagal, Gaia, and Galyna, they are the kind of Goddesses that wouldn't accept the ways of a Greek War God. That means it has to be either Lovisa or Aria. I don't think it's Lovisa, so that leaves Aria, Lioness of the Gods, beautiful and loyal; the kind of goddess a god of Greece would always fall for. Am I right?"

Viktor's right," he said, pushing her away, "you are a fucking bitch." He bent down and wrote 'seems' and again quickly erased it.

Thora now had the full sentence, 'all is not what it seems' she pinched his hip signalling to him that she understood what he was saying.

"I'd hate to be Uncle Odi," he said, "you're going to make his life a misery, aren't you?"

She immediately copped on and said, "He'll regret the day he was born." She again pinched his hip letting him know she understood there was to be no changes in her attitude towards her father.

"Ah, poor Odi," said Obelius, pretending to show pity, "don't be too hard on him, I like him."

"Ok," she replied, "I'll try control myself."

Back in the temple, after establishing the full story from Jacob, Eala went in search of Panya and Irina, planning to also let them know. When she found them they were comforting Lovisa who was really missing her brother. Eala hugged them and when she did, they felt a jolt that telepathically told them the full story.

Chapter 22

Evening was now falling and the War Gods, the wizards and the remaining pupils arrived back to the temple after another hard day's training. They were excited to see so many had arrived from Asgard. Magni, in particular, was delighted when he saw Odi; he hugged him with such a bear hug Odi struggled to breathe. Panya joined them, hugged Magni but totally ignored Odi.

"Oh. Is there trouble in paradise?" asked Magni.

"Never mind paradise," said Panya. "I'm more concerned for you than I am for HIM. I heard what happened to Marduk and my heart breaks for you. I hope you're OK?"

"Coming back to Olympus is helping," he replied, "but the pain never goes away. Only for my sons, I believe I'd have ended it all. They are a great comfort to me."

Thora arrived and as soon as she saw her father, she showed her distain by elbowing him in the ribs as she passed. Magni noticed the animosity and was about to call her back.

"Don't," said Odi, "I'll explain later."

Thora paused when she heard what her father said, turned back and aggressively yelled, "There's nothing to explain, you beat my boyfriend to a pulp, and I hate you." She then left.

When Odi and Magni were alone, Odi said, "Brother, I need a hug."

"It's been such a long time since I held you like this," said Magni, pulling him closer and holding him tightly, "I've almost forgotten how, when you were a baby, I used to bring you everywhere. Prudr and I always fought over who would look after you. I missed you, little brother."

Odi raised his hand to rest on Magni's head and at once Magni was able to see the whole story unfold before him. "You did the right thing," he said, "I'd have done the same."

Maximus arrived and introduced himself. "My father always compared us to you and Uncle Jacob," he said, "apparently, we are your clones. I see what he means." He then froze and took in a loud and deep breath, "Father, Isidra, she's in trouble. I need to go to her, now."

"Rest against this pillar and go," said Magni.

"No, not yet" intervened Odi, "take me with you. I want to see this place for myself." Heulwyn was nearby and heard everything.

"She's my granddaughter," she said, "and she will need the comfort I can give: Take me."

Maximus held both their hands and all three arrived just inside the rim of the cocoon. The relief in Isidra's face when she saw Maximus again showed how much she and he were in love. Odi immediately used his light to secure the cocoon. Although the cocoon was strengthened, Maximus noticed that the Shadow People were getting bolder and were trying different strategies to break through. This concerned him.

Odi was curious while moving his hands through a faint mist and asked, "Maximus! What's this?" Maximus shrugged and shook his head.

"It's a mist left behind every time Maximus leaves," said Isidra, "it was much stronger after Jacob left, and it seems even stronger since you and that lady arrived."

"Isidra," said Odi, "that lady is your grandmother." Isidra ran to hug Heulwyn but just fell through her.

"When last I saw you, you were but a baby of no more than two days," said Heulwyn, "I rescued you from the slavers, and during that rescue I fell to the poison of a prince of Hell. While in the tombs of Elysium I discovered a kink in his armour, giving me the ability to send my spirit to watch over you, but I never knew where you were. As time passed I became aware of another protecting you and I was happy. I never knew who that guardian was, but I'm so happy it's Maximus. When Drayce sang the 'Song of the Dragons' was when I regained my powers. His voice broke through the evil holding me and now I'm here for you."

Odi was getting more intrigued by the mist; he believed, that for Isidra, the way out was going to be through the mist.

He was about to send Maximus away when a portal opened close to the cocoon and twenty Shadow Riders came through. They were dragging a severely injured body. It was Viktor and he was savagely beaten, weapon less, bound, and naked. While being dragged passed the cocoon, Maximus reacted and tried to exit the cocoon but was held back by Odi who called out to Viktor.

Through his blood-soaked eyes Viktor managed to see Odi, and although tightly bound, he somehow found the strength to leap up and jump through the shield. As he fell through, his binds disintegrated. Six of his captors never made it, the Light ensured they suffered a very painful death while being dragged through the shield.

The remaining Shadow Riders were furious; they could see Isidra and Viktor talking to someone, but they couldn't see who it was. Isidra cradled Viktor, sharing whatever strength she had. Viktor had difficulty talking but made the effort. "My King!" he whispered, with blood spluttering from his mouth. "They knew of your plans and were waiting for me. They also know Modi and my father are out in the universe, and they've sent an army to take them. You must mount a rescue."

"Maximus!" said Odi, thinking on his feet. "Leave me here, take Heulwyn back to Olympus. Advise Magni of what's happening, then return with Jacob."

When Maximus left, Odi knelt beside Viktor. "I wish I could take you into my arms and comfort you," he said, trying to hide his devastation. "They've done some terrible things to you. I've never seen such damage; you're marked all over. I never thought you'd be caught. How did he find out? Are there traitors everywhere?"

Viktor was regaining some of his strength but still couldn't stand. "When you left," he said, "three men came to my aid, others nearby called for medics, but the three men whisked me into a nearby alleyway, it was protected by dark magic. As soon as I entered the alleyway, I saw it was another dimension, and then I heard his voice. It was deep yet rasping. He stayed in shadow; I never saw him."

He closed his eyes, falling into unconsciousness until Isidra vigorously shook him. "Stay with us," she whispered, trying to ensure Shadow couldn't hear, "help is on its way."

"My King," he said, trying to sit up, "he directed everything from the shadows, he had them strip and humiliate me. Every time they touched me, and did things to me, he cheered. He got immense pleasure in my pain. They used their claws to mark me. I heard him say, 'All loved by the Boy King and his imbecile brother will suffer'. He knew it was you who sent me to spy on his allies. He knows every move we make before we make it. It's as though he is a fly on the wall, listening to all our plans."

"It's some time since last I heard, 'Boy King' and 'Imbecile brother'. They are terms that were used by Lucifer to taunt both Jacob and I."

Maximus then returned, bringing Jacob who was shocked when he saw Viktor's condition. "Look," said Odi, pointing at the mist, "it appears each time Maximus left, today it appeared when we arrived, are you thinking what I'm thinking?"

"If the black mist was used to release Lucifer," said Jacob, pacing back and forth, "is it possible the white mist can be used in reverse, this time to rescue Isidra and Viktor? Is that what you're thinking?"

"That's exactly what I'm thinking," said Odi.

Jacob moved his hand through the mist; he closed his eyes and seemed to be listening to something, he mumbled, "Yes, my Lord, I hear you, I understand."

Chapter 23

Maximus brought Jacob and Odi back to Olympus. They acted based on what they had heard and seen. Odi grabbed a Gjallarhorn and ran through the main doors where he blew a very quick and loud burst that made its way across the universe, calling Asgard to send an army. Jacob in the meantime summoned all the heralds from the friezes above. They quickly alighted and when he explained what he wanted they used their trumpets, drums, and bells, to send warnings about the advance of Shadow, and how it was now targeting all realms. Within a few moments a loud rumbling was heard.

"That's a familiar sound," said Magni.

"Yes," replied Odi, "the sound of our army, I've called for experienced Asgard warriors, I plan to send them in search of Modi and Thanases. Viktor has warned me that Shadow is searching, and intends to kill them."

"In that case," said Magni, itching for a fight, "I will lead them, its time I got my revenge on Shadow."

"Not so fast," said Jacob, "I need you here, your guidance is too important, you are the only one who will see any flaws in my plan, you must stay. Right now, Isidra and Viktor are the priority, go back with Maximus and see for yourself how things have changed, look at the mist."

Magni bit his lip, trying not to explode, but deep down he knew Jacob was right. He joined Maximus who at once blinked, to bring both their spirits into the cocoon. Magni assessed what was before him, finding it difficult to watch the build-up of Shadow soldiers, especially when he recognised some of them as part of the group who killed his beloved Marduk.

He spoke briefly with Isidra, then moved his hand through the mist. "This seems to be brighter than what I was led to believe," he whispered.

While his hand was still in the mist he thought he heard a voice, he thought he heard someone call him and request he jump into the Light. He did, only to disappear and reappear outside the front door of the temple; he ran inside and rejoined his body. He woke Maximus and said, "Take me back, take me back now!"

On arrival back into the cocoon he quickly encouraged Isidra to use whatever strength she had to help Viktor to his feet and walk him into the centre of the mist. She did have difficulty, but she managed, considering it would seem some of Viktor's bones were broken, his pitiful grimacing, then screams, showed how badly he was suffering. Isidra aided him as best she could, but together they found the strength, struggled, and made it. Within seconds they were whisked out of sight, to re-emerge from a newly formed mist in the Great Hall. Isidra rolled into the waiting arms of Obelius, but poor Viktor was not so lucky; he tumbled the length of the hall before smashing against the steps beneath the throne of Zeus. Magni and Maximus returned to their bodies to ensure the plan worked, and when Magni saw it did, he insisted on going back to watch Shadows reaction to the disappearance of the captives. Maximus wasn't interested; he just wanted to be with Isidra. He didn't get is way, one look from his father and he knew it was best to comply. Their spirits arrived just outside the now fading cocoon, and the anger and bile was palpable, prompting Maximus to say, "They can't see us, but I think they know we're here."

It was then when a rasping and sinister voice reached their ears. They looked around, unable to see its source, the voice began to turn into a frightening and sneering laugh; then it became clear. "I smell Asgard warriors," it said as its anger grew, "one I've met before, it can only be Magni. The other is young and tender; one I will taste as my dessert. Show yourselves, cowards."

"Son!" said Magni, trying to reassure his now alarmed son. "It's ok to be afraid, always remember I'll always be close by."

"Father," said Maximus, "he was there, I sensed him again today. It's the same sense I felt when Marduk was killed. He's been targeting you, why?" Magni looked concerned, he too wondered.

In the meantime, Odi reached an unconscious Viktor and while cradling him, he kept repeating, "Come back to me, warrior of Asgard. Come back."

Fafner took Isidra into his arms then whisked her off to Apollo who began working his magic, aiding her recovery. Irina ran through the Great Hall and on reaching her son she pushed Odi away. She took her son into her arms and gently rocked him, just as she did when he was a baby. Her tears flowed, and then dropped onto his face allowing her Light to revive him.

"Hi mother," he said, trying to smile, "bet I gave you a fright, any chance of covering my bits, I feel very exposed."

"I can't believe your bits are all you are worried about," she said, wiping her tears from his face, "you're torn, lashed, black and blue, and look as though you have been to Hell and back. You must have a death wish."

"Mother," he said, "there was no death wish. I was working for King Odi, we had a good plan, but Shadow knew our every move. I didn't get a chance to imbed myself. He was waiting so our plan didn't work. Don't blame King Odi, I'd do anything for my King, and I was always aware of the dangers. We needed to find out who Shadow is and how bad the danger might get. Anyway, we saved her; we saved the beautiful princess Isidra." Irina then requested he be carried to Apollo's rooms.

Magni and Maximus returned to the temple and reported their findings. Maximus was distracted, he backed away and made his way to Apollo's rooms, where he finally, in real life, met Isidra. He stood back for a moment wondering was she real, he moved closer afraid to touch her. He just kept staring. "I'm seeing you with my own eyes for the first time," he said, hoping her feelings for him hadn't changed, "I feel the same as I felt each time I visited. I fell in love with you. Please tell me you feel the same way."

"That first time I saw you," she said, struggling to stand, "I saw what looked like a ghost, I was terrified. I thought you were a trick of Shadow. Then I saw a face full of compassion and eyes that oozed kindness. You're no longer a ghost, your face is still filled with compassion and those eyes, they draw me in just like they always did. You are what I hoped you would be, you are my saviour. You entered my dreams and sustained me. Now I need a real embrace."

He moved his hands to touch each side of her head and then gently caressed her hair and cheeks, before moving in to kiss her on her lips. She felt his power and became subsumed into his Light.

"Is this what real love is?" he asked.

"If it is," she replied, "I never want to lose it, hold me closer." He held her closer.

They were soon interrupted when Fafner, Heulwyn and Drayce arrived. Seeing Drayce, she lit up and reached across to embrace him. "I know you well," she said, "I know you blame yourself. Don't, Shadow manipulates everyone, finds our weaknesses, and uses them against us. Let today be a wonderful day for us, let today be a day our parent's pain is taken away."

"Well then, its decided," said Drayce, "We travel home and take our parents pain away."

"If you leave," said Maximus, "I too will leave, there's no way I'm allowing you out of my sight."

"So be it," said Fafner, "I'll meet with Jacob and make the arrangements."

Chapter 24

In Apollo's rooms, Viktor was making what looked like a miraculous recovery, all saw he was the kind of God who could take any type of abuse, and when it was over he'd just move on. He never suffered long term effects but with every experience he learned many lessons. He felt his recovery was hampered by the continuous attention Odi was giving him and eventually had to say, "My king. Stop! please don't feel guilty; I knew exactly what I was letting myself in for. It wasn't your fault. Go, and be with Jacob and Lord Magni, ensure all other plans are well hidden."

As Odi was leaving he saw Apollo stumbling, then slump back into his chair; it was as though he had lost all his power. "What is it?" asked Odi, getting genuinely concerned.

Apollo exhaled and gasped, "My connection with earth is gone," he replied, rapidly gasping and exhaling. "All ties are broken. I feel or see nothing, something sinister has happened and I fear for the Oracles."

"My Lord," said Odi, helping him to his feet, "you're trembling. Is there anything I can do?"

Apollo acknowledged Odi's concern; he said his plan was to leave at once to establish what has happened. When fully recovered he rushed to the Great Hall and spoke with the Olympus War Gods who were also showing signs of concern. Both Athena and Ares experienced the same loss of their oracular connection, but didn't suffer the same weakness.

Apollo briefly spoke to Jacob, then opened a portal close to his plinth, this allowed him to quickly enter the realm of man.

On arrival in the outskirts of Athens he transformed to pass off as human, his robes changed into modern clothing and his hair shortened to complete his disguise. He made his way into Athens and sought out the ruins of all temples. Nowhere did he detect the spirits of the oracles. He climbed the Acropolis, and on reaching the Parthenon, he quickly established that even the power of Athena was missing. He left, and made his way along the nearby motorway, towards the Gulf of Corinth.

When close to Corinth, he entered a small village where he met a fisherman who offered to take him across the gulf to the port of Itea. He sensed a threat but felt able to deal with any aggression. His senses served him well, hidden in one of the fish storage units were three more villains and they intended robbing him. He wasn't interested in engaging with them, far more important issues had to be dealt with. He used his power as God of Plagues to create a quick-acting bacillus. He raised his palm to allow his creation to rapidly grow before blowing it towards the villains. The bacteria acted so fast the villains had no chance. On their bare legs, arms, necks and faces, blisters suddenly appeared before erupting. From their mouths, nostrils, ears and down their legs poured their liquefied innards. Then they turned to messy sludge. The fisherman had no time to react, he was terrified and under severe threat, he steered the boat towards the port.

On reaching Itea, Apollo hurriedly made his way up into the mountains to reach the sanctuary of Delphi where he used his powers to gain unfettered access to the Archaeological Museum. Through wall-mounted mirrors he noticed he was being followed, and went on alert, but he needn't have feared. He was being followed by a loyal servant disguised as a museum attendant. She approached him. "My God," she whispered, "I am Selene, and for many years I've waited for you to appear. Have you not heard our cries? Are you here to help?"

"I heard no cries," he said, placing his hand on her arm, hoping to offer comfort. "It was the silence that alerted me to something sinister. Tell me, where is the oracle?" He noticed many more attendants and guides approaching, and sensed their excitement, but he was distracted, he again asked, "Where is the oracle?"

"The portal closed yesterday," said Selene, lowering her head in sadness, "Ever since we've been prevented from entering the sanctuary. We fear for her; we heard her scream and couldn't go to her aid."

He made his way out of the museum and walked up towards the ruins of his temple. He placed his hand on the first column and using his powers opened the portal which showed the whole complex in its structural pristine state but there was no life. He and the attendants entered, but soon realised the temple and sanctuary had been violated. Blood spatter and stains were everywhere. The bodies of priestesses lay ravished, with many half-eaten, there were bones stripped clean of all soft tissue, leaving only gnaw marks. After entering the private rooms of the oracle, they found her strung up, slowly being bled, her blood dripping into strategically placed cauldrons.

"They are still here," said Apollo, looking around for any signs, "they're not finished with her. Leave, you must all leave. I'll deal with this defilement." He undid her binds and laid her on the bed.

The oracle was still alive but very weak, she felt Apollo's presence and managed a few words while falling in and out of consciousness. "My God," she said, "I knew one day you'd return; we prayed in your honour. Please look favourably on me and comfort my servants."

"Tell me who did this," he said, placing his hand on her head, preventing her spirit from leaving, "who defiled this most sacred of places?"

"It was a Shadow," she said, struggling to say her last words, "I see it everywhere and when it does its deed it looks towards the heavens hoping the gods are watching. It wants Olympus, and I fear even the power of the God of Gods will not prevail against this new threat. It has no fear, and the power of this Shadow knows no bounds. It's relentless and merciless. I see it walking on your sacred meadows. Beware Shadow." She then passed away.

Apollo was devastated; she was one of his favourites. He closed her eyes, cleaned her wounds, and ensured she had the dignity she deserved. He then left to rejoin Selene.

"It seems, my lady, you are now my oracle," he said. "You bear the name of a good friend of mine; she is the Goddess of the Moon. As my oracle, my guardian of this most holy site, tell me what you need."

She took Apollo's hand into hers and they entered each other's minds. They knew what they had to do and knew never to speak loudly of their plans, Shadow had ears everywhere.

Apollo stepped back into the real world, and through the portal he watched as the new oracle raised her arms towards the heavens. calling on the gods to send their power. He watched that power arrive and surround the sanctuary, raising a mighty shield that was impregnable. He then watched Shadow soldiers arrive and bounce back off the shield, he smiled as they screamed in rage before disappearing, he was happy his sanctum was now secure.

He decided to investigate other sanctuaries before returning to Olympus. He made his way across the mountains, towards the northeast, where after three gruelling days he reached the temple of Zeus in the sanctuary of

Dodona. When he entered the ruins he opened a portal, wide enough for him to view the origins of the temple. The portal took him back to Thebes in Egypt where he watched the high priest release two rare black doves, one that flew towards Libya and the other, towards the northwest of Greece. He continued watching as one of the doves landed on an oak tree near Athens, he listened to it declare in a clear human voice that this location was to become a shrine to Zeus, with temples dedicated to Hera, Dione, and Heracles. He watched long enough to see local villagers put the finishing touches to four temples, as well as the oracular shrine.

He waited for the first oracle to arrive and after stepping through he listened to her prophesies. "Tell me, oh wise one," he asked, "who is Shadow?"

"Why does a god of Olympus visit such a lowly oracle?" she asked while scattering her stones, she then announced that the stones revealed nothing.

"Trust me, my lady, no oracle is lowly," he replied, "But my visit is urgent. Two thousand years into the future a silence will develop between man and the gods. This silence announces the death of the oracles. I search for answers, yet none come to me. I've stepped back in time to see your origins and witness the black dove command the villagers to build this sanctuary, still nothing comes to me. I wonder why Delphi has fallen, yet here in Dodona you still reign supreme."

The oracle stepped forward, took Apollo by the arm, and said, "Let us together walk through the portal and see what happens." They stepped through and immediately the oracle began trembling, "I fear my time has come to an end. Shadow is strong in these lands, but it's not man he's after, it's to kill a god. Killing the Oracles has got your attention. Who better to kill, then Apollo, the one known as the beautiful son of Zeus? The one who is of the sun, radiant and full of grace."

Just then, and out of nowhere, came two arrows. One was gripped by the quick reaction of Apollo just as its tip grazed his head. The second hit its target, and the oracle fell. Apollo placed a shield around himself while waiting for the next deluge of arrows to stop. When they stopped a malevolent voice was heard. "I am Shadow, soon all that exists between the gods and man will be forever broken. Look at her body, she is but one of many." The voice was then gone.

Apollo now knew he had no choice but to travel to all realms and save as many oracles as possible. He chose to visit the Asgard realm as a priority, where on arrival, he met with Prudr and Vidar, who arranged for all three of them to visit the Caves of the Oracles. When they reached the caves, they were met with a horrendous sight, the attendants were all dead, it would seem they were tortured, then bled. The oracle was still barely alive and hanging above her Cauldron of Mysticism. Her dripping blood infusing with the white mist that bestowed on her all prophesies she imparted. Behind her, on the back wall was scrawled in blood - WE ARE EVERYWHERE -. Prudr immediately put Asgard on alert.

Just as Vidar untied the oracle and laid her on her bed, she whispered, "There is another, find him, he needs to be taken to Olympus." The oracle then passed away.

Apollo had already sensed a presence, a connection to the oracle, one who is unused and untried, one who is powerful, and will be responsible for saving many lives.

Prudr and Vidar were on high alert with their swords drawn; they too sensed a presence. They searched everywhere but found no one; that was until Apollo pointed to a smooth area of sand near the cauldron. He used his foot to brush the sand aside revealing a very well concealed trapdoor. On opening the trapdoor, he found a twelve-year-old boy who was in deep meditation, slightly levitated with his eyes closed.

No words were spoken; the boy magically rose up to stand before Apollo and the Gods of Asgard. He was like an angel, perfect in every way. His long and curled blond locks draped past his shoulders, setting him apart from all other Norse oracles. He bowed, then announced his name to be Fitch, arbitrator to the Gods. He turned from Prudr and Vidar and bowed to Apollo. "Take me to Olympus," he said, in a soft boyish voice, "before you stands one who is the last of the Asgardian Oracles, one who needs the protection of the God of Gods. Shadow seeks me, fears me, it seems that I, like a son of Olympus, will be one of the last faces he will see. I have a message for the King of Asgard and it's for his ears only."

Apollo took Fitch by the arm, blinked, and materialised in the centre of the Great Hall where he spoke briefly with Jacob, then left in search of more oracles.

Fitch stood for a moment, taking in the grandeur of the temple. He oozed confidence and only moved when Jacob approached. "Do not be afraid," he said, surprised at how young this oracle was, "You are among friends."

"My Lord," said Fitch, "I'm grateful for your protection, I am Fitch, and within me is all the knowledge of old Asgard."

"Here," said Odi, "you will be safe."

"My king," said Fitch, while bowing, "they came in the night, hidden in shadow. They slaughtered all in our sanctuary. The white mist warned us, giving your oracles enough time to hide me. I heard them scream in rage, they fear me, I then heard them reveal their plans." He ushered Odi away to speak in private but was stopped.

"Feel free to speak," said Odi, "Jacob is my greatest ally."

"Asgard is in great danger," he said, "they mean to destroy our homeland by using a traitor from within the royal household. His identity his hidden from me, he is protected. Of one thing I'm certain, he's high ranking."

"Is there the slightest clue as to who the traitor is?" asked Magni, who just arrived, "tell me everything."

Fitch froze; he recognised Magni from images painted on the walls of Asgard. He was before his hero and was momentarily awe struck. "The shadow army fear you more than any other War God," he said after composing himself. "They know when you unleash your wrath, none will survive. But Shadow! Of you there is no fear. You've met in the past and he claims to see your last battle. He knows you are the one who will fall."

"I fear no evil," said Magni. "Those who believe the future is set in stone are delusional, we gods know the future has many paths,"

Meanwhile Apollo arrived in the lands of Danu where he materialised on the Hill of Tara. He remained there for some time, turning regularly to view across almost a quarter of the sacred Celtic lands. He sensed a retreating evil, occasionally catching fleeting glimpses of Shadow. He feared he was too late. He focused his attention on the south where, as darkness fell, he saw a light that was significantly different to the light emitting from the many towns and villages that lay before him. He recognised the light and immediately moved to intercept its source. On arrival he said, "Oracle of Danu, douse your light, you're attracting the forces of Shadow."

"Who's there?" asked the oracle.

"I am Apollo, God of Olympus, and son of Zeus. I seek the last of the Oracles."

"I am Mug Ruith. High priest and druid, loyal to the Goddess Danu. I too seek my fellow druids, but none have answered. Once before I was the last, and I fear I again have become the last."

"If there are others where are they likely to be?" asked Apollo.

Mug Ruith placed his hand upon Apollo's head and shared the possible locations. They immediately left to search Newgrange, Glendalough, Drombeg, The Giants Causeway, The Rock of Cashel, St Patricks Cathedral, Clonmacnoise, Dun Aengus and the Cliffs of Moher.

Each visit brought more pain; druids were found beaten and savaged to the point of being unrecognisable; none were to survive. For Mug Ruith this was devastating

"With the assistance of the Ladies Danu and Eriu," said Mug Ruith, "as well as the power of Lord Lugh, I trained these druids to be guardians of the old ways, if anything happens to me all the knowledge of the ancients, and all that is natural will be lost forever. You must take me to Olympus now."

The words were barely out of his mouth when he was whisked away to materialise in the Great Hall alongside Jacob and his brothers.

Apollo remained in the temple for no more than a few moments. He briefed Jacob on what he was finding, then left, and this time, he began his search of the African realm.

❦

He arrived in Giza and made his way towards the sphinx. On his way he noticed the plateau security watching him. They saw him as different to all other visitors, no backpack, no water; he had nothing needed for a safe trip to this ancient site. He had decided to present as he was, no longer prepared to negotiate, hide or be clandestine. The search was now so urgent it needed the rules of the gods be discarded.

The plateau guards approached, with their weapons drawn, and challenged him. He reacted by flicking his arms from left to right, knocking all to the ground. Those guards who fired their bullets were incinerated, he showed no mercy. He reached the Sphinx and bowed.

"Lord of the desert," he said, "waken, answer the call of Olympus."

A slow rumble rolled through Cairo towards the plateau, where visitors were shocked to see the sphinx move then take on its full form. All blemishes, pock holes, scrapes and scratches disappeared. The colours used by the ancients appeared, giving back to him the grandeur he deserved. He opened his eyes and asked, "Why is it, a God of Olympus, wakens me from my deep slumber?"

"Time is not on my side," replied Apollo. "Tell me of the oracles, have they passed, or do they hide. Olympus senses nothing, and it worries us."

The Sphinx closed his eyes, and after a few moments began to speak, only to be stopped by Apollo. "Remember, my lord," he said, "even the sands have ears."

The sphinx understood and used his powers to enter Apollo's mind.

"All but the remnants of the ladies of Isis are dead," he announced. "They've been slaughtered by a Shadow that still creeps across this land. It threatens the deserts, woodlands, rain forests and the mountains. No village oracle has been spared; none have survived. The high ones still live. Hidden, but their powers wane. Shadow is close, it still searches. Seek out the Sibyls. They know the way. You must hurry."

Apollo quickly made his way south, and deeper into east Africa, he knew it was there where the Sibyls had their main temple. When he arrived, he was horrified to find they were subjected to constant attacks leading to the desecration of their sanctuary. Priestesses were sold into slavery, forced to worship gods of temples in Greece, North Africa and in Rome, gods who were alien to them.

While in the main temple Apollo waited. He saw a gathering of ten more rare Black Doves, and when he was sure there were no more, he called out, "Sisters of Isis, carriers of the Holy Spirit, answer my call." When there was no response, he called out again, "Prophetesses of the Black Diana, I am Apollo, a friend. Do not fear the power of Olympus, come to me."

The doves flew down to join him, taking their human form while landing. The oldest and most revered among them was the high priestess. "We are in mourning," she said, "many of our sisters have been murdered or enslaved. They came like a shadow in the night, condemning us as false seers. They called us harlots, infidels, and witches. Their treatment of those whom they captured was straight from the bowels of Hell. Their cries of pain will forever ring in my ears. Tell me, Lord of Olympus, why now? Why so late when so many are dead?"

Apollo acknowledged their sorrow and offered his apologies. He told them of the new threat stalking the universe. He enquired as to the whereabouts of the remaining Sibyls to be told that what was before him were the last. He offered to take them to Olympus, an offer they readily accepted and before leaving, they presented him with an ornate urn containing amulets, each one encasing a powerful crystal.

"These amulets were born among the stars," said the high priestess, "look to the two mountains and see how between them one star shines the brightest. From there came the ancestors of the Dogon, and they've passed through the generations, a message for the Children of the Gods. These amulets will show them the way and from them will shine the brightest of light." Apollo accepted the gift, wondering what lay ahead for the Children of the Gods.

"The way of the Sibyl will not die," he said trying to reassure them, "worry not about the murder of your sisters, or the destruction of your temples; they are but flesh, bone, sand, and stone. All lost will forever be remembered when the images of the Black Diana and the African Earth Mothers show themselves. Those who remember will rise up to be a powerful force for good throughout your realm." He then brought the Sibyls to Olympus.

After introducing the Sibyls to the gods and securing the amulets in the vaults he immediately left to continue his search in Africa. He visited the homelands of the Asante, the Maasai, the Obi, the Tutsi, the Yoruba, and the Zulu among others, and found all oracles were gone. He then went in search of the Dogon.

It was while moving towards the southeast of Mali when he reached a cliff face village peppered with stacked mud huts. The village was built by the Dogon peoples and had been in existence for over a thousand years. In the centre of the village, close to the base of the cliff, the inhabitants were conducting a council of the elders. They were robed in the most vivid colours and were all wearing the iconic masks of their nation.

Apollo was invisible and was able to make his way to listen to what they were discussing. He heard the chief medicine man discuss the fall of the oracles and then express his concerns for the future of the gods. He was intrigued by how they were aware of the gods being under threat. He chose to materialise and was further surprised to find they showed no fear.

Ah Apollo," said the supreme elder, "Lord of Olympus. One who is most welcome into our humble homeland."

"How do you know of me?" asked Apollo as he bowed.

"We are aware of everything," was the reply, "we are of the stars, and we always see what's coming. Look to the mountains and see how today Sirius glows so brightly. From that system did come, the Nommos. They arrived in an 'Ark' while spinning and creating a violent wind. They walked among our ancestors and gave us vast knowledge. Not only is there a connection between them and us, but there's also a connection between them and the Mer-nations. The lady Isis, Goddess of Egypt is also of Sirius."

"The gods are aware of the Nommos," said Apollo, "we worked with them during the cosmic wars. They've spread their knowledge throughout the universe, many realms benefited. Their world was attacked during the advance of The Darkness and many lives were lost. We believe that the threat before us now is more sinister and focused. Today it targets all oracles and seers; I need to take you to Olympus before all connections between the gods and man are severed."

The elder thought for a moment and then declined Apollo's offer. "We will not be leaving," he said, "the Dogon peoples need us as their guides and oracles. We've ways of hiding; absorbing ourselves into the very fabric of nature. Do not worry for us."

"The gods respect your decision but ask for one concession," said Apollo, not giving up, "allow one of your seers' travel with me. The wisdom of the Dogon will be invaluable at any future Council." This request was granted, and he at once left to deliver the seer, known as Mirembé, into the safety of Olympus.

∞

The next realm to visit was the land of the Anangu tribes of Australia and he immediately made his way to Uluru, their sacred mountain. He tried to contact the elders only to find their oracles were missing. He sensed no evil presence so decided to investigate their disappearance himself. He examined the gullies running from the summit while looking for clues but found none; he made his way to the caves dotting the base of the rock, only to find nothing but the still intact carvings and paintings, created thousands of years ago. He continued searching and was horrified to find the decomposing remains of what looked like several elderly ladies. He knew by the tattoos, clothing, and jewellery, that they were the missing oracles. He had no choice but to move on.

∞

He arrived at the foot of Mount Osore in Japan and immediately sought out the Itake. Initially he had difficulty, but knew to watch out for blind, or very near-sighted elderly ladies. He made his way to the site of where the renowned Buddhist festival of Obon was being held, arriving just in time to witness the Itake become possessed by the spirits of the dead, before imparting their prophecies. He never understood how easy it was for some families to bring their twelve-year-old daughters to be brides of a local deity, hoping she would become an Itake conduit between the gods and man.

He continued watching and was impressed by the accuracy of the events they were prophesying. It was then when he felt a hand rest on his arm and when he turned, he was greeted by an incredibly beautiful young woman. "Forgive me my Lord," she said, "even through my blindness, I see your Light. I am Mieko; named after the brightness of the Light that shines through you. Tell me, who are you?"

He was taken aback to be seen by a blind woman. "I am Apollo," he said, "God of Olympus. I seek out the oracles of the Fire Islands but only those who are true. I see you carry the black cylinder and wear the beaded necklace. You are the first, why are there no others?"

"It is said my sisters heard a calling and answered," she replied, lowering her head in sadness, "I didn't answer. My visions showed me the rising of the ancient Yamabushi Monks of the Kumano Mountains. It showed me their consorts selling amulets, inviting the living to communicate with the dead while they sit in trance. I then saw the sanctity of the trance being violated; a Shadow is rising while the dead speak. It surrounded and swallowed my sisters. All have fallen to this savagery. Tell me my lord, why have the gods forsaken the true Itake? Why have the gods left me to stand alone?" She began to weep and through her tears she managed to say, "Through my visions I saw the black cylinders fall, releasing the spirits of the beasts; I saw the beaded necklaces lie shattered and broken around their gnawed bones. They're all gone."

"Come, my lady," said Apollo, "there's a sanctuary within the home of the gods; there you'll be safe under our protection."

He and Mieko arrived in Olympus and were greeted by Jacob and Odi.

"My lady," said Jacob, "the power of the gods is used for many things, allow it be used to give you sight." He didn't wait for a reply; he just raised his hand and called on the Light. When it arrived, it quickly entered Mieko giving her, for the first time, her sight.

Apollo then left for China where he met up with very distressed gods who had lost all contact with their oracles. He travelled to Mongolia, before crossing over into the Russian Federation, he again failed to sense the presence of any seers. He checked all across India before making his way through the Middle East and it was then when he began to feel dejected; it would seem none had survived.

He thought of the Americas and travelled to Mexico, where he was delighted to sense a presence, one to the north and the second to the south. He opted to go south, into the rain forests, where he knew the true oracles of nature dwelled, the ones who had the power to meld into the trees and hide. These were the only oracles who, by placing their hands on any tree could view all of history, allowing them to learn from the mistakes of the past before calling up the future.

Like all gods, Apollo had the power to walk on water, and this allowed him to use the Amazon River to take him towards Peru and into the Andes. On reaching the foothills of the mountains he felt his connection with the oracle growing and summoned her into his presence. He waited, and soon he watched a majestic tree, heavily weighted with fully opened leaves, each branch carrying vines that reached the ground. It was moving towards him, and as it got closer, he knew it was someone incredibly special to him. As it approached it began transforming to become the most beautiful woman Apollo always remembered her to be.

"I know how in the realm of the gods 'Time' means nothing," she said, after excitedly running to embrace him, "but it's been too long. I've missed you so much. Please tell me you can stay this time."

"I'm afraid not," he said holding her tighter, "you must leave this place, Shadow creeps across the universe and relentlessly seeks all oracles."

"I'm aware of Shadow," she said, enjoying his embrace, "it stalks the forest, wiping out all oracles, seers, and healers. It shows no mercy and yes, it is relentless. I've been powerless against its onslaught."

He looked deep into her eyes, remembering the times they spent together, then continued, "My beautiful Tayanna, I've never forgotten our time together. No other woman captured my dreams the way you have. Throughout the ages I searched and all I found was emptiness until the chatter of all other oracles stopped, only then did I hear your voice telling me where to search. If I can find you, so will Shadow. You must come to Olympus."

"Yes," she said, slightly backing away, "I will go to Olympus, but before I go there's something I need to say." She paused, took a deep breath, then said, "Through the ages the trees spoke of your many lovers, both men and women. I know of those consorts; the men are powerful, and the women incredibly beautiful. Others have asked as to why a God of Olympus would give up all for a lowly oracle such as me. Is there a future for us?"

"My future shows you are everywhere," he said, reaching in to kiss her waiting lips, "there's a loose end, but it'll be sorted before this day is out."

She went very still and then slightly moved her head to the right, "The trees are speaking of danger." Just then she managed to grip two arrows that came out of the shadows. Apollo was furious and immediately raised a shield, surrounding both of them. He waited for the next volley of arrows before releasing the plague, wiping out the soldiers of Shadow hiding among the trees. Their screams, as their bodies painfully decayed, echoed through the forest.

Apollo and Tayanna arrived in Olympus, and much to the surprise of the Gods Apollo stayed a lot longer than earlier visits. He introduced Tayanna to each god individually causing a lot of gossip. "She's special to him," said Panya, whispering to Eala, "see how he glows. Never before has he been so attentive to anyone."

"I think you and I should rescue her," said Eala, "and have some interesting girly time."

"My lady," said Eala, after reaching her, "you are most welcome into our realm. Come, I know a place where you can freshen up."

"You're just being nosey!" said Apollo.

"Of course we are," sniggered Panya.

Apollo watched them walk away and when he turned back, he was met by a wall of eyes staring back at him. "Brother," exclaimed Ares, "In the name of Zeus? You've never spoken of her. Tell us everything. Who is she?"

Apollo just smirked, bowed to Jacob, and disappeared to arrive on the west coast of North America. He again felt an extraordinarily strong connection with an oracle of the north. He made his way across California and stayed in Sacramento before travelling south into the canyons where he reached the Sequoia National Park. When he arrived, he sought out the tallest and most ancient trees where he sensed the last of the Native American oracles had chosen to live. He found a clearing and waited.

"Welcome, God of Olympus," said a strong voice.

"Why still hide from me?" asked Apollo. "Why are the oracle voices of these sacred lands silenced?"

He looked around and focused on one tree where he thought he saw a slight movement, he did, and as the moments passed a shape formed and then stepped out from its trunk. What was before him was a Blackfoot Skin-Walker, one who was wearing multi-coloured and frilled moccasins, deer skin breaches, and a full body bear skin. He was also wearing, as a mask, the head of a wolf showing its teeth, nose, eyes, and ears. On his back draped a cloak made from the skin of that same wolf. He had his medicine spear in one hand and a snake rattle in the other. Bear claws dangled from his wrists and ankles, and he wore a bobcat medicine bag around his waist.

"You cannot fool me 'Skin-Walker'," said Apollo, "show yourself, shapeshifter and oracle of Olympus."

The skin-Walker knew he was caught and at once transformed into an Olympian, "You were always the one I could never fool. Tell me, Lord Apollo, why are you here?"

"My friend Hyacinthus, reclaim your status as a god," said Apollo, "your banishment ends now, come back to Olympus with me."

"Has Zeus forgiven me?" asked Hyacinthus, "will he allow me the freedom to walk the meadows of his realm?"

"Zeus no longer rules Olympus," replied Apollo, informing him of the changes, "his grandson Jacob, is now the God of Gods."

"Where are all your pupils?" enquired Apollo. "Where are the oracles you trained? What happened to them?"

"It was strange," replied Hyacinthus, lowering his head in shame. "This is my domain, and the pupils came in their hundreds, they said they heard a calling and that calling showed it was from me. It wasn't, I never called them. I trained them in the ways of the seers, yet they didn't see their demise, they were all deceived. Then it happened, I could do nothing; they came like wraiths in the night and savaged all before them, showing no mercy. I heard them ask as they beat my friends, 'Where is the Olympian?' Where is the lover of Apollo?' I was not betrayed, no oracle in the northern lands survives."

Apollo pulled him closer, embracing him in a way that showed how close they once were. "I can only offer you a small comfort," said Apollo. "Tayanna is back in my life and there'll be no room for others."

"I understand," nodded a subdued Hyacinthus.

They immediately left for Olympus where on arrival, they met with Jacob, and after their meeting they left the Great Hall. Magni couldn't contain himself. "Poor Apollo," he sniggered, "his two lovers in one place, one female and one male, he won't know which way to turn."

Jacob, Odi, and Modi all froze, then slowly moved their heads forward in unison before turning to stare at Magni only to be met with a grin. "I'm just saying," he said.

Chapter 25

The following morning Jacob was first up, and as always he went out into the meadows for his morning run but this time he was not alone, Maximus had joined him. Little was said until they reached the lagoon. "Ok," said Jacob, "my curiosity's killing me. What are you after?"

"Uncle!" he said, hoping not to overstep the mark, "There's no point in asking my father for permission to leave Olympus, he'd never agree. I need your support in standing up to him. I'd like permission to travel with Fafner, Heulwyn, and Drayce on their journey to the Dragon Realm. Isidra will be joining them, and I don't want her out of my sight."

"I wasn't aware Fafner planned to leave so soon," said Jacob, "I again need him, this time to help in the search for Modi and Thanases. I respect his desire to leave but other things, right now, are far more important. With regards to you – if the one I loved was leaving, I would make sure I was with her. Leave Magni to me, I will remind him of how well trained you are and I'm sure when he sees the passion you have for Isidra, he will remember his own passion for Marduk and relent."

They continued training and when finished, they made their way back to the temple. Jacob met with Magni and informed him of the decision to allow Maximus leave; he didn't give Magni time to respond. He then met with Fafner who after listening to his request, delayed his departure, agreeing to help. He asked that Isidra be guarded, preferably by Drayce and Maximus.

It was now time to begin the search, which began when four chariots were placed at the main entrance to the temple. Each chariot had a charioteer and was fitted out to carry three gods. The first chariot was for Magni, Fafner, and Heulwyn, the second for Odi, Panya, and Apollo. Ares, Eris, and Irina were on the third, and Jacob, Baldor and Eala were on the last.

Obelius held his counsel until he saw Maximus approach Jacob, loudly expressing his fears. "Why are you leaving Olympus under the protection of eighteen pupils?"

"Maximus," he replied, "You must trust us. The temple is safe in your hands, you are all well trained and will still be under the guidance of Athena," Maximus continued with his concerns, "I smell Shadow, it's the same odour I detected after the attack on our palace."

Obelius then intervened. "Father," he said, "I agree with Maximus. I too smell a foul odour. Apart from that, how can I be your guardian if you are out of my sight?"

Jacob dismounted and placed his hands on both Maximus and Obelius.

"Look at the chariots," he said, "The God of Gods, War Gods of Asgard and Olympus, the King of Asgard, the Emperor of the Dragons, the Goddess of Chaos, and Goddesses of the Light, and not forgetting Apollo. How much more power could we need? Trust us, we'll be safe."

The charioteers then flicked their reigns, and the four chariots moved into the sky, making their way towards the southwest. This was the last known direction towards which Modi and Thanases were travelling, and it was assumed they would continue with that plan. When the chariots left the earth's atmosphere the four goddesses created spheres, allowing them to move faster than the speed of light.

Within an hour they knew they were travelling in the right direction; they reached a debris field that included the bodies of many Shadow soldiers. On investigation it was agreed the causes of death were hammer blows that could only be meted out by Modi who was, since the great battle, a custodian of the hammer. There was also evidence of rope burn marks and again it was surmised that this form of war-weapon could only be the work of Thanases, his new skill with using ropes as weapons was renowned in Asgard. Magni got excited by the sight of so many vanquished adversaries and was delighted his brother, and Thanases, seemed to be in control. Having said all that, he went on full alert, never taking his eyes off the wide-open spaces before him.

Although they were prepared for any attack, they couldn't help but take in the beauty of the Milky Way. Passing many planets that circled old suns was a pleasure, especially as life was returning into the cosmos. The starlight they met, highlighted the cosmic dust, and created the most amazing spectrum of colour that was so enchanting it held their gaze, while the many pulsars, comets, meteorites, and the assorted white, red, and black dwarfs all provided a backdrop to a star filled sky that can only be described as spectacular.

They met ancient Sun Deities who were using whatever powers they had to help with re-igniting extinct suns destroyed by The Darkness, but unfortunately those sun deities were unable to help with a sighting.

The search was taking longer than expected causing concern for the safety of Olympus. Jacob discussed his worries with Magni who reassured him and reminded him of how well the young War Gods were trained. It was then agreed to continue searching for another few days.

They travelled further out into space and soon they stumbled upon more evidence of battle, causing them to conclude they were getting close. The dead Shadow soldiers they met were fresh kills indicating Modi and Thanases had to be close by.

It was soon after when the Asgard army came into view, and it was obvious they too had just been in a battle, there were many casualties. Odi joined them and was thrilled one of his greatest allies had survived. He leapt across to join him.

"You are one of my most trusted allies," he said after using his powers to enter his friends head, "and what I'm about to tell you is so important it could cause your death." He waited a few moments for his friend to absorb what was said, then continued, "I need you to promise me that my warning, and my instructions, will be delivered to Prudr and Vidar. Tell them to secure the perimeter and prepare for battle. Also, tell them of a traitor in the royal household. They must tell no one of my suspicions." The Army left and the four chariots continued on their way.

After travelling for a further few hours they found themselves close to an active battle, they saw flashes of light and could hear the clashing of steel. Magni raised his clenched fist for them to stop, allowing him to focus on the battle. He could see the Sun Gods were seriously outnumbered but in no danger, it was as though Shadow had sent an ill-trained army, obviously keeping his elites for an attack elsewhere, possibly the temple. He now became concerned and resolved to quickly finish the battle.

He already recognised the Sun Gods as a group of gods who have worked together since the beginning of time; their primary function is to patrol the rim of the Cosmos next to The Nothingness. He soon noticed Modi and Thanases, they were in the thick of the battle and they were enjoying themselves.

Magni lined up the four chariots, setting them a mile apart. He requested the goddesses release their light on his signal, and when he signalled, the Light came, and the spheres moved forward, at first slowly, then at a speed allowing them to reach the battle within seconds. The light from the goddesses was so strong it blinded the Shadow army allowing Modi and Thanases to travel between their ranks decapitating all before them. Any soldiers they missed were quickly dispatched by the Sun Gods.

When the battle was over, and that sector secured, the Sun Gods approached Magni and offered their sympathies for his loss of Marduk. They spoke of how they worked with him in the past, and of how he was held in such high esteem. Magni acknowledged their condolences then introduced them to Jacob. They all bowed before him and one said, "We saw the speck of dust sent by the Ancient One, and knew it was a spark of life. As it passed, we escorted it, ensuring its safety, we ushered it on its way."

Thanases approached Odi and shook his hand; letting him know he was aware that Viktor's beating was a ruse allowing him to become a spy for Asgard. "Did your plan work?" he asked.

Odi just shook his head causing Thanases to panic, Jacob intervened. "Don't fret," he said, "Viktor was betrayed, we don't know by whom, but he's now safe back in Olympus, a little worse for wear but recovering."

Thanases then saw Irina and leapt across the chariots to embrace her. When Modi saw Eris, he did the same, sweeping her off her feet. After a few tender moments Modi returned to his chariot carrying Eris in his arms, and using her powers as a Goddess of the Light she created a sphere to surround them. All five chariots were now ready to return to Olympus but before they left Magni said, "All is not right," he looked back and out beyond the stars towards The Nothingness. "Oh My," he whispered.

"Brother," asked Odi, "what is it? What do you see?"

"I see an army, millions, I see them. Shadow is massing an army; they're spread across the rim of The Nothingness and are baying for blood. They move in Shadow. He starves them, wants them to be ravenous, another of his plans before releasing them into the realms of the gods."

"I, like you, am one of the ancient gods," said Ares, "you and I have the same powers, yet I can't see what you see. Are you sure?"

Magni never liked being questioned and out of respect for Ares he didn't react, but Jacob did. He stretched across to rest his hand on Magni's head. He then saw all Magni saw and his face drained. "To be forewarned is to be forearmed," he said, "you, like Ares. Are the Goods of War. What is it you propose we do?"

On our return to Olympus," suggested Magni, "we must detour towards a small, isolated planet. It's no bigger than earth's moon but it's safe and hidden from the gaze of The Nothingness. It orbits Sirius, the brightest star easily seen from earth. From there we will plan a defence to be built across the cosmos, and the only defence strong enough will be a gathering of the most powerful of the Sun Gods, we must summon the Sun Gods."

"Only the ancient gods or the God of Gods has the power to summon them," said Ares, looking at Jacob.

"Then it's the Sun Gods we call," said Jacob.

Chapter 26

On arrival near Sirius, they made their way to land on the planet where they immediately prepared to summon the deities of all suns.

Magni, Modi, Eris, Apollo, and Ares being the ancient gods, knew what to do. They formed a circle; linked with Jacob and together they lowered their heads. Soon the Light came and when it did, it shot out in all directions, alerting all sun deities to a call from the God of Gods.

While waiting Odi showed a concern, he approached Jacob. "You've summoned the most powerful sun deities from across the universe to this barren rock, look around, this place is not appropriate. We must do something; we must recreate the grandeur of Olympus before they arrive." Jacob agreed.

Odi found a flat and wide plateau, permanently shaded from the direct heat and light of Sirius. He stood at the western end and raised his arms. Almost immediately a walkway formed, one that was laid with the most ornate marble slabs, wide enough for large chariots drawn by multiple horses. By the time it was finished it travelled from north to south and east to west. The outer rim of the plateau was then clearly identified by fifteen-meter-high columns made from red sandstone and supported by lintels that were intricately etched with amazing carvings respecting all the different sun deity's realms.

Between each walkway Jacob created seating that tiered to ten high. Each seat was padded and had arm and back rests, generously quilted for maximum comfort. He was preparing for several thousand visitors.

In the centre of the arena, he placed a simple throne that was set in such a way it continuously rotated allowing all gods to feel equal in his presence.

As the arena was set in an almost permanent twilight, he placed bronze sconces on each column to emit the brightest light when needed.

Everything was now prepared and all that was missing were the Sun Gods. Jacob sat on the throne and waited while Eala, Panya, Irina, and Heulwyn, split up to take positions at the entrances to greet the expected visitors. Fafner, Baldor, Thanases, and Odi prepared to assist each arrival to their seats which was based on a first come first served basis. Jacob had earlier expressed a concern about the seating arrangements and put in place a plan that would involve the creation of emergency seating close to him if very senior gods or goddesses arriving at a later stage.

It wasn't long before the first gods arrived, they were queuing as each one was individually greeted before being directed into Jacob's presence.

Each god wore their full ceremonial attire, with both male and female deities dressing identically to each other. They wore robes created from the finest golden silk, heavily embroidered along the lapels, sleeves, and skirt rims. Their capes were a lighter shade of gold that shimmered as they walked to meet with Jacob. Their ornate crowns were created to look like sun bursts. Over five thousand attended and after been greeted they were escorted to their seats. Jacob said nothing, he sensed the impending arrival of more senior and very ancient gods.

His instincts were correct, soon several chariots arrived, and they were carrying some of earth's most esteemed sun deities. Each chariot was golden in colour and drawn by two powerful white winged horses. The first chariot was carrying Lords Ra and Atum of the Egyptian realm, the next was carrying Shamash, God of the Sumerian realm who was sharing with Mithra, God of the Persian realm. They were followed by two incredibly beautiful Goddesses, Surya, and Savitar of the Hindu realm. Behind them came two chariots carrying Lords Dazhbog and Khors of the Slavic realm as well as the Ladies Saule and Sunna of the Baltic and Nordic realms.

A short gap developed before two more chariots were seen to be approaching. The first one was carrying Yan-Di, the Chinese God of Fire, and his arrival was spectacular. From his arm rests, wheels, and horses' hooves, shot fierce and intense flames. Around his head his halo of sunbeams glowed, lighting up the whole arena. He was greeted by Irina before making his way to meet with Jacob. "Way back at the beginning of time," he said while bowing, "I was close by when the Ancient One blew a speck of dust out into the Cosmos, I knew it was the spark of life and, like many others, I escorted it on its way. It pleases me to know that that spark of life has become the God of Gods. My power is your power."

The second chariot landed at the western entrance to the arena. It was Lord Lugh and this time he was not dressed as a Celtic warrior god; he was dressed not that unlike the other gods, but it was obvious he was one of the most powerful. He showed his delight when he was greeted by Fafner and Heulwyn by hugging both in turn. "It broke my heart," he said, "watching the spear penetrate your armour that fateful day, I wondered when I saw the spirit and knew all was not what it seemed. Now I know. You are both blessed by the Ancient One and were destined to return to assist the God of Gods in his endless defence of the Light."

He backed away and walked the length of the western passageway, acknowledging many of those present as he passed. Jacob had turned his throne to face him and was getting very emotional, he didn't see Lugh walking towards him, he saw his best friend, Shane. The same height, same build, same walk, every movement made by Lugh looked to Jacob to be Shane.

"My lord Jacob," said Lugh on reaching him, "I see tears gathering. You still see Shane in me; it must have been some friendship."

"You do see tears," Jacob replied, "he was my closest friend and always had my back. I really miss him. When the Ancient One made your mould, he didn't discard it, he waited for the generations to pass, used it again and gave the world my best friend, my Shane."

Lugh bowed and took one of the seats set aside for the late arrivals. Jacob still didn't stand to speak; he knew there was one more to arrive.

He didn't have to wait too long because a chariot, this time drawn by four flying stallions, arrived and it was carrying the most powerful Sun God of them all. It was Helios, son of Hyperion, Titan God of Light, and Theia, Titan Goddess of Sight. To Jacob he presented as most impressive and certainly matched the image he had of the long-gone Colossus of Rhodes.

Jacob was surprised at how young he looked for one so ancient; his bright and fair curly hair was shoulder length and held in place by his golden crown of shooting sun rays. His piercing eyes glared at all before him confirming the legends of his all-seeing gaze. His fine-spun robes were those that could only be fit for a god of such high esteem.

"As his chariot slowly makes its way along the passageway," said Magni, whispering across to his brothers, "see how he shines his golden rays upon the deathless gods, see how they look on him in awe, he is the only one born of the Titans." He then noticed Eris inching closer to Ares.

"Brother," she whispered, noticing her brothers anger grow. "Don't even think about it. You must learn to forgive. Helios is all seeing as he crosses the sky. He saw what you and Aphrodite did, remember, it was you who betrayed Hephaestus by sleeping with his wife. He cannot speak other than tell the truth. He cannot be blamed for what you did wrong."

Magni also noticed Ares take on an air of hostility and went on alert, he moved and stood beside him, "If you attack, trust me, and I am aware you are the God of War, but so am I, and I won't allow your anger wreck this most important gathering." Ares was about to respond when he felt the point of Magni's sword rest against his ribs. "Promise me," continued Magni, "you won't do anything stupid; promise me."

Ares looked around at Odi, Eris, Apollo, and Modi and could see the tension in their faces, he then said, "I promise."

Magni backed away, stood beside Jacob, and said, "Trust me, you don't want to know."

"I do want to know," snapped an unhappy Jacob, "you drew your sword in anger against the God of War. What in the name of Zeus are you playing at, you drew your sword before thousands of Sun Gods."

Eris and Apollo joined them. "It's time you knew of a scandal unspoken of for millennia," said Eris. "It was soon after the birth of the first stars, a time when Olympus was in its infancy and many unacceptable things happened. You've seen how beautiful Aphrodite is, why she is known as the Goddess of Love? In the beginning she was also known as the Goddess of Lust and Procreation, this she did with abandon. It was arranged for her to marry Hephaestus who at that time, although powerful and brutish, like now, he was also ugly and lame. He was unloved by his mother leading him to a mistrust of women. As time passed he was unable to satisfy her, so she reverted to her old ways. She took many lovers, both men and gods, but there was always only one she really wanted, and that one was Ares. He was her greatest lover and fathered three children by her; their love was real and pure. They managed to keep their affair a secret for many years, but one night, after much ecstasy, they went into such a deep sleep they never noticed the dawning of the day. It was too late. Helios had hitched his golden chariot to cross the skies and bring forth the sun. On his way he looked down and saw them naked and embraced. He had no choice but to tell Hephaestus what he saw. Hephaestus forged an unbreakable bronze net and secretly attached it to the posts of his bed. He deceived Aphrodite into believing he was travelling to the Far Lands but later that night he arrived back to find her and Ares naked and confined. His net had trapped them. He continued the humiliation by inviting all the Olympus gods to visit and view the shame of the naked and helpless couple. Ares has never forgiven Helios for betraying him. He doesn't except that Helios is bound to always tell the truth."

Jacob summoned Ares to join him. "I now know what happened between you and Helios," he said, "and, as far as I am concerned, you were a free god, it was Aphrodite who broke her vows. I want you to make your peace with Helios and then focus on the battle that's coming. You may not like him, but you are the God of War, and he is the most powerful of all the Sun Gods, together you two will be unbeatable. I need you both as allies. Do you understand me?"

Helios finally reached Jacob and greeted him as an equal. "We finally meet," he said, surprised at how young Jacob was. "Tell me of this Shadow." He paused, while looking around at the gathered Sun Gods. "So few have come," he said, "has The Darkness really caused this much damage? There should be thousands upon thousands."

"There are thousands more patrolling the outer rim," said Jacob, momentarily leaving his throne, "they succeeded in forcing The Darkness back into The Nothingness, but weaknesses are showing, and this new threat is more devious and powerful. It has abilities that allow it to enter all realms by using any shadow available to it. Even in this gathering the very shadow of my throne could harbour a spy."

Helios walked the full circuit of the throne and when he reached the shadow he stopped and stared. His gaze was fixed on one spot and then he released his power. He sent two beams of an intense light that highlighted a soldier of Shadow cowering against the rear of the throne. Jacob was furious.

"Tell me spy," he yelled, "how do you bring what you find to your master?"

"I am everywhere and fear no god," said the spy with a sneer, "that speck of dust, that spark of life; I too was there, Boy King. You will rue the day you travelled across the Cosmos."

Jacob reached for his sword and lunged forward but was outsmarted when the spy disappeared but not before announcing, "Fool, I am Shadow."

"I heard that voice before," said Jacob, looking across at Magni and Modi, "tell me it cannot be, we all saw the black mist rise. Are we, yet again, being deceived?"

"Evil is evil in all its forms," said Magni, trying to reassure him, "we must forget those we fought in the past and fight those before us now. Today we fight a new threat, and that threat is Shadow and Shadow alone."

Helios agreed then said, "Tell me, God of Gods, what is it you seek of the sun?"

"Time," replied Jacob, after thinking for a moment, "we need time. We need you to strengthen the outer rim using the combined power of your light. We need you to enhance your beams so that Shadow has nowhere to hide. Never again allow its foulness near me."

"Your wish is our command," said Helios, acknowledging his request. He raised his arms, and all other Sun Gods followed. Through their palms they released their golden light. It travelled in all directions. Shadow had nowhere to hide, and the gathering now felt safe.

The council of the Sun Gods then began with Jacob first to speak. "Deities of the Cosmos," he began. "Bearers of the flame and carriers of the first light, listen on to me. A new terror is coming, one that knows no bounds. It stalks The Nothingness and waits to break through. Trust me, it will, and the devastation of the cosmos will begin. My friends: let it be known that your part is our first line of defence. You will delay the on-slaught by using the power of your charges; you will nurture the solar winds before releasing from the sunspots your powerful flares. Let your sun's energy-bursts come from your coronal heating and allow your solar eruptions to be unleashed showing the fury of the Sun Gods. When you see the Shadow army approach and then pass, it will be your time. For me, do your worst."

Helios then stood to speak. "The God of Gods has spoken," he said, "go now and spread the word across the universe. Tell all of what has been commanded. Do what we were born to do, bring forth the power of the suns. To War! To War! To War!"

Within seconds streaks of golden light shot out deep into the universe, and soon, across the cosmos, plans were put in place to prepare all suns.

Helios himself travelled to where the Big Bang begun and ensured all newborn suns had an escorting god. The arena was now disintegrating, and the planet returning to its original formation leaving the Olympians, the Dragons, and the Asgardians alone. When the gods were satisfied the restoration of the planet was complete, they recommenced their journey back to Olympus.

Chapter 27

Back in the temple the young gods continued with their training, which only ended when an unexpected slow-moving eclipse of the sun began. The light slowly faded causing Athena to take up a protective stance at the main doors. She summoned the young gods back to the temple fearing something sinister was afoot, she also instructed the stewards to place unlit torches strategically around the outskirts of the temple.

By the time the young gods returned the eclipse had reached its Totality but what was strange, the light wasn't returning. It wasn't total darkness, but it was dark enough for the stewards to become uneasy and go light the torches. Obelius joined Athena and while watching the stewards light the last torch, he said, "This is unsettling, see how the sun remains hidden, see how the wildlife have sought cover, even the crickets have gone quiet. It, in a way, reminds me of one of those warm and balmy nights spent beside the lagoon.

"Yes," agreed Athena, "it does, but those warm and barmy nights will become just a memory if we don't find out who Shadow is."

Obelius decided to recheck the perimeter and said when he returned, "I feel no threat; it seems safe. I'm tired and need some sleep; I think we should take advantage of this unexpected dark night,"

The young gods nodded in agreement; they too were tired; they had completed several gruelling days training and felt drained. Thora was delighted; she felt unusually weak and really needed to rest. On her way to her room, she noticed she was beginning to show.

Athena still felt uneasy, choosing to remain at the temple entrance for a while longer. After watching the stewards light more torches she decided to retire for the night, but her sleep was troubled.

In the girl's bedroom Thora decided to hide her growing bump by pretending to be asleep when the other girls arrived. When the girls finally fell asleep she found herself getting more uncomfortable, she was twisting and turning until she was suddenly startled by what felt like a powerful kick, her bump had grown quite a bit in the previous few hours and the more she caressed it the bigger it got. She struggled from her bed to make her way towards the door; there she noticed Aria was sitting upright and seemed to be in a trance. This bothered her but she was so uncomfortable she decided to say nothing and leave the room.

She moved through the quiet corridors, using the walls for support. On exiting the temple, she ignored the advice of the stewards, choosing to make her way into the gardens to sit near the statue of David. There she got a slight relief just by sitting on the cold stone bench. She received another kick and then felt her bump grow again causing her to become very agitated. Her need to walk became overwhelming, in fact the only relief she received was when she walked.

Her walk eventually took her to the hill where the folly sat. On her way she looked up at the stars, noted how bright they were and was taken aback that the eclipse still hadn't passed. She also wondered had Thanases and Modi been located. As she approached the folly, she felt a sinister threat but couldn't figure out if it were real or was it her imagination, caused by the baby making its presence felt. The pain was now becoming unbearable.

After reaching the folly, she stopped for a moment, certain she heard a voice. She listened intently and this time she definitely heard a voice. "Light the torches," it said, "light them now, time is not on your side." She raised her hand and blowing gently, she created a flame. She then quickly lit the torches ensuring the folly was completely illuminated. It was then when she saw them, Shadow People and they looked terrifying, worse than what Drayce and Maximus had described; she also noted them shielding their faces, suggesting they feared the torchlight.

Her breathing was now erratic, and she was really struggling. Her waters broke; her baby was soon to be born. "This can't be," she cried out, "It just can't be." She called for Viktor, but knew he was too far away and would still be in a deep sleep. She tried using her godly powers to reach any god, but the numbing pain was so strong it suppressed her abilities. She sat against the folly seeking respite, but there was none, she was totally alone.

Her contractions were now almost continuous, each one starting as a mild inconvenience, before rapidly intensifying to become severe and intolerable. Beads of sweat gathered on her brow before trickling down into her eyes causing her to be temporarily blinded to the threat that was now all around her. During those intervals when the pain subsided, her awareness as a Goddess of War would kick in, allowing her time to put in place plans to defend herself. At times, the flaming torches would flicker wildly, revealing the faces of the Shadow People, showing how close they were getting. Some of them were able to get their arms under the protective light to tear at her feet causing excruciating pain. She knew then that she and her baby were in mortal danger. Her contractions were now so frequent, they'd increase, reach their maximum, recede only to start all over again. No matter how bad the pain got she remained alert to the danger she and her baby were in. She placed her hand across her bump offering reassurance. "Fear not little one," she whispered, "I'm a War Goddess of Asgard, granddaughter of the mighty Thor. I promise to protect you."

It was when she mentioned her grandfather she remembered the Hammer. She raised her arm, lowered her head, and called it to her.

Out in the Cosmos, Modi was still enjoying the embrace of Eris when he felt a tug at his back; the Hammer vibrated, and then pulled away. It shot across space at such speed it soon landed in Thora's hand. She closed her eyes allowing it take control, it unleashed a torrent of blows giving her the protection she needed. As the hammer unleashed its fury a crystal amulet magically appeared round her neck, giving her the power of starlight to temporarily blind her adversaries.

Back in the temple Aria woke from her trance and made her way out into the corridor. There she found Zane leaning against the wall. "Do you sense it?" she asked.

"Yes," he replied, "I woke to the sound of a lion's roar. The white lions of the desert prides know you are the Lioness of the Gods and are awaiting your call."

"Strange how my dreams also heard a lions roar," she said, "I too hear their call, their patience grows thin."

Zane took her hand, and together they made their way towards the Great Hall. On their way they encountered a wafting mist that thickened into what seemed to be an impenetrable fog. They met Mirembé, the Dogan Seer, and she was holding the urn given to Apollo by the Sybils. She moved her hand across the mouth of the urn and within seconds, two amulets rose up and floated across to rest around both their necks giving them a new confidence. Zane hesitated for a moment before placing his hand into the fog, he looked at Aria and without fear, together they went through.

They stepped into the fog as scantily clad youngsters, still in their skimpy thong-style night attire, only to exit on the far side, not as teenagers but as two powerful Warrior Gods, dressed almost identically. They were wrapped in knee length calf-skinned skirts held in place by gem encrusted belts. The amulets were still around their necks, but they had changed, they were now star shaped, and in the centre was a glass compartment, storing the first Light, giving absolute protection to its bearer. Their body armour was emblazoned with the head of a lion and on their heads were head-dresses made from hair taken from the mane of a white male. Their arms and legs were adorned with bracelets and anklets designed in the forges of the mountain elves. Their shields carried the etchings depicting the images of their most powerful gods. Below their knees were two scabbards holding daggers that had been dipped in the volcanoes of Sirius.

They exited the temple and made their way to the grass terrace from where they saw the burning torches surrounding the folly. They could also see a struggling Thora. They bowed their heads and closed their eyes to call on the prides, and in their hundreds they answered. Within seconds a distant roar was heard.

In one of the boy's rooms, Obelius was resting his head against the headboard, looking startled, and confused. He too heard something calling but couldn't work out what it was saying. He looked around the room to see his brother, and his three cousins, all twisting and turning in their beds and to him they seemed to be having nightmares. He called them but they didn't respond.

In the adjacent room, Drayce, Hemish and Viktor, showed signs of the same restless sleep. It was Viktor who woke first; he leapt from his bed, calling out Thora's name. He was seriously agitated, and by the time Hemish and Drayce awoke and reached him, he was in total terror. "Thora's in danger," he yelled, "they're targeting her; they plan to kill her and take my baby."

"Thora's baby's not due for several months," said Drayce, trying to reassure him, "we have time to prepare her protection."

Viktor was having none of it. "No," he said, getting more agitated, "it's happening right now, I sense it. She's in pain. Don't you hear her screams? We have to find her."

Hemish stumbled back against the wall and went noticeably quiet; it was as though he was falling in and out of sleep. He went listless then slowly recovered. "Lord Shiva has spoken," he said, while making his way towards the door. "I must go to the gardens and prepare for war."

"Don't leave me," yelled Viktor, "Thora needs us, I don't know what to do." He ran to look out the window and got more agitated. "I can't see beyond the torches," he cried, "the flickering flames are causing shadows, help me somebody, please help me."

When he got no response, he looked back to find Drayce had left the room. He looked again towards the folly and focused a little harder. It was then when he saw Thora and was horrified to see she was in some kind of battle against an invisible force. He grabbed a sword from the wall before smashing his way through the window and leapt fifteen feet to the ground. He wasn't dressed, he was almost naked and didn't care; all he wanted to do was save his baby and the one he loved. He ran like a god possessed and seemed to know where Shadow was. Although he could barely see them, he was able to use his skills to leap and summersault above their heads, he even used some of their heads as springboards to his next destination. He eventually reached the folly and began using his combat skills to keep Shadow at bay, the torches came in handy; he too noted Shadow feared their light.

Back in the corridor Hemish was briskly walking towards the Great Hall with Drayce following close behind. They met up with Galyna who told them of her troubled dreams.

"I feel a fire burn in my throat," she said, taking Drayce's hand, "it gets stronger the nearer I get to the door."

"I too can feel its heat," replied Drayce, "it tells me we are going into battle."

As they reached the wall of fog they were greeted by Mirembé who again passed her hand across the mouth of the urn just before three amulets rose up to rest on their necks. Hemish, without fear, briskly walked into the fog and soon disappeared. Drayce and Galyna followed, and they too were gone.

On the other side Hemish was first to exit, he was transformed and looked to be a true God of the Indus. He appeared as 'Lord of the Earth' wearing a deep beige, heavily embroidered knee length sherwani over gold coloured palazzo pants. The silver thread embroidery was so ornate it could only have been created for someone who is a favourite of the Ancient One. His gold-coloured turban stood proud upon his head and was emblazoned with strings of pearls; the fan, sitting at the rear, was embedded with sparkling crystals. He wore earrings of ivory, and eye shadow to enhance his handsomeness. His shoes were of white leather with soles of many colours raised a little higher than normal to give him an appearance of grandeur befitting a god of India. His amulet glowed as he climbed the steps.

He continued his walk towards the doors and moved through the ornamental gardens to arrive on the grass terrace leading to the meadows. He looked across at the folly and watched Viktor fight off an invisible force. He wasn't alarmed, he was about to take control.

The mist was still in place and soon Drayce and Galyna exited, they too continued to walk towards the doors. They arrived, not as young dragons, but as powerful Gods of the Dragon Realm. They were taller and were wearing gunmetal grey coloured armour made from what looked like enlarged fish scales, armour which travelled from their feet up to their necks and was so figure hugging it highlighted how perfect their bodies were. Their hair was no longer shagged or curled but long and straight with sides held back into a ponytail. Upon each of their heads was a metal band with two spikes placed to look like horns. They were unarmed; all they needed was their fire.

They made their way out of the temple and soon joined Hemish, Aria, and Zane. All five never took their eyes off the folly.

"I think Viktor needs our help now," said Drayce, "he's fighting with his eyes closed, he seems to be weakening."

"No," replied Hemish, "his eyes are closed so as to enhance his hearing. He knows we can't see who he's fighting, he's telling us he can hear them. We must use our hearing instead of our eyes."

"He's ripping the hem off his thong," said Aria, "he's using it as a blindfold. If he's not careful, he'll soon be naked."

"I don't think he cares," said Galyna, "he'll do anything to protect Thora. Hemish, you need to do something now."

Hemish called on his Light and when it came it lit up his sherwani and turban releasing an amazing spectrum of coloured light that was so strong it travelled out into the meadows, highlighting the whereabouts of the soldiers of Shadow. It didn't last long; it wasn't strong enough and soon began to wane.

Back in the boy's bedroom Obelius was still in bed, sitting against the wall. He was listless, as though being held in a trance. He only snapped out of it when Demetrius leapt from his bed and ran towards the door.

"Where are you going?" he asked.

"I've no idea," replied Demetrius, "It's the Earth Mothers. They're calling me, telling me to meet with Gaia. They say there's a task only mystic gods can perform."

When Demetrius left the room Gaia was waiting. They made their way to the Great Hall where they too were greeted by Mirembé who again gifted amulets to each of them. They walked through the wall of fog without fear. When they exited they were unrecognisable. They had become Gods of the Earth, protectors of man and guardians of the Astrals.

They were dressed in full length black hooded robes; not that unlike the cassock of a priest, buttoned from their necks to their feet and tied by a wide leather belt secured with a rectangular crystal where the buckle should be. Their hair hung freely from the back and sides and was held in place using a leather band that was clasped by a bronze buckle. Their amulets stood out against the blackness of their robes, ready to release its Light. They were unarmed but for the staff they carried, and embedded in the head of the staff was another large crystal. They were transformed and oozed a new confidence.

While walking down the steps and through the ornamental gardens it was noticed how their Light brought forth the flowers, even in the semi darkness. Buds suddenly burst open, flies took to the sky, and birds chirped loudly, all knew that Gods of the Earth had just passed. They joined Hemish, acknowledged him and waited for his next move.

"Demetrius," said Hemish, "When I signal, I'll need you and Gaia to call on the Earth Mothers and bring forth the tremors, but only around the folly, can you do that for me?" Demetrius and Gaia bowed and backed away to stand just behind him.

Back in the temple the goddesses began to stir and although slightly catatonic, they managed to make their way through the corridors. As they reached the Great Hall they too were greeted by Mirembé who used her magic to rest the amulets on each of their necks. They then without fear walked through the wall of fog.

On the far side they exited as four of the most beautiful goddesses ever to grace Olympus. Helena was first to appear, followed by Sofia, then Sagal, and lastly Sunniva. Their beauty far exceeded that of Aphrodite. They exited as though walking a fashion catwalk. Helena, Sofia, and Sunniva all appeared as true descendants of the Norse Gods. Their flowing blonde hair fell in soft layers to rest around their bare shoulders. Their make-up was subtle as it wasn't really needed. Their eye shadow helped to show how their eyes were inviting and spellbinding.

Their gowns were made from a delicate and very pale cream silk satin material, moderately embroidered with intricate designs, produced using silver and gold thread. Around their necks the amulets matched their exquisite earrings bringing on a dazzling sparkle.

Sagal stood out; she was of Africa and looked exotic, her cream dress accentuated her dark and flawless skin. Her hair, although in an afro style, was shaped to highlight her perfect high cheek bones giving her the appearance of an Orisha Goddess. Her amulet, which was resting against her ebony chest, enhanced her great beauty.

They acknowledged Hemish before making their way towards a high terrace where they had a full view of the folly. Sofia remained behind. "Beware the Shadow that's still hidden from us," she said. "When your light dims, look for the grasses swaying from side to side. Ask yourself as to why they sway when there's no wind. Trust me, that's where they hide. Little do they know that your kaleidoscope of colour combined with the power of the Earth Gods, will soon highlight all of them: When the lions arrive send them in two directions, let them be the executioners. Let the War Gods bring the white light and the Earth Gods, the quick sands. Let the dragons patrol the sky; then use their fire, they will be your eyes and ears. The Goddesses of the Light will finish this army of Shadow." She then made her way to the high terrace.

In the meantime, Obelius leaned across and shook Maximus awake. "That power allowing you to be in two places at once, can it be shared?" he asked, devising a plan, "we're your cousins, and of the same blood. Can we too gain that power?"

"Yes, I think so," he replied, rubbing his eyes, "Tonight, in my dreams, I saw all of you, including Lovisa, and you had the power, place your hand on my head and see what has come to me." Maximus lowered his head and allowed Obelius, Magnar and Tristan place their hands on him. They discovered they all had the power.

They left their room, walked the corridors, and met up with Lovisa, who was anxiously waiting for them. Together they made their way towards the Great Hall where they were met by Mirembé, who, like for the other gods, used her magic to rest the amulets on their necks. Without fear they stepped into the wall of fog, and on exiting, they too were transformed.

Lovisa led them out to present as a most powerful Warrior Goddess of the Norse Realm. She stood tall and was exceptionally beautiful. Her flowing, almost gold coloured hair, was secured in place by a silver band clasped by the laurel leaf. Her ocean blue eyes were set against her perfectly chiselled cheekbones. Her armour was the colour of bronze, equally as strong and created to fit her perfect form. On the breast plate was an etching of the Hammer of Thor. From her shoulders fell a full length free flowing elk-skin cape: Her weapons, fashioned in the forges of the Ice Elves, were a perfect fit for her petite, yet extraordinarily strong hand!

Behind her came Maximus, Magnar and Tristan and they were a remarkable sight. Three young and extremely handsome Norse Gods who looked almost identical, they were tall, broad, and highly muscular. Their blonde tousled hair fell in thick layers to rest just above their shoulders and was held in place by a similar silver band to the one worn by Lovisa. Their baby blue eyes and flawless skin showed how they were also favourites of the Ancient One. They too wore the bronze-coloured armour emblazoned with the etching of their grandfather's hammer, and they were draped with a similar elk-skin cape as worn by Lovisa. Like her, their weapons were designed to be a perfect fit for their strong manly hands.

Within seconds Obelius appeared, he was now taller and broader than his cousins; he was also much darker from his years spent in the sun kissed meadows of Olympus. His deep brown wavy hair fell to his shoulders and was held in place by a golden crown made for a prince of Olympus. His deep chestnut-coloured eyes were mesmerising and showed a determination and stoicism becoming for a true Grecian God. His armour was the colour of gold and carried the etchings of Zeus and the Olympus realm; from his back an ivory coloured, heavily embroidered cape, draped to reach the floor. His weapons were also designed to perfectly fit his hand. All five of the War Gods had their amulets secured to their breast plates.

Obelius quickly moved to join Lovisa and his cousins, and when he reached them, he said, "I'm the last to pass through, yet there are many more amulets in the urn. Are there others to come?" They then made their way out to the steps and were acknowledged by Hemish.

Athena had arrived, wondering why Shadow would attack at this time. She was concerned for the safety of Isidra and the seventeen Oracles under her care and wondered was their presence the reason for the attack. She instructed a steward to escort them into a concealed room where they would be securely hidden from the gaze of Shadow.

She then turned her attention to the battle between Viktor and what looked like an invisible force; what she could see was alarming, prompting her to act. She stood before the main doors and took her colossus form to stand at over twenty feet tall. She then stretched out her arms and created a number of full-length metal shields, shields that stood high enough to reach the roof. When she flicked her fingers they, one after another, spread in both directions. They then slotted into place, interlocked, to form an impregnable defence by surrounding the temple. Nothing could now enter without passing her.

The Wizards took up a position standing before Athena, their task was to use their magic to protect the Goddess of War.

Chapter 28

Four hundred meters west of the temple five chariots carrying the search party exited from a portal, and immediately found themselves watching what looked like preparation for a major battle. Jacob was first to react, he leapt from his chariot, going into shock while trying to take in the scenes before him. He glanced around at the young gods and noted them standing in strategic positions, prepared for an attack. He looked towards the temple and satisfied himself that it was secure when he saw the metal cocoon, he surmised it was created by Athena. He was pleased to see the Wizards standing as though protecting Athena at the main entrance. He then looked towards the folly and immediately moved to assist Viktor, only to be restrained by Magni. "Not so fast," he said, "learn to read the signs, the young gods seem to have a plan, we're not part of it."

All could see how horrified Jacob was; to him it was inconceivable that anyone would dare desecrate these sacred lands, lands that were supposed to be protected by him. He turned to his brothers and yelled, "For thousands of years these meadows have been a peaceful refuge for all gods. Zeus ruled, and no one dared sully his realm. He hands the throne to me and within such a short time it's seriously breached, tarnished by the putrid stench of Shadow."

While Jacob was venting, Magni observed the folly and saw that Thora was struggling, he could hear the pounding of the hammer and knew that at some stage she would tire. He released Jacob from his grip and climbed back onto his chariot for a better view, all the time devising a plan. After viewing the efforts of Viktor, he gestured to Ares, Modi, Apollo, Fafner, and Baldor to move behind Jacob, Odi, Panya, Thanases and Irina. He anticipated Odi attacking when he saw Thora, he knew all Hell would break loose. He also saw that Thanases was near breaking point. His worst fears were realized when Odi did see Thora and the condition she was in. Odi began to run, with Thanases close behind.

Magni signalled for Odi to be stopped by Apollo, and Thanases by Ares. Jacob tried to intervene, but Modi managed to hold him. Baldor and Fafner gently held Irina and Panya. Eala, Heulwyn, and Eris were shocked but backed away.

Magni moved to stand before the now secured gods. "You've got to trust me," he said, "look at our children, they're in total control, and from what I can see they've been given all their powers. They're working as a cohesive unit and seem to be fully aware that there is something out there although they can't see it. Look at the Folly; see how Viktor valiantly fights while at the same time he protects Thora. Look at the War Gods and see how they are ready to go into action. Hemish is in command, see how the light surrounds him, look at how he's itching to release his light and allow the battle to begin."

"Magni," yelled Odi. "I'm going to kill you. My Thora is in trouble, her baby is being born, and she needs us; I swear I'll break your neck."

"If he doesn't kill you," said an equally angry Jacob, "I will. Release us now."

"You will be held secure until you calm down," said an unflinching Magni, trying to hold his nerve, "they cannot afford for you to react and endanger their plan."

Thanases struggled but couldn't release himself from Ares' grip. "For Odin's sake," he cried, "let me go, my son's being torn asunder."

"No," Magni calmly said, "you've got to allow the Children of the Gods use their newfound powers to do what they are trained to do."

"Who's that standing behind Hemish?" asked Modi, still trying to restrain a struggling Jacob.

"It's the spirit of Lord Shiva," replied Jacob, beginning to accept Magni's strategy. "It seems he has come to help his grandson. It looks like their battle is about to begin."

The battle did begin. Hemish stretched out his arms and accepted the support of the Gods of the Indus. He felt the strong, yet invisible hand of his grandfather rest on his shoulder and this led to his turban taking on a new glow. The gems, set into his turban fan, lit up and sent out their powerful coloured light. The remaining gems, embedded among the embroidery on his Sherwani, also began to glow. He became more powerful when Demetrius and Gaia used their staff crystal to strengthen his light.

From the woodlands emerged two majestic and rare white male lions. They joined Zane and Aria before moving in two directions to lead an attack of the felines. This was the most challenging time for Zane and Aria because the prides could smell the sickly stench of decay coming from their prey. They could also hear the baying groans and sinister screeching coming from all around them, but like the gods, they too couldn't see its source.

The arrival of the male lions was the cue for Drayce and Galyna to take to the sky and prepare for their attack. From their positions high above the woodlands, they saw the desert prides stealthily pass trees and scrubs to creep up and prepare to pounce upon their unsuspecting prey.

Hemish felt he was in total control, and just to satisfy himself, he turned to face the temple and was in awe of the sight before him. He was pleased to see the five War Gods and the four Goddesses of the Light were ready and waiting. He returned to his original position and continued emitting his light in search of Shadow. He intensified his light and soon the Shadow army was again revealed. This was the que for Demetrius and Gaia to use their power.

The War Gods then went into action; they called on the source light and it came. Maximus used his power and then there were ten, five Gods and their five spirits, one of which was the spirit of Lovisa. For this battle she was granted the same power as the grandsons of Thor. All ten levitated before floating across the meadows towards the folly. On their way they faced the threat of arrows, but they had nothing to fear, they knew the dragons were ready and waiting. The arrows never reached them; they were incinerated by dragon fire. Drayce and Galyna swooped, ensuring the safe crossing of the War Gods.

On reaching the folly the War Gods saw Viktor was frantically fighting off the now illuminated Shadow soldiers who were continuously clawing at both him and Thora. They immediately assessed the situation, and their training kicked in; they went into action. Before they landed, they noted how Viktor was seriously struggling and his strength waning. They could also hear Thora's screams as each contraction intensified and soon, they heard the first cries of her baby. Viktor didn't see them; he was too engrossed in battling a far more aggressive foe. His despair was now so acute he fell to his knees and called out, "Ancient One, help us."

Out at the rim of the universe, close to The Nothingness, a white cloud of cosmic dust floated, in its midst was a bed and, on the bed, lay on elderly man, white haired and bearded. He was restfully sleeping until he heard the call of despair. He woke and turned to The Nothingness. "Why do you keep trying?" he asked. "When will you learn you cannot win?"

"I am the first," replied the Nothingness, "you usurped me and brought forth the light, you blinded me and destroyed my power. I am always in the Shadows and will try and try again. The pain I bring will destroy all you create."

The old man raised his hand and sent a ball of light out into the universe; it travelled at such speed it arrived, within seconds, to rest high above Viktor's head.

"Ah," said Magni, still observing from the rim of Olympus, "that I didn't expect, it's a light only once before did I see."

"What are you talking about?" yelled Jacob.

"It's a different birth light," replied Apollo, "it's a very special Light, one that has only shone eight times before this night. This is certainly a magical time."

Using Hemish's light the gods now had a full view of Shadow's army, an army that was about a thousand strong, and the main body was moving towards the temple. At the same time a more lethal force was moving to join those already fighting around the folly.

The young gods never wavered, they had a plan, it was a plan being shared telepathically and controlled by Hemish.

Drayce and Galyna were continuing their attack, flying low above the heads of Shadow, and releasing their fire, but it had a negligible effect until they doubled back to release a stronger and more lethal flame. This time it burned through the ranks of evil that were heading towards the temple. What was odd, Shadow didn't seem to care about how many soldiers fell; it was as though this particular attack was a distraction. The Shadow army was too close to the temple causing Jacob to get concerned, but he held his nerve especially when he saw Demetrius and Gaia go to their knees, he listened to them call on the Earth Mothers and was delighted with the response. He saw them release the tremors that brought on liquefaction, followed by the quick sands causing the Shadow Army to sink, chest deep, into the now liquefied soil. He relaxed when he realised this was what the prides were waiting for. The majestic males let out a terrifying roar and the lionesses went on the attack. It was pure savagery, and the sound of crunching bones, the tearing of flesh, and the stench of the putrid black blood will forever be imprinted on the minds of the gods. The Shadow soldiers that were stuck in the mud had no chance; they were ruthlessly savaged and sent back to the bowels of Hell. Thanks to the lions the attack on the temple was averted.

Back on the folly Lovisa led the War Gods on an onslaught of power against the elite soldiers of Shadow, they used their skills to keep evil away bringing great relief to Viktor and Thora. The attack by Shadow around the folly was so relentless it confirmed the attack on the temple was a distraction, it was really the baby of two young gods they were after. Their success came close on several occasions when they successfully grabbed the baby only to be thwarted by the skills of Viktor. He fought for the lives of his family and at one point he fought using one hand while cradling his baby with the other. He finally got relief when Obelius and Lovisa arrived and rested back-to-back with him.

The greatest threat came when a portal opened close to Viktor, who was now drifting into a trance, being held by the power of the Light that settled high above his head. From the portal two hands reached out and grabbed the baby. Obelius was alert to the danger and used a power only his grandfather had, the speed of light. He reacted so fast he rescued the baby while leaving two Shadow hands severed and resting on the ground.

Magnar, Maximus, and Tristan moved up the folly to protect Thora allowing her time to recover. A recovery that didn't take too long. When she stood everything changed, her amulet emitted a brilliant white light to form what looked like a mist that surrounded her. When the mist cleared, she was wearing the robes and armour of a War Goddess of Asgard, and she was seeking revenge. When she attacked, her vengeance against Shadow was felt across the heavens.

The spirits of the War Gods were fighting at a lower level and as spirits they were untouchable. They alone prevented the remaining elite soldiers from climbing the folly. The lions, when finished with the soldiers near the temple, turned their attention to those around the folly. This time they didn't have the help of the quick sands but with the power of the War Gods and the fire of the dragons they were able to totally subdue the remaining soldiers.

On the patio the goddesses called on their light and together they released it across the meadows, it was so intense it incinerated any remaining soldiers of Shadow and soon any vestiges of the battle disappeared. Demetrious and Gaia, alongside the goddesses, then used their earth powers to restore the grasses and the meadow flowers, bringing balance back to Olympus. The cause of the eclipse then disappeared.

Chapter 29

Jacob was relieved and pleased to see everything dear to Olympus was restored, he began making his way towards the temple when Magni stopped him. "Not so fast," he said. "All but one of our children has gained their powers. Viktor still stands as though frozen in time. Look at him, see how the Light shines above his head." Jacob waited.

The ball of light that was sent by the Ancient One continued to pulsate above Viktor's head and as it got brighter it caused him to close his eyes and involuntarily raise his arms. He seemed at peace and was oblivious to all around him. As time passed it was noticed that the light continued to brighten before emitting an even more powerful beam, this one illuminated all of Olympus. What no one knew was that Viktor was listening to the voice of the Ancient One.

Thanases again tried to run to his son, but Magni intervened. "Wait," he said, "you need to watch. Only once before did I witness such a birth, there is nothing you can do to stop this."

"He's my son," retorted Thanases, "my heart's breaking, and my temper's rising. It hurts me to see him suffer."

"Trust me," said Magni, trying to reassure him, "he's not suffering, watch."

The light continued growing in intensity and began to raise Viktor to hover fifteen feet above the folly, allowing all to see what was happening.

He floated and slowly rotated with his arms and legs just dangling, and as he continued rotating, the remains of what covered his dignity fell away. Everything about him began to change.

Thora called out and for a while he didn't respond until finally her plea's reached his ears. He momentarily opened his eyes, and a smile crossed his face. She saw his eye colour was now the palest blue, and his skin was now perfection.

He again closed his eyes, and she watched as his blond hair became wavier and grew to reach his shoulders. He placed his arms across his chest and from behind him, grew two enormous wings, the whitest of white, causing her to shield her eyes. He was still naked with only a light white mist wafting around his legs, torso, and chest, and from behind the mist formed an armour plating that wasn't gold, or silver, metals normally used by the War God's; it was armour made from titanium covered in a coating of a pure white alloy, it was an unheard-of metal, shiny and strong. Soon his transformation was complete, and he presented as an Archangel destined to be more powerful than Michael.

When fully transformed he slowly descended and when he reached Thora he said, "The Ancient One came to me and told me of a new journey. He has made me an Archangel and a guardian of the Heavens."

"Does this mean you'll be leaving me?" she asked, getting alarmed.

"No," he replied, taking his daughter into his arms, "I will always be by your side, I now have the power of an Archangel, but I wasn't given the knowledge. I must listen and learn from the wizards. I'm afraid you won't get rid of me that easily."

Thora tightly hugged him showing the love that existed between them, and they remained in their embrace for a short while before Viktor again opened his wings to fly to the roof of the folly. When he landed, he opened them wide to show the gods the power of an Archangel.

Across the meadows the young gods, the lions, the plants, in fact, all of nature bowed before him. When he rejoined the War Gods, they were in shock, especially Obelius who was showing a few gathered tears.

Thanases and Irina could wait no longer, they raced to the folly, with Panya close behind. On reaching the folly they were greeted by the wonderful sight of their son cradling his daughter. "Father," said Viktor, "I was so worried, even though I always knew Jacob would find a way. He's the greatest."

"Never mind me," said Thanases, reaching in to hug his son, "what about you?"

"Look at her, isn't she the most beautiful," said Viktor, "I can't believe she came from me. Are you proud?"

"Proud?" laughed Thanases, "I've been proud of you since the day you were born. Even during those times when you were your usual obnoxious self. I can't believe you're an Archangel."

Irina took the baby into her arms, and like all grandmothers she quickly became besotted. Panya was anxious to get her turn but waited patiently while all the other gods and goddesses arrived to share in the excitement. That was except for Jacob and Odi.

While the baby was being admired Thora and Viktor discreetly slipped away to take a little time for themselves. They sat on one of the benches near the ornamental gardens and just held each other while enjoying the now bright and starry night.

"I've never been as happy," said Thora, reaching across to get a long-missed kiss.

"If this is what it's like with one child," said Viktor, responding with his own kiss, "imagine what it'll be like when we have more? Look at how happy our families are."

Thora slightly pulled away, looking very confused. She thought long and hard then finally said, "Viktor, love, Archangels can't have children, you must know that. They're neither man nor woman. Your bits, they will be gone."

Viktor froze and the colour in his face drained, she felt his panic rise and tried to comfort him. He went noticeably quiet, and it was obvious he was in shock. After a few minutes he stood to leave. "I, I, I need to be on my own for a while," he stuttered, trying to keep himself composed. He went looking for Obelius and Drayce, and when he found them, they could see he was very distracted.

"What's bothering you?" asked Obelius, "you should be the happiest god here in Olympus. Your father is home safely. You're now an Archangel and you have an amazing partner, but most of all, you're a father with an absolutely beautiful daughter."

"All you say is true," said Viktor, acknowledging Obelius's kind words, "but I can't help feeling all this will soon be lost. I now have a problem I didn't expect." He turned his head as though hiding his pain.

"Please tell me you haven't met someone else," said Drayce, trying to get him to speak, "have you fallen out of love with Thora?"

"For fuck's sake, you prick. Are you looking to finish our fight?" said a very annoyed Viktor. "And no, I haven't met anyone else. I'm still mad about Thora, it's her love for me that's in danger. I think I'll never be able to satisfy her again."

"For Zeus's sake!" said Obelius, "are you for real? Magnar and I saw you in action, you are a master. We shouldn't have been watching but we were, and we were breathless after what we saw."

"You pair of fucking perverts," said a shocked Drayce, "you watched him and Thora, oh my Zeus; I'm ashamed to know you...but tell me, I want to know everything."

"Enough," yelled Viktor, pushing them away, "enough. I've a problem and I need you to join me at the back of the temple where we'll be out of view."

The boys were intrigued, their curiosity getting the better of them. They quickly made their way to the rear of the temple and when out of sight they waited anxiously. There was just enough moonlight, as well as several burning torches for what Viktor wanted.

"I'm going to ask you to look at something and you're going to think this request very weird. I'm terribly upset and really embarrassed, please treat me kindly. I'm very worried, and can I remind you that you are my best friends, I expect your support."

"For Zeus's sake," said Obelius, "tell us? I'm losing my patience. Is everything all right? Do you have an illness? Are you...dying?"

Viktor closed his eyes out of embarrassment; he unbuttoned his tunic and raised his skirt.

"Is everything gone?" he asked, "Thora said Archangels have no bits, they're neither man nor woman. Are my bits gone? I can't feel anything." He opened his eyes.

"I don't know what to say," said Drayce, sucking in his breath and shaking his head, "never before have I seen such...emptiness. I'm really stuck for words."

"No more babies for you," said Obelius, trying to suppress a laugh by covering his mouth as though in shock, "you're not even half the man you used to be. Poor Thora she'll have to go elsewhere to satisfy her needs. Now I know what you're worried about." He paused for a moment then continued, "YOU STUPID PRICK! Thora has set you up, she's teasing you. Everything's intact; in fact, and judging by Drayce's face, we're both impressed. It's probably bigger than when last we saw it, and that was only last week."

Viktor fell back against the wall and knew he'd been had; he made his way back to the gardens to be greeted by a smirking Thora. "Do you forgive me?" she coyly asked.

"Nice one," he replied, "but always remember, some dishes are best served cold. Beware my revenge."

Obelius and Drayce passed them and as they did, they raised their arms, allowing them to dangle from their elbows. Viktor retaliated by showing them his raised middle finger.

When again alone, Thora snuggled closer. "This revenge," she enquired, "does it entail you taking me out into space and having your wicked way? Because if it does, I'll have to arrange a babysitter."

"Are you hinting at something?" he replied, trying to act horrified. "For Odin's sake, you only had a baby while at the same time fighting a vicious battle. Where will you get the energy?"

"I am a War Goddess of Asgard," she said, "and the Light is my friend, I've already healed and now I have needs, you're the only one who can satisfy them."

She stood, took his hand and together they made their way towards one of the vacant chariots. Obelius was watching and nudged Drayce.

"Look at that pair," he said, "they're up to no good. None of us will sleep tonight."

They mounted the chariot and after flicking the reigns, they quickly made it out to be among the stars. They found a remote planet, one that was bathed in a soft and warm sunlight, preventing any shadows from forming. At first, they just sat by a lake, which appeared as if by magic, and enjoyed the dancing sunbeams bouncing across its surface, sunbeams that created a most mesmerising display of light. The surrounding sand was golden and inviting. There were no sounds other than the occasional chirping of songbirds, apart from that, it was as though they were immersed in the stillness of the vaults in Elysium. The scent of the wildflowers was intoxicating, so much so that Viktor said, "I'll be unable to walk through the wildflower meadows of Olympus in the future without wanting to have my wicked way. There's these amazing sensations swirling around my body, and you haven't even touched me yet."

"I haven't even touched you yet?" she said, turning to face him. "You've another thing coming if you are expecting me to make the first move."

He got the message and immediately moved in for a kiss, then said, "How do you feel about getting into the lake and doing a Jacob and Eala?"

"That's some passion killer," she said, gently punching his shoulder, "Jacob and Eala are my uncle and aunt, that'll be a difficult image to get out of my head."

"I know a way to get rid of that passion killer thought," he said, easing her on to her back.

"Never mind the passion killer," she yelled, "you've forgotten to remove your armour, you're crushing me."

He quickly leapt to his feet and unbuckled all straps, he removed his tunic and then his skirt, to stand there in all his nakedness. "I look down on you and can't believe that after all these years, it's me who's with the Asgard Goddess of War who just happens to be the most beautiful woman in the universe."

"Are you going to stand there talking," she said showing her frustration, "or are you going to take me back to those magical places we shared that day while travelling to Asgard."

He got the message and leaned forward to kiss her again, ensuring his lips fitted perfectly with hers. She was pleased he had taken control and decided to completely surrender to his every whim. At this very moment in time, he felt her unconditional love, it was the way her eyes lit up and her back arched each time he moved his hands to caress every part of her body.

He, while kissing her toes, excited her, but nothing prepared her for the sensations she felt as he moved up her leg, gently massaging, sensually kissing, ensuring their souls were about to mingle. When she arched her back again in anticipation of where his fingers would next touch was when she felt the first probing push. She wanted to take back control but found she had become helpless causing her breathing to change with each new thrust.

She liked the new assertive Viktor especially when his arms reached around her back to tighten his grip, allowing their silk-like skin to continuously touch but she was totally unprepared for the magic touch of his fingertips; they were electric and sent skin-tingles racing through her body, completely taking her breath away.

When she finally managed to take back control, she flipped him on to his back and straddled his hips, allowing him to penetrate deeper. Their moans of ecstasy travelled across the universe, and as predicted by Obelius, they were destined to keep Olympus awake that night. Thora and Viktor didn't care; they'd become one, slipping gracefully into each other's minds and bodies. Their dreams, thoughts, and wishes were now shared for they were totally and utterly in love.

Chapter 30

While Viktor and Thora were out in space the excitement around the new arrival continued in the meadows. No one missed the new parents except for Obelius and Drayce. Thanases eventually noticed his son was missing and made enquiries.

"I wouldn't worry about him or Thora," said Obelius, suppressing a smirk, "they knew their daughter was safe and going to be well looked after. They decided to take a little time alone; they'll be back soon."

"Yeah right!" said Drayce, smirking while turning his head, "they'll be at it all night; my dragon ears can hear the grunts and groans, and they are light-years away."

"What was that, Drayce?" enquired Thanases.

"Oh, nothing, nothing," was the reply.

Obelius sniggered. Thanases furrowed his brow, thought for a moment; realised what his son and Thora were up to, and threw his eyes to the heavens.

In the meantime, Jacob sat on the lowest step of the temple, still in shock, not believing how under his watch, and for the first time ever, Olympus was attacked and infiltrated by an army of evil. He was devastated while thinking about how his stewardship had failed, he made a few decisions about his future.

He made his way up to the entrance to find Athena was still in her colossus form, maintaining her protection of the temple.

"My Lady," he said, "the danger has passed, go to the meadows, and enjoy your victory." She was unsure but took his advice and went to the meadows.

Jacob entered the temple and walked the length of the Great Hall to stand before the statue of Zeus. He went to his knees and with his sword placed across both hands, he said, "Grandfather, I've betrayed your trust and failed in my duty. I've let you and the ancient gods down and will now leave to go into exile."

He placed his sword on the ground and stood to back away but was stopped. "Brother," said a genuinely concerned Odi, "you're wrong! Olympus was always safe and that's because of your plans, they worked. Look around, see how your idea to create a school brought the young gods together. Your efforts ensured they were trained and prepared. They alone used everything they were taught to fight off an invisible army. Athena did her duty, Zeus chose her to remain, and she did what was expected of her, look at how she placed an impregnable shield around the temple and stood guard at the main door. Brother, Olympus was safe at all times, you did your duty." Jacob just stared at him and then moved away; he wasn't convinced.

Just as he reached the steps to leave, he was stopped by a loud and thunderous voice, a voice he recognised. He turned and was met with the awesome sight of three spirits standing just before the statue of Zeus. They stood as tall white shimmering lights and when he focused, he saw that one was his mother, and the others were Odin and Zeus. He also noted a very bright light shining behind them but couldn't work out what it was.

"My amazing grandson," said Odin, "pick up the sword; it's yours and yours alone. Before the next moon rises your power will again be needed to defend this sacred temple."

"My beautiful son," said Maria, "think back and remember all I gave you. All that makes you who you are. Your decency allowed you look on the pain of others with empathy, your strength of character allowed you control your passion, all gifts you nurtured. You were chosen at the beginning of time to be the God of Gods. This has always been your destiny."

"You are a Warrior King and a God of Olympus," said Zeus, "Odi's right, look at those in the meadows and see how your plans, using their skills, secured the safety of this most holy sanctum. Beware Shadow, the young gods may have won this battle, but the real war is coming. The gods have trusted you since that first day by the lagoon when you challenged me. It wasn't your weakness that showed, it was your strength. Today, rebuild that strength and let us have no more of this self-pity. Go to the highest steps and let all those in the meadows see who you really are."

They then disappeared but the bright light remained for a few more seconds.

Odi joined him, placed his arm around him, smiled, and said, "I think you've just been put in your place."

"Never mind me being put in my place," replied Jacob, "did you see the light behind them?"

"I did wonder about that," said Odi, "it faded almost at the same time as the spirits. Hey; my heart lifted when I saw mother, she looks well. Being a spirit suits her. I miss her, do you?"

"You've no idea how much I miss her," replied Jacob, "she was always there for me, and if what happened all those years ago didn't, she would've always been there for you. When I think back to the time I spent in Ireland, the dreaded teen years, those times when I broke her heart. I always knew she loved me, but those times when I'd catch a sadness in her face, I knew there was something else missing from her life. I thought it was our father she missed but no, it was you, it was always you. Did you see the way her spirit lit up when she saw both of us together, she was the brightest light?" Odi said nothing, he just reached up to kiss Jacob's forehead before leaving to go out and meet his new granddaughter.

Jacob remained in the temple. He made his way to sit beside his mother's statue. "Mother," he said, "I thought I was doing well. Eala really loves me. My sons have really matured and are doing well. My daughter is beautiful and has found love with someone I would trust with my life, but there's something missing, and I can't figure out what it is. It's while I'm training out in the meadows when I feel a deep sadness; and it's getting worse."

There was no movement, no comfort or peace. He received no guidance or inspiration, so he stood and made is way out towards the terraces. On reaching the highest steps he looked out across the vastness of his domain and could see all those present were staring back at him. It was then when the Light arrived to surround him.

To the Children of the Gods, he was presenting as a most powerful Warrior, and they continued watching as something magical began to happen. The Light intensified and appeared as though it was a sunburst, sending flames in all directions. Jacob's robes became pristine white. His golden armour tightened to become figure hugging. His cape draped for a moment, then fluttered gently in the soft breeze. Out of thin air, a gem encrusted crown appeared, to rest upon his head, and in his hand a crystal encased staff formed before sending continuous lightning bolts to illuminate all before it. At that moment, the brilliance of the first source light oozed from him.

The young gods had never seen him looking so powerful and were awe-struck. They always knew he was their King of Kings, now they were seeing him as their God of Gods. It was then when, all together, they bowed before him.

For Jacob it was good to feel his confidence return, he knew there was still much more to be done, and it would need to be done very soon. His instincts told him that what happened in the meadows earlier that day was just a skirmish, organised to test the resolve of the gods. He also knew that what happened was not big enough to draw out Shadow whoever or whatever Shadow is.

He momentarily closed his eyes while receiving a vision, a vision that was showing him the fall of Olympus and this rattled him, he said aloud ensuring all in the meadows heard, "Tonight there's a peaceful calmness resting across this magnificent realm." He paused for a moment before continuing,

"Trust me, I see it. It's a false calmness."

The End

Jacob

'Jacob - Journey of a God is the first in a gripping series of five books. It chronicles the journey of a troubled youth who, since his twelfth birthday, has been haunted by disturbing visions showing horrific events set in the past. As the visions escalate he learns of a future filled with turbulent and violent times.

Its 2016, and although living the normal life of a Dublin teenager - school, studies, rugby and girls, he soon discovers his true identity. His mother tells him the story of his birth and her efforts to protect him from forces beyond his comprehension. He begins to understand his extraordinary abilities especially when he realises those abilities are actually the powers of a God.

Amidst the unfolding drama of his life, Jacob's visions show him to be leading a battle against two malevolent forces - one is The Darkness and the other, the nefarious 'Prince of Hell'. Both have made him a target of their venom, they know he has been chosen to be the defender of the Light and they fear his power.

Why does The Darkness loathe the Light?

What fuels the Prince of Hell's hatred of Jacob?

In the face of these existential questions, will Jacob embrace his divine destiny and become the God he was born to be?

Journey of A God
Eamon Blake

Jacob

Throughout the ages there were many heroes, and the common thread weaving its way through their lives was honesty, bravery, chivalry and the protection of the weak. Nothing exemplifies this more than the heroism the four Messengers of the Gods and their formidable guardians showed while delivering Jacob's message during their journey of eighteen hundred years.

Jacob - Walk of the Messengers - is the second in an exhilarating series of five books, and this one tells the story of those same messengers and guardians. How on every road they walked, every river they crossed, every mountain they climbed, they were met by an onslaught of brutality from the forces of Hell that was relentless. With each attack their confidence grew and their skills enhanced, and as the years passed they continued to mature to become powerful gods in their own right.

Will they survive the relentless attacks by the forces of Hell?

Will they succeed in their task of creating the mightiest army ever assembled?

Will Jacob keep his promise and intervene when all seems lost?

Walk of The Messengers
Eamon Blake

Jacob

For centuries, there've been epic battles fought across vast battlegrounds. There've been empires that rose and then fell to the sound of powerful armies using weapons designed for mass killing. None of that compares to what is put together for the battle between the forces of the Light and the servants of Hell.

Jacob - War of the End Times - is the third book in a riveting series of five and tells the story of a monumental battle that threatens the very fabric of all existence. Apart from open battlefields, it also takes the reader into villages, towns and cities to witness the destruction of all infrastructures that makes those cities function.

Defence of the Light is led by Jacob, and using the power of the Gods, he brings together those of myth and legend. He also calls upon the overwhelming might of the Carriers, the millions of Carriers assembled over the centuries by his messengers.

Opposing Jacob is a massive army of pure evil led by Lucifer, the Prince of Hell, and Cain, the first murderer. Both of whom are being manipulated by the stifling shadow of The Darkness.

Does Jacob possess the strength to successfully command the armies of the Light?

Will humanity survive the relentless onslaught from the forces of evil?

Will the well-planned tactics of the Olympus and Asgard War Gods be enough to defeat Hell?

War of the End Times
Eamon Blake

Jacob

A mysterious and frightening shadow has been skulking its way through all the realms of myth and legend. Its sinister presence is always followed by an attack of such evil violence that few survive.

Jacob - Battle for Olympus - is the last in a riveting five book series. It concludes the story of his battles against the Dark side. In this instalment he finally establishes who Shadow is and quickly learns it can only be defeated with the assistance of the Ancient One.

Jacob's heart breaks on learning of attacks by Shadow on the Dragon, Elf and Yeti nations and is devastated when he discovers many of his friends and allies have been killed.

When Asgard is destroyed he concludes that Shadow's plan, just like that of The Darkness, is to destroy all that has been created by the Ancient One. This emboldens him to awaken the defenders of Olympus who have, since long before the time of Zeus, been sleeping deep in the caverns below the temple.

Can Jacob rescue the remnants of those of myth and legend?

Will the Ancient One come to Jacob's assistance?

Is the Battle for Olympus to be the battle to end all wars?

Battle for Olympus
Eamon Blake